PRAISE FOR

GRIM UNDERTAKINGS:
BOOK 1 OF THE GRIMFAERIE CHRONICLES

"Loved this book, I couldn't put it down!
A great take on the genre, & the main characters are awesome. Full of action, adventure, & humor, it's a fun book." RM

"…an interesting story with lots of twists and turns that will have you flipping pages all night long…" Patricia S

"As always, I expect the fight scenes in Whit's books to be done well -- but was so pleased to find out how extraordinarily well done they are!" Joey R

"It's kind of a cross between Batman, Angel and Jim Butcher's Dresden files –but also so much more. It's well written, with great characters and is just a fantastic read, full of action, twists and surprises. It packs a punch and kept me turning the pages to find out what happened next. It's just great, well-written fun. Can't wait for more. This would make a fantastic movie. Hollywood, take note." Simon B

"Hate that I have to wait for the next book in this series. I especially enjoyed the strong female main character which is par for the course with this author." Ruth R

"There's probably 20 pages in the entire novel that aren't action filled. There isn't a single wasted word. Every movement builds into the next then BOOM, heart racing action. The tension is high and the pace swift. The characters are well thought out and easily became friends in my head." JSH

BY WHIT McCLENDON

EPIC FANTASY

THE FIRE OF THE JIDAAN TRILOGY

MAGE'S BURDEN
GART'S ROAD
A MAGE AWAKENS

THE FORGE BORN DUOLOGY

REYANNA'S PROPHECY
REYANNA'S FIRE

URBAN FANTASY

THE GRIMFAERIE CHRONICLES

GRIM UNDERTAKINGS
A GRIM SITUATION

NON-FICTION/INSTRUCTIONAL

THE JADE MOUNTAIN WORKOUT SERIES

SHORT WORKOUTS FOR BEGINNERS
MORE BEGINNER WORKOUTS: THE NEXT STEP
KETTLEBELL TRAINING FOR BEGINNERS

A Grim Situation

The GrimFaerie Chronicles Book 2

By Whit McClendon

Copyrights

A Grim Situation
The GrimFaerie Chronicles, Book 2

ISBN-13: 978-1-7326300-5-5

Cover Art by: Wicked Smart Designs
Copyediting by: Michelle McClish
Published by: Rolling Scroll Publishing, Katy, TX
Website: www.whitmcclendon.com

To join my mailing list to be notified when a new novel is published, go to
http://www.whitmcclendon.com/contact

You can also Like my Facebook page!
http://www.facebook.com/whitmcclendonauthor/

Or Follow me on Instagram!
https://www.instagram.com/whitmccauthor/

Acknowledgements

Writing can be a very solitary endeavor. Fortunately, I have a crew of people who encourage, support, and help me as I get words on the page, and I appreciate them mightily. Tara Wood (look her up on Amazon), thanks for being so grabby about my stories. Michelle, thanks for your fabulous edits, and helping me remove all the extra *that*'s. Kathryn, thanks for your comments and ideas…they always help. Christina, thanks for constantly reminding me that I'm capable of doing this whole writing thing. RJ Batla, thank you for helping me with nuts and bolts along the way, and no, I'm not going to outline anything, so there. Thank you Larry for getting me to start attending conventions. I never would have done it without your urging and now I love them. Special thanks to Dennis L McKiernan, whom I count among my friends, and has always encouraged my writing. And thanks to Brian for cheering like a crazy person for me on occasion. They're a good bunch. Really.

~Whit McClendon

A Word from the Author

This is a work of fiction. I figure you knew that, but since I'm delving into Native American mythology a bit here, I figured I'd remind my readers that I'm not an authority on Native American culture. I've pulled elements from different traditions and tribes with the intent of simply entertaining you. I mean no disrespect whatsoever to any part of Native American culture, which I find absolutely fascinating. I'm just making this up as I go.

~Whit McClendon

Chapter 1

Katy, Texas used to be a little country farm town. Several miles west of the center of Houston, it had once been separated from that bustling city by vast expanses of prairie grasses and rice fields. It had been quiet back then, but the last two decades had seen both cities grow until they met somewhere in the middle. Now, Katy was a bit of a metropolis in its own right, and it was hard to tell where Katy ended and Houston began. The last few years in particular had seen an explosion of growth, and Katy swelled near to bursting. That meant more subdivisions, more apartments, more *everything*.

In spite of its rapid growth, there were still some quiet areas and lots of big trees in the older neighborhoods. That appealed to me. And since I'd been spending a lot more time with Ariana, the witch who lived on a family homestead west of Katy, it seemed logical for me to find lodgings close by. I don't need much. I'm equally at home sleeping under a bridge or in a soft feather bed, though I'll admit that I prefer to be under a roof. Keeps the rain out, as well as protecting me from winged creatures that might want to rip my head off while I doze. In my line of work, that's just an occupational hazard.

I'm not human, by the way. I'm known as Kane, and I'm a GrimFaerie. I'm faster, smarter, stronger, and sneakier than humans in general, and I have other abilities that come with being born of the Faerie race. There are lots of Faerie creatures, some big and some tiny. I'm man-sized, and although I'm built like a man, you'd rather not see me without my glamour in place. Without the illusion that makes me appear as an ordinary, forgettable human male, I've been told I'm...scary. I don't know if it's the claws or the fangs, but I have to think it's something in my eyes. Faerie are from this world, yes, but it's not exactly the same world you know, my friend. We're different. And yes, some of us are frightening. I could kill you before you realized your head was missing. In my true guise, I look like I can do just that. To move among you, I hide my unusual features with a glamour. It keeps unwanted attention away from me so I can do my work unmolested.

I'm an assassin by trade, and a darned good one. But I'm a peacekeeper...a good guy. Granted, it gets pretty messy when I get called in, but hey...peace comes at a price. I don't come out for shoplifters or jaywalkers, though. The Goddess only sends me up to the plate when things get serious. Deadly serious.

There's a balance, and it's delicate. You've heard of the never-ending battle between Good and Evil? Yeah, that's not just in the movies. It's right under your noses, folks. Mostly, we leave it up to you humans to do as you will. But when a sorcerer gets ambitious, or a creature that shouldn't get loose from one of the Etherworlds somehow does just that, I'm the guy that gets called in.

It had been quiet lately, though. I'd made a deal with a human that allowed me to live in a tidy little home in the middle of town in return for keeping up the place. He might have been looking to rent it out rather than have me live in it for free, but I might have used a touch of magick to influence him into our current arrangement. Even so, I would keep up my end of the bargain to the letter, so I repaired anything that even looked like it needed work. The place looked better now than it had when I moved in.

The house backed up to a hike and bike trail that followed a drainage canal which fed into Mason Creek. When I wasn't following up on a command from the Goddess, I often walked or ran along the trail, reveling in my love of movement. I can move blindingly fast if need be. More often, I'd just walk so that I could feel the breeze and listen to the birds. Super casual, that's me.

One afternoon, I stopped to sit on a green metal bench alongside the trail. Ordinarily, I don't do that, but it seemed the thing to do at the time, and I tend to follow my instincts. Directly opposite me, across the canal, was the back side of a new apartment complex. It was gray and blocky, not very pleasing to the eye, but it was built with all the modern conveniences a young professional could want. Not many cars took up spaces in the lot on that side. I didn't know if that was because it was late afternoon and everyone was at work or because the place was so new they hadn't rented out all the units. It looked pretty deserted out there, either way.

The wind brushed against me and I relished the feel of it on my skin and in my hair. Beneath my glamour, my hair was long and dark, and I shrugged my head to keep it out of my face. *I should braid it*, I thought. *Get it out of my way.*

I reached my hands up behind my head to follow the impulse when I heard a woman scream, a short, sharp sound that was quickly silenced. I bolted to my feet, trying to pinpoint its source. It came from the apartments across from me, but beyond that, I couldn't tell anything more.

As I watched, a glass door on one of the fourth floor balconies opened up and a man backed through it, dragging something. When I saw that the object in question was a woman, feebly struggling against him, I burst into action.

Grass grew all the way down the slope until it met the concrete riverway, where steep concrete banks channeled the waist-high water through its course. I covered the distance to the canal in a blink and leaped over the twenty-foot wide river with about as much effort as you might use to step up onto a curb. I climbed the opposite slope and reached the iron fence that surrounded the complex. I put one hand on the top railing as I sailed over it to land on my feet in the parking lot.

The man on the balcony was a pretty ordinary looking guy. Not big, not fat, not skinny either. Strictly dad-bod. He looked in his thirties, had dark hair with a receding hairline, and wore a blue polo shirt and khaki pants. However, the frightening, crazed gleam in his eye didn't bring any sitcom dad to mind. Something was very wrong in there. As I watched, he grabbed the woman's neck with one hand and her leg with the other, and easily lifted her still-struggling body over his head like a barbell. With a grunt of satisfaction, he flung her out over the parking lot and towards the unyielding pavement below. He chuckled maniacally to himself as he went back inside.

I knew the fall might not kill her, but it would certainly break bones. I jumped up to intercept her falling weight as carefully as I could to avoid giving her whiplash. Her limbs were loose and flopping, but I gathered her close to my body to keep her under control. As I landed, I flexed my knees to absorb the shock, then I set her down in a patch of manicured grass nearby as gently as I could. I moved her hair out of her face with my fingers and tried to reassure her.

"Hey," I said, injecting a sense of comfort into the words with my magick. "Hey, I've got you. You're safe. What happened?"

She coughed, working around the swelling in her throat. She was in her early thirties, as best I could tell. Shoulder-length blonde hair that needed brushing, no makeup to speak of, but cute. I could already see the bruises left by his fingers appearing on her neck. Her eyes opened and finally latched onto mine. "He," she began, "he's insane!" Fear shone in her eyes as she continued in a hoarse whisper. "Andy's not like that," she shook her head side to side. "He's never laid a finger on me. Today, he just went...crazy!"

At that point, I heard something that froze my black heart. Andy was laughing, but it wasn't Andy. I knew the sound of human laughter, and this was not it. The sound crawled through the air and up my spine, chilling me to the bone. It was a high-pitched, hysterical giggle that wasn't human at all. I knew what it was, though. And it had no business here.

"You're safe now," I reassured the woman. "Just stay here and rest easy. Someone will be along to get you." I poured restful energy into my words, and the woman relaxed, curled over on one side, and went to sleep. I turned my eyes upward. A vicious, delighted giggle floated down to me and turned into a singsong chant.

"GrimFaerie, GrimFaerie, won't you come up and plaaaaaay?" Then that eerie, hateful laughter again.

Oh, you bet I will, asshole.

I let my claws slip out of my fingertips, and my fangs began to ache the way they do when my body is anticipating combat. I leaped to the third-floor balcony and landed inside its protective railing. The door that led into the apartment was open a crack. I heard something shatter inside. And more laughter. I dimmed myself and stalked through the back door.

I was about to fight for my life. Who says Mondays aren't fun?

Chapter 2

Blood has a sharp, coppery smell you can taste. It hangs in the air, thick and cloying. The smell hit me the moment I entered the apartment and my mouth began watering.

The thing was in the kitchen when I entered, standing with its back to me and hunched over at one of the counters. It chewed at something, ravenously, and I could see a faint spray of blood across the ivory colored cabinets in front of it. The noise was awful as it chomped and slurped. I caught sight of something black and furry in its hands and noticed that a tail dangled from the small carcass. A cat, most likely. Suddenly, as if it had caught my scent, the creature that had been Andy froze. It canted its head slightly in my direction but did not turn to face me.

"Want some, GrimFaerie? It's fresh." Its voice was harsh and shrill, and sounded like it had to hurt Andy's throat to come out like that. It slowly turned its head farther so that it could see me. I wished it hadn't. Andy's eyes were unnaturally wide, and shot through with blood, the irises nothing more than pinpricks in spheres of sickly yellow. His gory lips were skinned back so I could see all of his teeth in an awful death's-head grin. "Or have you become too civilized?" A low chuckle escaped it, grating through Andy's tortured vocal cords. It stared right at me, as if seeing right through my dim glamour.

Only a creature from the Etherworlds would have known what I was. There were many such worlds, some hellish, some enchanting beyond your wildest dreams. Almost all were dangerous to humans. I knew this beast, all right. Although it was a huge surprise to come across an incubus these days, the demons weren't unheard of.

"No thanks, I'm trying to quit," I snarled.

The thing that had been Andy whirled with unnatural, freaky speed and hurled the grisly carcass at my face, then grabbed a pair of kitchen knives and came at me in a screeching, horrific blur.

I dodged the cat easily enough, and heard it thump wetly against the wall behind me. As much as I love wet work, that was just gross. I flipped a coffee table out of the way so I'd have more room to move and crouched, waiting for it to attack.

Animated by the incubus, Andy came flying out of the kitchen. Creepy fast as he was, he was still slow by my standards, so I had a blink or two to decide how to deal with him. Incubi are nasty creatures. They jump into a human's body and shove their consciousness into a tiny little corner of their mind. Sometimes, the human can still see, hear, and feel everything their body does, but can't do a thing about it. If the incubus stays in the body too long, the original owner dies. Normally, they would bide their time, hide in plain sight for days, even weeks, until the owner's spirit winked out and the demon gained full control. Then they'd just ride out that body's lifespan, causing trouble of one kind or other until they died of natural causes or misadventure.

Judging from the crazy that oozed out of this one, though, I was willing to bet it had only just made the leap, crammed the real Andy into a deep hole, and started partying. Patience didn't seem too high on its list of virtues, and it wanted to have some fun right now.

It lunged at me with one knife, the other coming in an instant later as the incubus tried to gut me. Staying calm, I lashed out, grabbed it by the wrist, and spun on the ball of my foot. I saw its already wide eyes switch from crazed attack-mode to surprise as I swung it around and hurled Andy's body horizontally into the nearest wall. He impacted on his back, destroying the sheetrock and bending the lightweight aluminum studs behind it, but not

7

going all the way through. Fortunately for Andy, there was a couch against that wall, and his body flopped onto it amidst a hail of chalky rubble and dust.

I was in a spot. This incubus was already murderous, and likely to take as many innocent human lives as it could before someone put him down. The simplest thing I could do would be to slash its throat, but for all I knew, Andy was a perfectly normal guy until less than an hour ago. He was probably still in there. I don't mind killing humans when they deserve it, but chances were that this guy'd been minding his own business before this happened. I sighed and shook my head in disgust at myself as I watched Andy-demon trying to crawl out of the debris on the sofa. *I must be going soft,* I thought to myself as I decided to do things the hard way and let Andy live. That meant getting the demon out of him, pronto.

You might wonder if I was going to call a young priest and an old priest to expel the demon. Nah. They have their magick, I have mine. It all comes from the same place, no matter what words you use. Mine was more elemental, more immediate. The land of Faerie was not far from the Hell that this thing had come from, metaphorically speaking. I knew its kind. And I knew what could get it out of Andy without a cross and fancy robes.

It was starting to recover, so I punched poor Andy hard enough to stun both him and the demon, and they fell back to the sofa, raising a cloud of sheetrock dust. While the thing was rattled, I yanked a curtain off the rod hanging over the sliding glass door and used my claws to rip it into usable strips. Using my Faerie speed, I quickly bound Andy's body at the ankles, thighs, and wrists before also tying its arms tightly to its sides. The incubus did not like that, not one bit.

"Release me, Faerie!" he howled as he struggled against the makeshift shackles. "You don't know who I am! I'll kill you and everything you've ever loved! The witch will die screaming, and…" I smacked him in the head sharply, and when he opened his mouth again, I jammed another piece of curtain in there. Much better.

"Sorry, Andy," I mumbled. If he survived this, he'd probably need to spend some time in the hospital, but better that than the alternative. "You'll thank me someday. Maybe."

I grabbed the bindings at his arms and legs and picked him up like a bale of hay. The sliding door to the balcony was still open, and I carried him out into the daylight with me. As the sunlight hit him, he screamed behind the gag and squeezed his eyes shut, thrashing as best he could underneath his bonds.

On the balcony, I scanned the area and saw that in spite of the noisy battle in the apartment, no one had ventured out to look. I could hear sirens in the distance, though, so someone might have already called it in. *Figures,* I thought. Even so, the fact that there wasn't a crowd to deal with was a huge relief. I looked over the edge of the balcony, and the woman was still down there, dozing under my spell.

I hefted my struggling bundle and leaped over the railing. With him wriggling like that, it wasn't easy to keep Andy's head from slamming into the concrete when I landed, but I managed. I hoped he didn't get whiplash. The instant I hit the ground, I started running towards the back fence where I had initially entered the complex. Thankful I had minimized the chance of getting bitten by the Andy-demon by stuffing that fabric in his mouth, I slung the body over my shoulder, then jumped up and over the fence. I cleared it easily enough, and then I was on the grassy slope beyond.

Andy-demon's thrashing intensified as he figured out where I was headed: the river. Running water grounds out many kinds of magick, and both he and I knew that the incubus would never be able to stand being in the water for any length of time. Bound and gagged as he was, the demon had very little to say about it. At least until he managed to spit out the gag. I should have used a bigger chunk of curtain.

"You can't stop us!" he screeched. "Our time has come! We'll take all the humans and then the Faerie will be next! We know you, Kane! We know you..."

Always with the delusions of grandeur, the incubi. Dangerous, yes, but generally far too disorganized to pose that kind of a threat. Annoying, though. Its gibbering ceased when we hit the thigh-deep water. It was cold, and the current was strong, but I'm pretty solid, so I managed to stand against the chill rush. I shut the Andy-demon up by plunging his head and torso under the water's surface. I held him down there for a long handful of seconds, then yanked him up. He sputtered furiously, gasped for air, then started screeching at me again in the demon's voice.

"Nope," I muttered, and held him under again. His body whipped and thrashed about like a man-sized salmon under my hands, but my grip was firm. Gradually, its struggles slowed. I thought about pulling him up, but figured it was better to be sure. I waited another half-minute, then was rewarded by an ugly yellow and red flash of light that blazed from within Andy's body, turning him into a human jack-o-lantern. "Gotcha, you asshole." I waited ten more seconds, then yanked Andy out of the water and dragged him up onto the concrete bank of the canal. His body hung limply in my arms, all the fight gone out of him along with the demon.

I slashed open the lengths of curtain and freed his limbs, then put my hands on his sternum. I leaned over and began pumping. His ribs cracked under my hands, and I eased up a bit so I wouldn't break them entirely but kept pumping. Just when I started thinking about where to hide the body, he finally convulsed, spewing water everywhere. He struggled to pull in a decent breath, only to cough it out again along with more water, then repeated the process. Hacking and sputtering, Andy pushed himself to a sitting position. I slapped him on the back a few times and remained silent while he gathered himself.

"Hey," I said as I touched his shoulder. "You OK, man?"

"What...in...the..." his face contorted with shock and pain as the results of the last several minutes registered. He clutched his chest in agony as he cleared his lungs and sat there, curled around his pain. When he groaned, I sent a touch of magick into him to lessen his discomfort. I needed some answers, and if he was worried about everything that was broken, I'd never get them. He sighed with relief and sagged back into the grass. "Who are you? Oh, man...what happened?" His eyes drifted to mine. They were a normal blue now, the pupils back to their usual size. The demon was gone, for certain.

"What do you remember?" I asked in return. I could get a lot from him if I went into his mind a little deeper, but he'd been through a lot. I figured I'd start easy.

He furrowed his brow as he thought. "I..." he began, "I was making a sandwich. In the kitchen." He looked around, taking in the drainage canal and the grass that surrounded us. "How did I get out here? Where's Lisa?" Concern edged into his voice as he started to realize that something big had happened.

I spoke in a soothing voice, hoping to keep him calm enough to give me a few answers. "You kind of lost it there for a bit. Went a little crazy. Did anything else happen, anything at all?" I was surprised that he didn't remember anything. I guess the demon had shoved him down deep.

His eyes flicked away from mine and I caught his embarrassment. He stared at his feet for a moment before confessing. "I...I tried a few pills a friend of mine gave me." His gaze returned to meet mine, his voice pleading. "He said it would help me focus and keep me awake. I needed it! My work is running me into the ground and the night classes I'm taking are killing me! I took the afternoon off so I could get some sleep, but I've got a report due in class tonight, so I...I tried the pills." He looked around, as if finally understanding that he was no longer in his apartment and was instead lying in the grass next to the canal. He slowly started to shake his head. "How did I get here? Where's Lisa?"

"She's fine, you just rest a minute," I said. "Who gave you the pills?"

He frowned for a moment, thinking. "I can't remember. But that's crazy, I just saw him yesterday! I know him! But I can't remember what he looks like. His name is...what is it? I can't think of that either. What's wrong with me?"

He was becoming more distressed, which wasn't going to help anything. "It's OK, just relax. It's all right, buddy, just rest." I encouraged him to lie back in the grass and sent a bigger dose of calming energy into him. His eyes closed and slumber claimed him. He was exhausted, not only from the weeks of living on so little sleep, but from the possession itself that had wrung him out like a dish rag. He'd hurt like hell when he eventually woke up, but he'd be alive, and without a demon giving orders to his body. I figure that's a win.

The sirens were almost on top of us, so I knew I needed to get moving. Leaving Andy asleep, I jumped the fence again and went to check on Lisa. The exhausted woman was still dozing where I'd left her, so I figured she'd be all right. I hopped up to the balcony and slipped into the apartment. The place was a wreck, but then,

12

dealing with demons was often a messy business. At least there were no entrails to clean up this time. Well, except for the cat.

I went into the kitchen and looked around but only saw the usual kitchen stuff. The apartment was a small one, only a bedroom and a living room, and I found what I wanted in the bathroom by the sink. A small amber pill bottle sat there. It was anonymous, having no label, although it looked pretty standard. I shifted my perception so that I could see in a different light and was taken aback by the play of energies that surrounded the remaining pills. An ugly glow surrounded the bottle, a sickly yellowish light streaked with red. Not good. These were no run of the mill uppers, no common stimulants to keep someone awake and help them focus. Someone had definitely used magick to make these, and with focused ill intent.

I picked up the bottle, twisted off the cap, and looked inside. To the naked eye, they looked like regular pills, oblong and beige colored. But the power that seethed around them was potent. I twisted the cap back on and turned to make my way out of the apartment.

The sound of feet pounding up the stairs outside and the voices of police officers reached me, and I knew the cops would be in the apartment in moments. Not wanting to deal with that kind of nonsense, I dimmed myself and bolted back out to the balcony. From there, it was another easy jump to the parking lot below. The police cars were there, red and blue lights flashing, but the few officers remaining looked right past me at another officer who was waking Lisa up. I dodged around one of the cars, jumped the fence yet again, then leaped over the rushing waters of the canal. I glanced at Andy as I went past, but he was still slumbering in the grass. He would awaken soon enough, and although I knew he would be beside himself when someone told him what he did, I didn't have time to help him with that. He and Lisa would have to deal with that on their own. I had more important things to do. It was surprising to me that the goddess hadn't given me a more specific vision regarding this incident, but then again, I was pretty sure she had suggested I park my butt on that bench in the first place. Mysterious ways and all that.

The pills rattled in my hand as I ran down the hike and bike trail towards my house. If there were more of these bottles around, that meant trouble, and a lot of it. If they somehow made the victim more susceptible to demon possession, that was going to get ugly in a hurry.

Although I could see and feel the magick in the pills, I could tell nothing of their origin. Fortunately for me, I knew someone who could. And I would bet a ton of money that she would be happy to help, especially if it meant she got to strap her guns on. Drugs of any kind were a rough business, and if the malevolent aura surrounding these pills was any indication, I might need her to bring extra ammo.

I reached the house and slipped in the back door. The landline, as Ariana had called it, was on the kitchen table with a pad and paper next to it. There was only one number written on the pad, as I'm not much of a talker. I picked up the handset and pushed the button that awakened it, and the dial tone erupted from the tiny speaker. If Ariana lived a little closer, I might have been able to reach her with my mind, but the distance to her house in the country was too far for me. I carefully punched out the numbers from the pad and waited for her to pick up, hoping she wasn't busy. Not that I cared. This was far more important than whatever she might have been up to.

"Kane?" her voice held a note of concern. "What's wrong? What happened?"

"What spell did you use to know it was me?" I was genuinely interested.

She laughed a little, "It's called Caller ID, you dummy. It tells me who's calling based on the phone number. I recognized yours."

I blinked at that. Technology was getting closer to magick all the time.

"I just yanked a demon out of some guy," I explained. "He had taken some pills, and I think they made it possible for the demon to get into him. I need you to figure out where the pills came from so we can stop them from making any more."

"Wow," she laughed again. "Magick pills, demons, and drug dealers, oh my. You sure know how to show a lady a good time."

I ignored her joke. "Are you at home?"

"Nope," she answered. "I'm actually in town. Had to pick up some stuff from Costco, but I just finished. Want me to swing by and pick you up? I'm in the Jeep."

That made me smile. Most of the time, Ariana zipped around town in a tiny little car, a mini Cooper. Occasionally, she broke out the fortified, souped up, anti-zombie Jeep she had inherited from an uncle. Against my better judgment, I liked it. It was a brutal and vicious machine, a weapon in its own right. I could relate.

"Yes, you know where I am."

"Be there in five," she said brightly and disconnected the call.

I pushed the button to send the phone back to sleep, set it back in its cradle, then sat down in one of the two kitchen chairs to wait. It seemed fortuitous that Ariana was already in town, just a few minutes away. Just as it seemed quite lucky that I had chosen to sit on that bench at that particular time. I shook my head again. Mysterious ways, indeed.

Chapter 3

"That's the third one this week, right?" Detective Jim Kaley asked as he jotted notes on his notepad. He still used the same battered little black notebook he'd had since he was a rookie, even though refills had become harder to find.

"Yep. Third one." The woman that knelt on the carpet was Jim's opposite in almost every way. Where he was tall and lanky, Detective Avery Lynne was a smidge over five feet tall and sturdily curved. He was slightly older at forty-six, his hair was thinning and blonde, while hers was jet black, cut in a stylish bob that hung an inch above her shoulders and swished when she turned her head. Jim favored cheap brown suits while she preferred to be more stylish on the job, though she favored men's slacks because of their useful pockets. The detective badge clipped to the left side of her belt glinted against the deep blue of her blouse, and a well-used 9mm rode on her right hip, its slim holster worn from daily use.

Avery examined the remains of the dead cat, and although her face was neutral, she was thoroughly disgusted. She had seen a lot in her time as a police officer, and even more as a detective, but stuff like this still managed to surprise her. She shook her head and stood. With a nod in the general direction of the suspect, Andy Dembrow, in the parking lot down below, she turned to Jim and asked, "How does he seem to you? Pretty normal, right? Just like the others."

"I don't know," Jim answered with a typical shrug of the shoulders. "What's normal these days? He seems like an ordinary guy, by the looks of it. Day job with heavy hours, going to school at night, lower-middle class apartment. Until we talk to his friends and family, we won't know if he was prone to this kind of thing." He raised an eyebrow at the bloodied carcass of the cat Avery had been examining. "Domestic violence, I mean. Something tells me that eating cats was not a usual thing for him, regardless."

"I have to agree with you on that one, Jim." Avery slowly scanned the room with eyes that shifted from grey to green depending on the light and her mood. Jim kept quiet. He had seen her do this before and knew better than to interrupt her. She took a deep breath, closed her eyes for a few seconds, and then opened them only to repeat the process. Her voice was quiet when next she spoke, as if she were speaking more to herself than to her partner. "There was a third person in here."

Jim nodded and jotted something in his notebook. He had seen no evidence of a third person in the room, but he knew Avery's tone. It didn't matter what he thought, when the forensics guys went over the room, they'd find evidence of a third person, no doubt about it. Even if they didn't, something would come up later to prove her correct. He never knew how she did it, but after three years as her partner, he knew to trust Avery's instincts implicitly. Beside him, she let out a huff of frustration

"This is weird. The door wasn't forced. It was locked when we got here. The only way in or out was through the sliding door on the balcony." She turned her intense gaze on the other detective. "We're four stories up, Jim. That's a hell of a jump."

"Well," Jim began, "you know these kids and their parkour these days. They do some pretty crazy stuff."

One side of Avery's mouth quirked up in a smile. "That's true, yes." She surveyed the extensive damage in the apartment and sighed. "Even so, why would some parkour-running kid jump up here and throw down with our guy? It doesn't make any sense. And the guy's story? Making a sandwich one minute, then waking up outside, soaked to the bone and beat to hell with no memory whatsoever of what happened? I've heard some wild ones before, but he believed every word."

Jim nodded. Again, he trusted Avery's assessment of the perp's story. It had been crazy and irrational, but Andy had believed it completely. Jim flipped back in his notebook and checked his notes. "I don't know what to think. He mentioned some pills, but there were no drugs stronger than ibuprofen, cough medicine, and some muscle relaxers in the medicine cabinet. Nothing in the trash, either. His story is flimsy as hell."

Avery looked around the room again and frowned. A stack of papers had been scattered across the kitchen table, and she walked over and glanced at them.

"Where was he going to school?"

Jim tugged at his faded brown tie to loosen it and flipped a couple of pages in his book to check his notes. "Houston Community College. Looks like he was working on an HVAC certificate." He looked up from his notepad. "Good money in that."

Avery laughed. "In Texas? You can say that again. If my air conditioning goes out, I can't call a repair guy fast enough." Her eyes wandered over the papers and something tugged at her attention. Scanning them more carefully, she noted that most of the assignments were for the same class. "You've got his work information?"

Another couple of page flips and Jim responded. "Affirmative. It's not far from here, actually."

Avery stared at the top corner of one of the papers, noting the instructor's name at the top. Something there was important, though as usual, she had no idea what. "Same for the college, but in the other direction." She frowned slightly, then asked, "Didn't one of the other guys work at Vitamin Shoppe?"

Jim flipped a few pages back. "Yep. Second one, Arturo Diaz. He was the manager, but he wasn't there when he freaked out. He was at home in Cinco Ranch."

Avery nodded, assessing the information. "Vitamin Shoppe is just around the corner from the college. That's just a few miles away from here. Let's check the school out first." She took out her phone and snapped a picture of a few of Andy's papers.

"You got one of your hunches?" Jim leaned over and copied down the same info, knowing that anything she captured would end up being important. One of the reasons he enjoyed working with Avery was the fact that her intuition was surprisingly accurate. Not only that, but they'd run into some tough scraps as a result of her ability to chase down a lead, and the smaller detective was fun to watch in a fight. Everyone underestimated her because of her build, her height, and the fact that she was a woman, but that always ended up being a mistake. Sometimes, he wished he had popcorn so he could better enjoy the show.

Avery shrugged. "Nothing so solid. Just filling in the details."

Jim closed his notepad and tucked it away. "Well, that's always how it starts. I'll drive."

"Like hell," Avery laughed.

"Please? You know I love to drive." Jim pleaded half-heartedly. It was a game they always played.

"You nearly killed us."

"That was a long time ago," Jim reasoned.

"Nope."

"You're no fun, and you know it," Jim elbowed her lightly as he ambled towards the door.

"More fun than you could handle, Jim," Avery quipped as she scanned the room one last time. "You're not my type, though." Something was nagging at her. It was that third person she felt in the room. Whoever he had been, he left a strong impression, so strong that it was rubbing up against her senses even now. It was dark, but not evil. She'd run up against some crazy stuff, but this...this was different. Not only that, she couldn't shake the faint sense of recognition she felt, as though she'd encountered it before. That intrigued her the most. She suddenly found herself hoping she could run him down, come face to face with him. Her heart fluttered at the thought, surprising her. *What is that?* she thought.

"Aw, Avery, don't be like that," Jim monotoned from where he now held the door open. "You know you're my one and only true love." He propped the door with his foot and pulled out his phone to check his messages while he waited for her.

Avery finally disengaged herself from the energy of the room. Something interesting was starting up. She could feel it. Shaking her head to clear it, she briskly headed out the door. "True love, huh? Get me some tacos and you might have a shot." She swept past him and headed outside.

Jim let the door shut behind him as he followed her, still staring at his phone. "I'll have to ask my wife. She says hello, by the way. And I'll only get tacos if I can drive."

Avery sighed dramatically. "Fine. You can drive, but get me tacos. I like the brisket ones with jalapenos and cheese."

Chapter 4

Ariana carefully twisted the top off the medicine bottle and shook the tiny brownish pills out onto a mat on her desk. The flat leather was inscribed with a pentacle, a five-pointed star enclosed in a circle and surrounded by elegant symbols. Using a pencil, she moved the pills into the center of the star, then looked them over. To the naked eye, they appeared to be ordinary ibuprofen pills, but Ariana had felt the sharp tingle of dark magick the moment she opened the bottle. When all of the pills were visible, she set the bottle aside and examined them closely.

"Wow, these were definitely created by someone with skills," she began. With a subtle gesture and a quiet murmuring of words, she infused the circle on the mat with her power, creating a small force field to enclose the tablets. When it was complete, she looked over her shoulder at me and shrugged. "Hey, you can't be too careful with stuff like this. If it turned your guy into a raving demon-loony, I don't know that I want to get too touchy-feely with these things."

I moved away from the wall where I had been leaning with my arms crossed. "No, you're right to be safe. Whatever else they can do, I know for a fact that they can render a body open to possession by a lesser demon, and those are pretty nasty. At best, they leave your body feeling like a hotel room after a fraternity party. I could get it out of you, but since there isn't a stream running nearby, it would be a lot more work."

"Gee, thanks," Ariana muttered dryly. "Your concern for my safety is almost overwhelming." She turned her attention back to the seemingly innocent pills. "OK, I'm pretty sure I can enchant a vessel to keep these in safely until you want to destroy them." She shook her head in frustration. "Beyond that, I can't really tell you very much. Their maker was pretty slick. I can't get a trace on them at all." She paused for a moment, then brightened, "That said, I can easily recognize the feel of this magick if I come across it again. We may not know where to start, but at least if we bump into it, I'll know."

I frowned and started my heavy thinking. My first inclination was to ask the Sprites to look around, but the last time I did that, they ended up getting hurt. I was reluctant to put them in that situation again. I could recognize the particular feel of the dark power that surrounded the tablets just as Ariana could, but I needed to know where to start.

Before I could say anything, Ariana spoke up again. "What happened to the guy that had the pills? After you left, I mean?"

I thought about that for a moment. "Sirens were approaching. I am sure your police have him by now."

"Hmmm. If anybody could get to him in jail to ask more questions, I'm pretty sure you could." Ariana knew well my ability to move undetected beneath the cloak of my magick. Unless someone knew exactly where to look when I held myself dim, they wouldn't see me.

"True, but I already questioned him. He didn't know anything. Whoever gave him the pills also clouded his memory. He couldn't recall who gave them to him or where, just that it was yesterday."

Ariana swiveled in her chair until she faced me directly. Her eyes were almost as blue as her aura, although probably no one knew that but me. "Well, where was he yesterday? Work? School?"

I thought about that before answering. "From what he said, he probably spent time at both. He mentioned the long hours. My guess is that it was someone he knew. It's doubtful he would've taken pills from some stranger."

Ariana stood and walked to the opposite corner of her conjuring room, to her other desk. The computer that sat there was much more impressive than the one that had been there when we had first met. The new machine, a black desktop with a stylized golden wolf's head logo on one side and red and green LEDs that pulsed like a heartbeat, was powerful enough to run something called the Death Star, according to Ariana. She flicked a switch, and the machine powered up with a deep, rumbling hum that I felt in my feet. The two enormous monitors flashed to life as she sat in the big chair, and Ariana tapped her password into the keyboard.

"What are you doing?" I asked. I've been around for centuries, but as much as I hate to admit it, computers are still something of a mystery to me. I can understand what Ariana shows me if she takes a minute to explain it, but the way she flits from screen to screen and travels the web eludes me.

"I'm looking up your boy, Andy, on Facebook. There's a good chance we can find both his work and his school there."

I had no idea what she was talking about, and I peered over her shoulder to watch. She quickly found a blue and gray screen and typed Andy's name into a little rectangle near the top. A list of Andy Dembrows came up with little pictures to the left of each listing. One of them showed the man I knew smiling next to the woman he had thrown off the balcony.

"There," I pointed at the image, "that's our guy."

Ariana clicked on the image and the screen changed to bring up a larger version of the small picture, and another picture of him standing next to a flashy car across the top. She moved the screen down a little bit, scanning the information that was there.

"Lucky for us, his profile is public, so we can see pretty much everything there." She pointed one finger at a section of the screen. "This says he works at Foster Brothers Manufacturing. That's on the west side of Katy, closer to where we are now. Hold on a sec," she said as she began to scroll down the screen. "There it is." She clicked somewhere on the screen and a large picture of Andy and another man appeared, the entrance to a building right behind them. "He was going to school at Houston Community College. That's not that far from your place, and his apartment." She turned around, folded her arms, and smirked at me. "And you're welcome."

I had to admit that she was good at ferreting out information. That had been a lot easier than canvassing the neighborhood for the next few nights. "Good work," I said simply. I saw her raise an eyebrow and tilt her head a little, but I saw no need to stroke her ego any more than that. "His work is closer, but we could probably ask around at the school more easily without arousing suspicion. Let's try that first."

"Cool," she said, shaking her head. "Let me get some things together, and I'll drive you."

"Perfect, thank you." Then I remembered what she had looked like the last time we had gone out together. She had worn black fatigues, a tactical vest, a backpack with an incredible array of equipment somehow stuffed inside, and two rather impressive handguns strapped to her thighs. As effective as she had been, I wasn't sure that would be necessary. Yet. "Hey, we're not going to assault the tower here. I know that your laws allow you to carry those guns of yours openly, but we are trying to keep a, how do you say, low-profile here."

Ariana turned to look over her shoulder and smiled extra-sweetly at me. "Don't worry, Kane, I wasn't about to go full Terminator. I just like to take a few things with me in case we run into trouble. Is that OK with you?"

I smiled. I was never good at sitting through movies, but for a change, I actually knew what she was talking about, and I approved. "All right, then. I'll meet you out front."

Chapter 5

Jim backed the car into a parking space so they faced the side doors of the college. Avery knew he liked parking beneath the sheltering limbs of trees whenever he could so the car wouldn't be scorching hot when they got back to it.

"I've been around here for years, and I don't think I've ever noticed that thing behind us," he said, craning his neck to peer over his shoulder at the silvery geodesic dome that sat forty yards behind them.

"It's part of the college," Avery said without taking her eyes from the side entrance to the building. Students were ambling in and out, chatting with each other or glued to their phones. "Horticultural studies. You know, plants and such."

"Ah," Jim said wisely. "That explains the carved wooden Horticulture sign next to it, as well as the abundance of shrubs and cacti surrounding the thing."

"You don't miss a trick, do you?" Avery's voice was still distant, but Jim paid little attention. She was looking around, taking in everything and committing the details to memory. She tended to drift when she did that.

"Hey, that's why you love me," Jim teased.

"You're killin' me, Jim," Avery sighed, garnering a chuckle from her partner. One corner of her mouth quirked up in a hint of a smile, but she kept her eyes on the college. More specifically, she watched the students. Something was nagging at her, but she was having trouble putting her finger on the source of her disquiet.

Most of them were young adults, likely not long out of high school, while a few were older, more mature. They were coming and going, all with backpacks or bookbags or notebooks in hand. Nothing should have aroused suspicion, but Avery had a feeling. Jim unbuckled his seat belt and reached for the door latch, but she quickly stilled him with a hand on his arm.

"Wait," she said. Her words were soft and somewhat faraway, but their tone froze Jim in place.

"You got something?"

"I don't know," came her soft reply. "Just...just wait."

Jim made sure his seatbelt was out of the way and the door was unlocked in case he had to move in a hurry. He also undid the snap on his shoulder holster, as Avery's hunches often preceded a situation. He scanned the entrance just as she did, knowing that whatever she was seeing, he was probably missing it. He stayed quiet and watched.

"There," she said suddenly, nodding at the doors. A moment later, a man exited the building and squinted in the sudden brightness before turning his eyes back to the phone in his hand. He seemed to be in his 50's, average height, and wiry. His hair was pale and thinning, and his silver-rimmed glasses glinted in the sunlight. He had a prominent nose, and a strong chin beneath it, though his ears seemed too small. He carried a slim briefcase of brown leather that nearly matched his pants, and he stopped walking just long enough to slip his phone into one of its outside pockets. As he started moving again, he reached up to loosen the knot of his dark blue tie, pulling it away from the collar of a white dress shirt that looked a bit too big for him.

Before Jim could say a word, Avery had already exited the car. Sighing in exasperation, he followed suit, knowing that his long legs would help close the gap between them, but only if he hurried. For a woman as short and sturdy as she was, Avery could hustle when she wanted to, and she already had a head start.

"Sir?" she called out as she crossed the parking lot towards the thin man. "Could you help us, please?" Her voice was sweet and innocent, completely harmless. Jim had seen it work for her many times before, but it only took an instant for him to know that this was not one of those times.

Before the last word left her lips, the man's head snapped towards Avery, his eyes narrowed and his body hunched for either flight or combat.

"You! I know who you are!" he hissed, glaring at Avery, who blinked in obvious surprise. "And you're not going to stop me, no way!" When she opened her mouth to protest, the man surprised her by turning away and sprinting for the far corner of the building, looking like a startled scarecrow but moving faster than Avery would have thought possible.

"Jim!" she yelled, but her partner was already sprinting after the man, his longer legs pumping as he tried to catch up.

"I've got him!" he huffed as he blew past her. Avery knew that Jim hit the treadmill just often enough that a chase wouldn't kill him, but he'd be feeling it for days. At a glance, she could see that he was too far behind the perp, and he'd not reach him in time. She had a few ideas of her own, though, and she burst into action as well.

The man slipped on the grass as he tried to make the corner but recovered quickly enough that he was back on his feet before Jim got close enough to grab him. He threw a look over his shoulder displaying wild eyes and an insane grin, nothing like the absent-minded professor he had seemed to be only moments before. "Stop! Police!" Jim yelled between wheezing breaths. A crazed cackle was the only response he got. Jim cursed as he struggled to keep up.

Moving with surprising dexterity, the man leaped over the walkway that led to the east entrance and began weaving through the round concrete tables and benches, surprising the few students who had spread out to enjoy the spring breezes. He was gaining speed, his tie flying over his shoulder like a pennant in the wind, and Jim was hard-pressed to stay close. Jim knew if the runner made the corner, he might make an escape. All he needed was a few moments out of sight and then he could be gone for good. Ignoring the burn in his legs and blinking sweat from his eyes, Jim tried to push harder, knowing that he was out of luck.

As the man reached the corner, a dark green Jeep came flying out of the unseen parking lot on the far side of the building and screeched to a stop in front of him. The fugitive slammed into the side of the vehicle and dropped the briefcase to the ground. He wobbled, but recovered quickly, then snatched up his case and bolted to his left. Ignoring a bloody nose, he sprinted away, leaving the Jeep idling in place.

"Stay there! Police!" Jim yelled at the driver, trying to keep his eyes on his target. He rounded the corner and saw the man racing down the parking lot, picking up speed. Despair washed over his face as he gauged the distance and knew he'd never make it. It seemed the man knew it too, as he turned and threw the detective the finger as he ran.

As he passed a van parked next to the north entrance, Avery slammed into him like a linebacker. Airborne, she drove her shoulder into his exposed ribs and knocked most of the wind out of him as she took him down. The rest came out in an explosive wheeze as Avery crushed his body into the pavement, and he gasped like a fish as he struggled to draw a breath. Blood oozed from the new holes in Avery's slacks where she had scraped her knees, and her palms were also abraded, but she felt no pain as she rolled him over on his face and pinned him with a knee in the small of his back. She efficiently yanked his hands behind him as she reached for her handcuffs, a faint smile appearing on her face.

She hadn't been sure that cutting through the building would get her across in time, just as she hadn't been certain their target would be close by once she emerged, but her gut had told her it was worth a shot. Once inside, she had to skirt the fountain and several students, but her instincts led her unerringly along the shortest path to the exit door. She had burst through it, skipped across the uneven steps, and honed in on the man's harsh laughter. She'd launched herself through the air before even seeing him. He hadn't had a chance.

"You have the right to remain silent," she began, silently adding, *you asshole.* The man struggled beneath her and managed to catch a pained breath, which he released with a moan of bewilderment and pain.

Jim staggered over to them and bent over, hands on knees, heaving for breath. "That," he began, pausing to suck in a few more lungfuls of air before continuing, "was beautiful." He swallowed as he began to recover. "I need to buy you tacos more often."

"Damn straight, you do," Avery muttered between lines of the Miranda warning. She finished informing the man on the ground of his rights. "Do you understand these rights as I have explained them to you?"

The man groaned, then stopped and began muttering something under his breath.

"What was that?" she snapped. He muttered again, a faint chuckle weaving its way into the quiet syllables that floated out of his thin mouth.

Avery tried to focus on the sounds...and then she blinked her eyes and realized that the man was gone. She was still on her knees, her handcuffs lying on the pavement before her. Puzzled, she turned, only to find Jim standing where he had been before. He was silent, his

30

eyes wide and unseeing, his mouth hanging slightly open. She lurched to her feet.

"Jim!" she exclaimed, alarmed. "Hey, Jim! What happened? Hey!" She slapped him lightly on the face, and he jerked as if he'd been startled awake from a nap.

"Wha...? What the hell?" He looked around, his eyes slowly coming into focus. "Where's the guy? What happened?"

Avery sighed heavily. "I was just asking you! I had him there, right there!" She pointed at the spot on the pavement at her feet. "Where could he have gone?"

Jim shook his head. "I don't feel right," he said, putting one hand up to his forehead. "Everything's fuzzy."

Cursing, Avery scooped up her handcuffs, holding them daintily. "Hey, you have one of those evidence bags on you?"

He patted himself down, a look of muddled concern still on his face. He reached into an inner pocket of his suit jacket and produced a plastic bag. He held it open and Avery dropped the cuffs inside.

"With any luck, we might get something." Even as she said it, Avery knew that would not be the case. Something strange had happened here.

Jim carefully sealed the bag, wrote on it, and tucked it back into a pocket. "Well, we can ask around inside, at least. Someone should know that guy. He looked like a regular. At least, before he went all cuckoo on us. Did you hear him cackling at me as he ran?"

"No, I missed that, sorry." Avery shook her head. "This whole thing feels very weird, Jim."

"And you're going to run it all the way down to the ground, aren't you?" Jim said as he pulled out a handkerchief to wipe the sweat from his face and neck. He was thoroughly unsurprised by her terse nod. "Thought so." He glanced at her hands and added, "Let's go get those scrapes cleaned up. I'd hate for them to get infected." Suddenly, he looked over his shoulder for a moment before turning back to her. "Damn," he muttered.

"What?" Avery followed his gaze, but saw nothing.

"A green Jeep pulled out in front of the guy. Fast, too." Avery's head snapped up. "He slammed into it. That's what sent him your way, I think. I told them to stay put, but they're gone now."

"A green Jeep?" Avery asked warily. Jim nodded. "Four door? Tough looking?" Jim nodded again.

"Yeah, I guess. Looked like it was ready to go zombie hunting, if you like that sort of thing."

A shock of cold ran through Avery's veins. Those kinds of vehicles were common enough in Texas, where folks either worked on a ranch and needed one or just wanted to be ready for the apocalypse. Something about the mention of that particular Jeep, though, pinged her deeply.

"You got another one of them feelings, dontcha?"

Avery looked down at the spot on the pavement where she had recently pinned a bad guy that had somehow vanished into thin air, and then in the direction of the Jeep Jim had seen.

"Yep," she declared. "I sure do."

Chapter 6

The muffled thumping from the small cargo area of the Jeep had finally stopped, but only because I went back there and bounced the guy's head off the floor hard enough to daze him. Then I used a bit of Faerie magick to ease him into dreamland. Trussing him up had been the easy part, thanks to the duffle bag full of what amounted to kidnapping supplies that Ariana kept in the back of the Jeep. She had it all: zip ties, handcuffs, rope, duct tape. You'd think she'd done this kind of thing before.

The hard part had been snatching the guy from underneath the noses of the cops and a few nearby students back at the college. Ariana had enspelled some of them while I handled the others. While I eased into their minds, sending them into a sorcerous pause that stretched a single moment into several, Ariana threw one of her own spells. There had been a burst of chanting and gesturing from her, and I caught a few old German words meaning *sleep*, and *wait*. Whatever spell she threw had worked beautifully, allowing us to drag the weirdo out from under the lady cop and into the Jeep. He hadn't been too thrilled about that, but neither of us really cared what he thought. He'd been casting his own spell as we approached, but a sharp kick to the head from Ariana had shut him up quite nicely.

He had been easy enough to identify the moment he slammed into the side of the Jeep. The stink of dark magick was all over him, and it had the same feel as the pills; oily, slimy, and ill. He'd already drawn the attention of the police, judging by the gangly guy with the badge clipped to his belt that was struggling to catch him, so we figured the best plan was to grab him ourselves. If we were lucky, we could get some answers out of him, make him forget he'd seen us, then kick him back to the cops. I had the sense that he wasn't the source of it all, but I couldn't tell you what made me feel that way, aside from the fact that it had been too easy to catch the guy.

We were making progress, which was all well and good, but what really had me preoccupied was the woman who had tackled our guy. She was...unusual. I had felt it the moment she had exploded out that door and into the perp, a tingling sensation deep inside me, a recognition of an energy that echoed something in my own. She was human for sure. But she was something more, besides. I thought about her grey-green eyes. Even unfocused as they had been under the influence of Ariana's hastily thrown spell, there had been something in them that kept tugging at me. I'd been so distracted, both by her and by the bad guy, I hadn't bothered to see what her aura looked like. I shook my head, disgusted with myself. Not like me to miss something like that.

"You think he'll tell us what we need to know?" Ariana's voice interrupted my train of thought, and I flashed back to the present. We were only a few miles from her house, and then we'd get answers one way or another. I caught her eyeing me somewhat warily.

"I can rip it from his mind if I have to," I said evenly. "I just don't care for that. Going that deeply into human minds, especially the ones who dabble in dark magick, isn't my favorite thing to do." There were dangers there, and she knew it. She turned her eyes back to the road but stayed silent. "What?" I asked.

"What's with that cop?" she replied, her voice flat. "You stared at her, like, forever."

"Barely a moment," I corrected.

"But you acknowledge that you were staring," she replied quickly, as though she'd caught me. "Do you know her?"

I turned my eyes to the road ahead as well. "I do not."

She waited for me to elaborate, which I of course refused to do. I didn't know anything about the woman anyway, just that she was more than she seemed. Finally, Ariana sighed and flipped on the radio, filling the air with what she thought of as music. Some of it was kind of catchy, but I still found it tedious.

We turned down the narrow road that led to her property. I always enjoyed that part, rolling down a tunnel of tall, sheltering trees. It reminded me of home. A few minutes later, we pulled into the repurposed barn that served as her garage. The huge farmhouse with a wraparound porch, barn, and a couple of smaller buildings sat in a clearing in the center of over a hundred acres of forest. That forest was an island in the middle of encroaching civilization. Houston had already swallowed up Katy and was heading west at a ravenous pace, chewing up all the green space as it went. It wouldn't touch us here, though. The land had been in Ariana's family for generations, since the 1800s, and although there had been many offers for the property, Ariana had no intention of leaving.

The barn we pulled into had long ago been renovated, some of its stalls closed off and made into storage rooms, but it still retained the smell and feel of a barn. Old traces of horses and hay lingered, and the scent was comforting to me. Ariana keyed off the engine and slipped out the driver side door without a word to me. Fine. We had a job to do anyway. I followed suit and came around to the back of the Jeep.

"Do you want to do the honors?" Ariana gestured to the Jeep with a little smirk, some of her good humor returning.

"No, you open it," I said. "I'll grab him and take him into the house."

"Oh, hell no!" Ariana laughed. "I'm not letting this crazy into my house!" I must have looked confused, because she pointed at one of the stalls that had been closed off. "Just drag him in there. I've got a summoning circle on the floor that will keep him from causing too much trouble." Then she shrugged and pulled a gun from somewhere. I had no idea where she had been keeping it, her shorts and tank top not exactly the best places to conceal a hand cannon, but she managed. She racked a shell into the chamber, flipped on the safety, and continued, "Of course, I have my gun, so I can just shoot him if he acts up." With a deft movement, she replaced the gun in the small of her back so that her hands were free once more.

I grinned before I could help myself. That was more like the Ariana I knew. "Good enough, then. I think between the two of us, we can handle this guy." I nodded towards the tailgate of the Jeep. "If you please?"

She took a step back and pulled her keys out of her pocket, and I heard the mechanism unlock as she pushed a button on the fob. She put the keys away before opening the back window of the Jeep, then she pulled the latch on the horizontal tailgate and opened it up. I half expected him to leap out at us because that's just how my luck usually runs, but he stayed quiet. Honestly, I was almost disappointed to see him still lying there, unconscious.

"He doesn't look too dangerous, does he now?" Ariana muttered as she reached in and grabbed his ankles, while I grabbed him by the upper arms.

That's when my usual luck came back in full force. His eyes snapped open, wild and wide, and his high-pitched scream was muffled by the gag. He lurched forward with far more strength than he should have possessed and head-butted me squarely in the face. Everything went white for an instant, and I fell backwards as I struggled to regain my composure. Dammit, that hurt.

36

I heard Ariana yelling next to me, and the scuffling sounds of combat followed by a grunt of impact as something hit her. I shook my head to clear it, and when my eyes focused again, I saw Ariana on the ground, unmoving. Our crazy had managed to get his arms free and gotten in a lucky shot to complement the one he'd laid on me a few seconds ago. He was frantically fighting the tape on his ankles, and I was glad we had taken time to bind them.

I snarled in anger and leaped, grabbing him by shirt and belt. He slapped and scratched at me as I yanked him out of the vehicle, but I paid it no attention. I was ready for him. I pressed him up over my head, and then simply slammed his body down on the dirt floor of the barn. I didn't want to kill him. Well, that's not entirely true, but I knew it wasn't a good idea, so I held back quite a bit. Even so, the impact stunned him again, and the crazed light went out of his eyes as unconsciousness reclaimed him. When I was sure he wasn't going to jump up and attack me again, I sighed in frustration and snatched a roll of black duct tape from the back of the Jeep. By the time I was finished, I had our guy's arms completely taped to his sides, and his legs similarly mummified for good measure. He was going nowhere.

"Dammit," Ariana mumbled from behind me. She was already sitting up, holding her head with one hand, her face crumpled up in pain. "That was embarrassing. He was faster than I expected, smacked me upside my head before I knew it."

"Sometimes that happens," I said matter-of-factly. "He snuck a good one in on me too." I felt the bones in my face arranging themselves back into position with subtle pops. I heal quickly. Being Faerie certainly has its advantages. Even so, it hurt. "You all right?"

She had already pushed herself to her feet and began to brush the dirt from herself. "Yeah, yeah," she

37

replied, annoyance thick in her voice. "I'll be fine. Let's get this guy into the circle and get some answers. I'm thoroughly pissed off now."

"That makes two of us," I mumbled as I grabbed one of the guy's ankles and started dragging him towards the room she had indicated earlier.

The room was small, only the size of the horse stall it had once been. Sheetrock walls had been added and the floor was wood instead of hard-packed earth, otherwise the room was empty. A summoning circle, somewhat less ornate than the one in Ariana's conjuring room, had been inlaid into the floor. It consisted of a length of tightly braided copper wire, pressed into the floorboards in a perfect circle, a pentacle of the same metal carefully enclosed within. I had to hand it to her, Ariana was a girl who liked to be prepared. She brought in a chair and we propped our guy up in it in the center of the circle. After some consideration, we threw a few more loops of duct tape around his mummified body to secure him there. Our guard was up, but there was no sense in taking any chances. He had slowly recovered from his "fall", and by the time we settled in our own chairs, he was glaring rather angrily at us. Ariana removed his gag, and though we expected him to start throwing crazy at us right away, this time, he remained silent.

"Who are you?" I began. I figured we should start with the simple stuff. His mouth remained tightly shut. I sighed, then employed a simple bit of magick, a light glamour, in the hopes it would get him talking. I gestured, a simple flick of my fingers to help me focus my energy in the right direction, and cast the spell. The effect was immediate. His eyes flew even wider than they had been, and he began frantically looking left and right. I allowed myself a faint smile as his fear began to override his desire to frustrate us.

What did you do? Ariana's voice echoed in my mind, fascinated. Being able to communicate without speaking came in handy for us more often than one would think.

Not much, I explained. *I just made him think he's gone blind.* The man's breathing became more frantic as his eyes darted around the room, unseeing. He started to panic, and began to whimper. I let him squirm a moment longer, then let the glamour fall away with a loud snap of my fingers so he would understand that I was in control. He blinked rapidly for a couple of seconds and then narrowed his eyes as he focused on me. Good. Now I had his attention.

"Let's try something else, then. Tell me about the pills," I asked. I kept my voice quiet, but let a lot of menace slip into the words. He felt it, and I saw him flinch, though he kept glaring at me. He clamped his lips shut and stayed silent.

"I can shoot him in the knee," Ariana proposed, somewhat loudly. She was pissed, but I knew she'd do no such thing until we figured out if the guy was a true villain or instead, just a hired gun of some kind. The guy's eyes flicked towards her warily, then back to me. He seemed to be calculating whether or not she was kidding.

"That won't be necessary...if he talks." I hoped he would make this easy for us and just tell us what we wanted to know. After so many centuries, you'd think I'd know better. Although he did start talking, it wasn't anything I wanted to hear. He started mumbling under his breath, and a steely glint came into his eyes. He was casting a spell. "Ariana!" I warned.

She was already on it. Casting a circle was a simple affair for someone like Ariana, who'd been training in the use of magick since she was a little girl. Magick is all around us. It's like electricity, except it doesn't need wires to move around. It's in everything, the air, the earth, the water, us. It's a natural thing, and it's immensely, unimaginably powerful. It takes years of training and discipline to manipulate it even a little bit, though some beings have an easier time of it than others. Some humans have a greater aptitude for it, though not many are worth worrying about. Goosebumps, hunches, premonitions, they're all part of it, and almost everyone can feel it to at least a tiny degree. For true witches like Ariana, people who combine natural ability with arduous training, magick becomes a potent tool. It's still a lot of work to use well, but the effects can be impressive.

Casting a circle is a way of focusing or containing energy. The circle is actually created from the caster's will and doesn't technically have to exist anywhere but their mind. However, it takes an enormous amount of discipline and focus to pull that off. I can do it, but I seldom resorted to casting circles, preferring more down and dirty endeavors. Ariana could do it too, but it's always easier to have a physical circle to work from, even one as simple as something drawn in the dirt with a stick. Sending energy into the circle creates a boundary, a barrier, an invisible dome of energy that can keep bad things out, or as in this case, keep them in. The moment Mr. Crazytown started mumbling, she gathered her will and slapped a hand down on the floor, fingers touching the copper wire that surrounded him. She poured energy into the circle, and I felt the barrier spring to life around him, enclosing him within a buzzing field of power.

He felt it too. He glanced around himself, realizing the futility of the spell he'd been about to cast, and fell silent again. He scowled at us for a moment, then grinned.

"I can't get you from in here," he growled, "but you can't get me either. Not without breaking the circle."

"Wanna bet?" Ariana held up her gun pointedly. "A bullet will break the circle, yes, but it'll shut you up long before you can throw anything our way. I'm a damned good shot, I've got a headache, and my patience is wearing thin."

His smile slowly faded and he stared at her appraisingly. He rightly judged her as being serious, then looked to me as if for help. I smiled, letting my human disguise fall away just enough for him to see my fangs and my eyes. That finally did it. He shrank away from us in his chair, his eyes growing wide with fear. "You're a Grim!" His voice was high-pitched and shaky.

"I am." I confirmed with a nod. "And you're currently on my shit list." I paused, then inclined my head towards Ariana and added, "You're definitely on hers."

He almost looked pitiful just then. For all the trouble he'd given us, his fear made him look like the scrawny, aging professor that he probably was, rather than some dangerous, demon-mongering bad guy. Even so, the fact remained that he was exactly that. "Let's try again. Tell me about the pills." He looked away from me, obviously terrified. It was nice to be respected.

"I can't say," he offered. Not helpful. Ariana snorted, and I rolled my eyes.

"You might want to try. We're not terribly patient just now." Ariana ejected the magazine of her handgun and made a show of checking the number of rounds inside before reinserting it. "Who are you?"

His eyes darted around a moment longer, then he sagged into the chair, defeated. In a thin, wavering voice, he said, "Raymond. Raymond Clark."

I nodded. "That's a good start. Now what's with the pills?"

He hesitated for only a moment before he got going. "They're an experiment. Something I've been working on for a while." He shook his head, "It took weeks to get it right. I hardly slept! The rituals are so complicated, and the ingredients nearly impossible to get.

Some of the mistakes I made in the beginning nearly killed me..." He cut his eyes towards me with a hint of triumph. "But in the end, I think I got it right!"

I just stared at him and said nothing. He held my gaze for a few moments, but when I remained silent, he faltered and lowered his eyes again. I let the silence stretch to build the tension, then I asked simply, "Why?"

Raymond started to shake his head, and Ariana thumbed the hammer back on her automatic. His eyes flicked to her and fear crawled back onto his face. "I...I can't tell you," he repeated, almost pleading now. "She'll kill me if I say anything." He paused, realizing what he'd just said, and all the color left his face.

Ariana picked up on it immediately. "She?" she said. "Your boss is a woman?"

Raymond clamped his lips together and shook his head, making Ariana roll her eyes. I waited a beat, then spoke up. "You need to tell us everything, Raymond. Tell us who she is and what she's up to. We might let you live. I'm not terribly inclined to do so," I watched him cringe a moment before continuing, "but we might work something out."

"No," he whined, "no, I can't do that." He stared at me, pleading. I dropped the rest of my glamour so he could get a good look at my true self. I did it quickly so Ariana wouldn't see, and was rewarded with a frightened gasp from Raymond. Ariana's eyes flicked my way but I already had the illusion back in place. Now shaking in terror, Raymond started sputtering. "Look, she told me what she wanted me to do, gave me a ton of money, and I did it. That's it. The last test is complete. I'm supposed to give her the rest of the pills tomorrow." He hung his head, defeated. "She warned me against *her*, but didn't say anything about a damned Grim!"

"What?" Ariana interjected, "You were warned about me?"

42

"No! The other one!" he stammered, "The one that found me."

Ariana and I glanced at each other and found no answers. *Do you have any idea who he's talking about?* Then insight struck her, as it occasionally does. She is a witch, after all. Her eyes widened and she thought loudly at me, *I bet he means that cop you were staring at.*

I thought about that. There had been something about the woman that had struck me...something unusual. Had we not been in such a rush to get Raymond tucked away in the Jeep, I'd have figured out what it was. If she was some kind of witch, specialist, or half-breed, that would make sense. Furthermore, if she was any of those things, it would figure that she might be involved in some way. Careful to keep my thoughts neutral, I silently replied, *It's possible. I did sense something from her, but we were in a hurry, and we left before I could figure it out.*

Ariana nodded, a slight frown creasing the space between her brows. She turned her attention back to Raymond, who was becoming increasingly agitated.

"You need to let me go! I've told you what I can; release me! If I don't report to her soon, she'll make me suffer. She said so!" He struggled against the tape, not getting anywhere.

"Tell us where we can find your boss. Whatever she's doing, we need to stop it." Ariana was leaning forward in her seat, intent on squeezing as much information out of the wizened little man as she could. "What's her name? Where can we find her? *We'll* make you suffer more than she will, I guarantee it!" she bluffed.

"You don't understand! You can't stop her! She's more powerful than..." The little man froze in place, going completely still. We tensed, waiting to see what he was up to, but he remained motionless, his eyes fixed and unblinking.

"Kane?" Ariana whispered, with a glance at me. "What's he doing?" I didn't have an answer for her. Then Raymond started to shake, his whole body vibrating hard enough to make the chair beneath him tremble and rattle. Ariana started to her feet and reached forward, intending to break the circle to get to him.

I lashed out and grabbed her arm, yanking her back down to her chair. "Reinforce the circle," I urged in a tight voice. "Now!" To her credit, she didn't argue this time, she simply trusted me and did as I suggested. I felt the tingle of her magick on the air as she willed more power into the protective circle that surrounded Raymond. The dome-shaped barrier between us became visible as she strengthened it, a wavering haze of energy that enclosed our captive within.

Raymond managed a pained groan before his body erupted into an inferno of intense flames that completely filled the space within the circle, a ferocious blast of fire that looked as though hell had arrived to consume his body. The heat was nearly unbearable, and I saw Ariana lurch to her feet with her hands before her, chanting frantically as she attempted to maintain control of the circle, struggling to contain the blaze.

The conflagration surged like a thing alive for about ten seconds, and then just as suddenly as it had appeared, it was gone. Ariana held the circle for a few moments longer just to be sure it was safe, then she lowered her hands, stepped forward, and broke the circle with the toe of her boot. It dissipated with a pop, the smells of burnt wood and melted plastic, along with the awful stench of incinerated flesh, spread throughout the room. Where Raymond had been just moments before, there now sat a mound of ash and the misshapen remains of his chair in an unrecognizable pile. Ariana stood still for a few seconds, then turned and walked out of the room. Moments later, I heard the sounds of her retching as she

44

spewed the contents of her stomach into the dirt outside. Yeah, the smell was pretty gross, and I wrinkled my nose at it as well. I'd smelled worse, though. I shook my head and sighed. It seemed like we had another heavy hitter to deal with. She must have set him up with a self-destruct spell of some kind, and a powerful one at that. Not easy to do, not easy at all. You had to have major skill as a magickal practitioner, not to mention a marked lack of morality, to pull something like that off. As I stood there, staring at the scorched floor and remains of the little wizard, a smile crept onto my face before I could stop it.

Looks like this might turn out to be fun! I thought. I picked up the late Raymond Clark's leather satchel from where I had set it on the floor. I flipped it open and found a couple of binders full of reference materials on some kind of machines, and folders filled with graded papers, the obvious supplies of a college professor. I dug deeper and found a small handful of envelopes, all opened but neatly tucked together in a bundle.

Ariana reentered the room with a disgusted sigh. "Sorry. That caught me off guard." She wrinkled up her nose. "Gaah…yeah, that's bad. I almost feel sorry for the guy." She saw what I'd fished out of the briefcase and her face brightened. "Whatcha find? Is that his mail?"

"I think so. That's his name on the front." I handed the thin sheaf of envelopes over to her and she flipped through it, scanning each before slipping it to the back of the stack.

"Yup. His address is right there, not far from the college. If that's his place, we should go check it out."

I stood up and nodded. "I agree. That's probably where he set up shop. I'm sure we could find something that might lead us to whomever he was talking about. The woman. The one who did *that* to him." I allowed myself a flash of anger. "And maybe we can do *that* to her, as well."

Chapter 7

It had taken the better part of the afternoon to ask around at the college, and after gathering all the pertinent information on Mr. Raymond Clark, Avery and Jim found themselves standing outside a little house barely a mile from the school. It was a quiet, older neighborhood, shaded by wise, majestic trees, and situated around a long empty field of grass that needed mowing. Jim looked at his notepad and checked the number on the house.

"1307 Windy Knoll," he confirmed. He folded the pad and tucked it into his jacket pocket. "This is it. Should we call for backup, do you think?" He patted his holstered automatic absently, wondering if he'd need it.

Avery's eyes scanned the front of the house. It sat on a wedge of land at a corner of the subdivision, so she guessed the back yard would be much larger than the narrow garage they could see in front. "No, he's not here," she said, her words solid with authority. "I don't know where he went after I lost him, but he's not inside."

"After *we* lost him," Jim amended for her, and Avery felt a surge of affection for her partner. He knew she was taking it hard. She'd had him completely under control, bought and paid for with skinned knees, hands, and elbows, and then...gone. Of course, she blamed herself, but Jim was having none of that. "I was right there with you, don't forget."

Avery sighed and cast an embarrassed but grateful glance at her partner. "Yeah, you were. Thanks." She looked back at the house. "Let's head in." She was moving before Jim could reply, and he lurched forward to catch up with her, just as he always did. They walked up the driveway and around to their right. The front porch was mostly hidden from the street by the branches of a shade tree, a fact which made both of them wary. Although

Avery seemed certain enough that no one was inside, Jim pulled his gun anyway, holding it down low, just in case.

Avery took up her station on one side of the door as Jim did the same opposite her. She pulled her own handgun, steeled herself for whatever might come, then reached up and rapped on the door a couple of times. "Raymond Clark!" she called. "Police! Come on out with your hands where I can see them!"

There was no response from within, and she repeated the process once more with the same result. Then she cocked her head to one side, as if listening.

"You hear that?" she asked.

Jim hadn't heard a thing, but he knew where this was going. "What, like someone calling for help?"

"Exactly. Probable cause. That means we have to check it out."

With a nod to Jim, who readied his gun, Avery turned the knob and pushed open the door. Jim slid inside with practiced ease that belied his lazy appearance. Avery rolled around the corner in his wake, both of them holding their guns at the ready as they entered a quaint living room.

It only took a few minutes to clear the main part of the house, as it wasn't large. The kitchen was orderly and somewhat austere, lacking decorations of any kind. Two of the bedrooms were empty, save a few boxes in one and a lonely desk in another. The master bedroom was simply furnished, its queen-sized bed left unmade, its attached bathroom unoccupied and decidedly ordinary-looking. An old Subaru sat quietly in the garage next to stacks of boxes and a mismatched washer and dryer. One door remained, and Avery and Jim sidled up to it.

"What's this, do you think?" Avery asked in a hushed voice.

"I would think it's a door to the back yard...maybe a covered patio or a sunroom?" He nodded to the windows on either side of the door, both neatly boarded up from outside. "See? Back porch, probably. But I don't like how it's boarded up that way."

Avery nodded and reached for the knob. Then she hesitated, her fingers frozen a few inches from the cold metal. They had begun to tingle, and not in a good way. She pulled her hand back a few inches and the sensation vanished. She tried again only to have her fingers prickle painfully before she even touched the knob.

"What's wrong?" Jim whispered.

"I'm not sure," Avery began, "something is definitely off, though. Give me a sec."

Jim frowned, looking very concerned. "What, is there a bomb?"

Avery immediately shook her head. "No, I don't think it's a bomb, but something bad will happen if we open this door without..."

Jim waited, but when Avery didn't respond, he prompted, "Without what, exactly?"

She remained silent as she listened to her intuition. It had yet to fail her, but although it often gave her surprising insight, it sometimes took her a while to understand the signals she was getting. Finally, she reached up with her left hand and ran her fingertips along the top of the door frame. A key had been hidden there, and her fingers tingled as they touched it. The sensation was different from that of the doorknob, but it also felt right, somehow. It felt safe. She pulled it down and held it up so that Jim could see it, then she slowly moved it toward the keyhole. The instant the key touched the metal of the lock, the tingling disappeared completely, and Avery let out a sigh of relief. Whatever danger had existed before had been nullified with the use of the key.

"It's safe now," she whispered, "but let's take this slowly." Jim nodded and held his gun at the ready while Avery turned the knob and gently pushed open the door.

She carefully reached a hand inside and flipped the light switch so they could see into the room beyond.

"Sweet baby monkeys..." Jim breathed in astonishment as he took in the sight. Then he snorted as the sharp smell of incense, herbs, and chemicals assaulted him.

A room had, indeed, been added where a porch used to be. It was about twenty feet square and had no windows. Another door on the far wall led to the back yard, and the otherwise plain walls were covered in corkboards. Papers and drawings were held up with pushpins, all arranged very neatly on the boards. A large desk sat in the corner to their left, a computer workstation with two large monitors that showed a beautiful forest scene as a screensaver. A small sink and countertop had been installed next to the desk, and the far wall also contained a similar workspace, covered in an elaborate array of vials and beakers in a rack that practically screamed 'mad scientist'. Shelves above and below the counter held carefully labeled bottles of various substances; some were liquid, some powdered, and some appeared to be natural herbs.

To the right of the door sat another small desk with several books piled on its surface. Some were new, but battered, and others were very large and old-looking, covered in cracked leather.

The most interesting feature of the room, though, was the corner to their far right. It was empty of furniture, but the wooden floor had been painted black. A pentacle had been embedded in the planks, a five-pointed star inscribed within a circle, all wrought with thick golden wire. Other symbols surrounded the circle, but they were nothing either detective had seen before. Avery gestured towards the circle, "Don't step there."

"Are you kidding?" Jim said, his eyes wide, "I wouldn't step in there if you paid me. I tried to play with a

Ouija board one time, and my mama slapped the hell out of me. I'm going nowhere near that thing."

Moving carefully, Jim crossed the room and unlocked the back door. He opened it, looked around to confirm that it led outside, and then closed it again. "Yep. Looks like a pretty ordinary yard. Needs mowing though. There doesn't seem to be a shed or anything out there, but we can still look around if you think we need to."

Avery stood at the computer, staring at one of the monitors. Moving deliberately, she holstered her gun and snapped on a pair of rubber gloves. She gently pressed the Enter key on the keyboard, and the password box appeared on one of the screens. She let her eyes go out of focus for a few moments, then she pecked in a series of letters and hit Enter again. The Password Denied box appeared, and she cleared it. She tried again and got the same result. On the third try, the screensavers vanished and an orderly desktop came up on one of the screens.

Jim shook his head as he holstered his gun. "How do you *do* that?"

"Just lucky, I guess," Avery muttered as she scanned the folders that were visible on the desktop. There were five of them, each simply numbered one through five. Not very helpful.

"I wouldn't open those," a feminine voice came from just outside the doorway. "And whatever you do, don't read anything you find on there out loud. That would be bad."

Avery and Jim whirled, guns out, but no one was visible in the doorway.

"Step out where we can see you, hands in the air!" Avery yelled, her voice firm with authority. Jim slipped over to put his back to the wall on the far side of the door, preparing to charge through it while Avery covered him.

"Look, we're here to help," the voice replied. "You're stepping into something that is way over your

50

heads. The best thing you can do is just walk away and let us handle it. This stuff is right up our alley. Seriously." There was a pause, and then she continued, "This is far more dangerous for you than you realize."

Jim glanced at Avery and nodded, then he rolled around the corner and disappeared into the hall beyond as he confronted the newcomer. He started to yell for the unseen stranger to put her hands up and get down on her knees, but there was a loud slap, a couple of thumps, and some grunting, and Jim reappeared in the doorway, scooting backwards on his butt. He scuttled back into the room like a wounded crab, his face contorted with pain. As soon as he was safely inside the room, he lay down on his side and groaned as he clutched his groin. Avery stared at him in disbelief.

"Where's your gun?" she asked tightly.

A whistle from the hallway brought her attention back to the open door, where a feminine hand daintily dangled his Glock. "You mean this?" Avery blinked in surprise and took aim at the wall, about to send a few rounds through it in an attempt to hit the unseen person beyond. The voice urgently spoke again as Avery's finger curled on the trigger, "Hold your fire please! Look, I'm giving it back. See?" The hand slowly placed the gun on the floor, then it was joined by another hand, fingers spread and palms facing Avery. "I'm going to step into the doorway," the voice warned. "As you can see, I do *not* have anything in my hands. We need to talk. I'm an expert on this stuff, and I'm trying to keep you from hurting yourself."

Avery's eyes narrowed, and she kept her gun trained on the doorway. She hesitated briefly, then followed her instincts. "All right. Step slowly into the doorway, and no sudden moves." The blonde woman that appeared almost made her gasp, but not because of the tactical vest and handguns she wore. Instead, a powerful feeling of recognition struck her. This woman was dangerous, but even though she had apparently dropped Jim like a bad habit, Avery felt no ill intent from her. Every fiber of her being was quickly telling her to trust this person. Nevertheless, she kept her gun aimed at the newcomer's center of mass. "Who are you? Start talking."

"My name is Ariana," she began, speaking carefully and evenly, "and it will take a few minutes to bring you up to speed. I doubt you will believe it all, but Kane says we should give you a chance." She leaned into the doorway slightly and glanced down at Jim, who was still curled in a fetal position on the floor. "Hey, sorry about the nut shot. No hard feelings, right?"

Jim groaned in response but did not get up. He did manage to extend his middle finger in greeting.

Ariana shook her head and smiled, unruffled. "Yeah, I don't blame you. I hear that hurts a lot. Here," she gently nudged his gun closer to him with her foot, being careful not to move too quickly. He reached over to claim it, then struggled to a seated position. He racked the slide to be sure a round was in the chamber, expelling the previous round, confirming that she had not tampered with it before returning it. Once assured it was in working order, he trained it on her and struggled to his feet. "You've got your gun back, and I'm sorry I threw a knee into your nuts. Now that's settled, can we all be friends?" Ariana said hopefully.

"Fat chance, missy," Jim growled. "Get in here and lie down on the floor, fingers laced behind your head."

"No, wait," Avery interrupted. Jim turned astonished eyes towards his partner, only to widen them further as he watched her holster her sidearm. "She's OK. I think we can trust her."

Keeping his gun on Ariana, Jim hissed, "Have you lost your *mind*? She's armed to the teeth, and in case you hadn't noticed, she assaulted a police officer! I'm not gonna walk right for a week!"

Ariana spoke up, "Hey, I said I was sorry! You came around that corner like Rambo! What's a girl supposed to do?" The slightest of grins touched Ariana's mouth.

In spite of her concern for her partner, Avery grinned a little as well. She put a gentle hand on Jim's arm, and he slowly lowered his gun. She whispered, "I've got a hunch."

Jim looked deeply into his partner's grey-green eyes, then looked back at the newcomer, his face still hard. Then he sighed, holstered his gun, and relaxed. Folding his arms, he muttered, "All right. But you are definitely taking the heat on this one if something goes wonky."

To Jim, she conceded, "Agreed. I'll take responsibility." To Ariana, she said, "All right, Ariana, tell us again who you are and what you're doing here." Suddenly she remembered something Ariana had said. "And who is Kane?"

A low, rumbling voice crawled up Avery's spine, raising gooseflesh along every inch of it.

"I am."

The owner of the voice stepped through the doorway and Avery gasped in shock and took a half-step back. She had trouble speaking for a moment, but finally found her voice, shaky though it was. "It's...it's you!"

Her gun was back in her hand in an instant.

Chapter 8

After cleaning up the remains of Raymond Clark, we gathered our wits and drove to the address on his mail. Twilight had arrived, making me feel more at home as darkness approached. Ariana followed the disembodied voice issuing forth from her GPS system and we found ourselves in an older neighborhood in Katy, north of the freeway and only a little way from the campus where we had snatched Raymond from under the noses of the police. We stowed the Jeep at a park at the center of the old subdivision and got out. She pointed her keychain at it, and it made a sharp chirping sound as she armed its security system. She could have used her magick to set a more interesting snare for would-be thieves, and I said as much, but she just gave me one of her looks in response. No harm done; I'd grown used to them.

"The house is down at the end of the street, at the corner," Ariana informed me with a gesture toward the homes south of us. "Are you getting anything yet?"

I shifted my sight to detect the auras of life and magick more clearly, and found the house right away. The physical structure wasn't quite visible from our vantage point, but I spotted a bloody yellowish radiance over the treetops the way you might see the lights at a baseball field at night from a distance.

"Yes, it's definitely where Raymond did his dirty work. Let's go."

"Hey, hold on," Ariana said, touching my arm to keep me from leaving. "I know it's Texas and all, but I'm a little conspicuous out here." She gestured to herself, clad in a black tactical vest, a semi-automatic pistol strapped to each thigh, and a backpack loaded with witchy goodies. She had a black baseball hat on, her long, blonde ponytail sticking out the back, and I knew there were several knives secretly stashed in her clothing. "A little help?"

I smiled as I focused my will, waggled my fingers for effect, and cast a spell to adjust her appearance. Ariana's SWAT team look wavered and shifted, then suddenly, she was wearing a flimsy sundress that left little to the imagination. Her lithe muscles moved smoothly under her tanned skin, and although built for speed rather than softness, even I thought she looked quite fetching that way. She looked down at herself and squeaked in horror, then gave me another hard look. "All right, just a moment," I surrendered. Another waggle of fingers and the sundress became a pair of casual shorts and a pale blue t-shirt, an outfit I had seen her wear on occasion.

She looked down at herself again, and the change apparently satisfied her. "Wiseass," she muttered at me, then she started down the street without checking to see that I followed. Still grinning, I decided to get a move on. I swept past her in an eyeblink and stopped a few houses away from our target, sheltering in the deepening shadows of a stately old oak tree that adorned someone's front yard. Calling on my power again, I dimmed myself so that I wouldn't be seen and surveyed the street. From my new vantage point, I had a clear view of the house that had formerly been occupied by the late Raymond Clark.

A car sat at the curb, its motor still running. As I watched, the driver cut the engine, and both occupants stepped out of the car. I swore as I recognized the tall fellow in the brown suit and the short woman in the deep blue top, the same police we had run into at the college. They would probably be trouble, especially if they got into Raymond's conjuring space. They could ruin our only chance to find additional clues. A forensics team would destroy everything that would be helpful to us. We had to get in there before that happened.

In spite of my concern for the situation, I found my eyes glued to the dark-haired woman, and I watched her draw her gun and disappear with her partner behind the cover of the sheltering shrubs that decorated the yard. I *listened*, and I heard them call to Raymond before entering the house. A few seconds later, I heard them go inside.

Ariana strolled past me on the sidewalk. She had seen the police as well but was making good use of my illusion to seem like no threat at all. She glanced in my direction and tilted her head at Raymond's house, though she kept walking as if she hadn't a care in the world. I sped ahead and stopped on Raymond's porch. I could hear faint rumbles from inside as the two police moved around the house. Ariana stepped onto the porch beside me, and I allowed her glamour to disappear so that she could see her guns and other equipment. To my surprise, she didn't draw one. She must have seen my questioning look.

They're cops, she thought at me, her voice clear inside my mind. *If I have my guns out, they'll shoot first and ask questions later.*

We could enspell them again, I suggested.

Ariana shook her head. *If they're on this case, they won't stop until they either get somewhere or they're called off the case. No telling when or if that might happen. I think we should talk to them. We need to stop them from making a mess in there anyway. They could get hurt!*

I mulled over the situation for a moment. Ordinarily, I'd prefer to magick them both into a stupor, do what we needed to do, then leave them with the suggestion that they found nothing. I thought of the female cop. Something about her called to me, something that felt like magick. What kind, I had no idea. But even so, I knew then that I couldn't just walk away. I had to talk to her, find out who she was.

All right. We'll talk to them. But if something goes awry, I'm enspelling them both. I paused before adding, *Watch out for the woman. She's the more dangerous of the two.*

Ariana gave me a quizzical look, but then silently opened the door and slipped into Raymond's house. I dimmed myself and followed closely.

The house was simply furnished, nothing special. Nothing screamed *ancient evil* at us. We heard low voices towards the back of the house, then the sound of a door being unlocked and opened. Silence fell, and I figured they'd found what we were looking for. We made our way down the hallway towards them. A door was open, and light spilled out of the room to splash on the wall opposite. Ariana pressed her back against the wall while I simply stood there, listening. After a minute or two, we heard the clacking of computer keys. Ariana's eyes widened. *If he has any spells on that thing, and they read them aloud, it could be trouble.* She carefully peeked around the corner. *Dammit, she guessed the password; she's in!*

Normally, it takes a ton of focus, training, and will to perform magick, to make it work as it is meant to. That doesn't mean that some knucklehead can't accidentally initiate a dangerous spell. Even toddlers can turn on the stove and cause a fire, and some incantations can be the same way; the simple act of reading the words aloud could bring catastrophic results. Before I could stop her, Ariana was already talking.

"I wouldn't open those," she called around the corner, "and whatever you do, don't read anything you find in there out loud. That would be bad."

I sighed and shook my head. We could have swept in there just as we had before, bewitched them both, and they'd have been none the wiser. But Ariana is an act-first, discuss-later kind of woman, and it was already too late. I just stepped back to enjoy the show.

When the male cop came around the corner, Ariana neatly grabbed his gun in both her hands, pushed it off-line, and twisted it. He instinctively pulled it back towards his body to keep her from getting it, and she just went with the motion, adding momentum to the knee she slammed into his groin. He grunted in agony and fell to the floor, clutching the ache that was rapidly gaining prominence in his nether region, and leaving his gun in Ariana's practiced hands. To his credit, he managed to escape, scuttling backwards and disappearing back into the room he'd come from.

Ariana examined the gun she'd just acquired. *Nice,* she said silently, *at least the guy takes care of his equipment.*

I heard the female cop ask her partner about his gun, and I froze in place. There was something in her voice that shouldn't have been there. I struggled to identify it, to put a name to the sensation that had blossomed in the pit of my stomach at the sound, but although it was strong, it was also elusive. The woman was no witch, I was willing to bet my life. Even so, her voice carried a hint of ancient power.

Before I could stop myself, I said to Ariana, *It's OK. Introduce yourself to them first. I'm not sure why yet, but we need to give them a chance. They'll work with us.*

Are you sure? Ariana's voice in my mind was uncertain, but willing.

Sure enough, I replied, *go ahead and show yourself. Be careful. And maybe give him his gun back first as a sign of good faith.*

Ariana carefully placed the gun on the floor where they could see it, then stepped into their line of sight.

Moments later, so did I.

Chapter 9

It wasn't the first time I had stared down the barrel of a gun, and considering my line of work, it certainly would not be the last. It wasn't entirely unexpected, as police officers tend to be a twitchy bunch anyway, but the genuine fear that rose in her eyes as she whipped her gun from its holster and pointed it at me was a surprise. My glamour was in place, so I should have looked like an ordinary human. I glanced at the male cop, who had also drawn his gun, but he looked more confused than anything. I looked back at the female and became aware of the intense power radiating from her. I raised my hands slowly to show I meant no harm, and sent a hint of calming magick her way to ease the tension. This time, it slid off her like water breaking on the rocks. She blinked a couple of times, and then glared at me.

Uh oh, I thought at Ariana.

Are you kidding me right now? Ariana's mental voice was awfully irritated. I couldn't blame her. She kept her hands raised. *Seems like she knows you. An old friend?*

Doubtful, was the best I could come up with. Ariana rolled her eyes.

"You..." the woman's voice was hard, and although her hands were shaking, her stance was firm. "What are you?"

At her side, her partner glanced her way in confusion, but kept his gun trained dutifully on us.

Ariana spoke up gently, "Look, let us explain. There's a lot going on here that you don't understand."

The cop ignored her, every fiber of her being focused on me. "I said, *what* are you? You're not human! You can't be..." her voice trailed off as she tried to make sense of what she was seeing.

As much as I hate to admit it, I was perplexed. If she were a witch, she might have sensed that I wasn't human, but witches were well-acquainted with the paranormal and the existence of magickal beings. That's Magick 101 stuff. But how could she possibly tell what I was? I focused intently on the cop, trying to gain a sense of her. Although I could feel the waves of power coming from her, there didn't seem to be any structure to contain it, none of the discipline that I often felt from a practiced witch. The answer slowly dawned on me. I released the breath I had not known I was holding as I came to the realization that she wasn't a witch at all. At least, not one who'd been trained. Her powers had to be innate, natural. Which probably meant that somewhere in her family tree, someone had done some dillydallying with one of the Faerie. I shifted my perception and was surprised by her cobalt blue and deep indigo aura, shining so brightly it rivaled Ariana's paler blue. She definitely had magick in her blood, and it was potent. Interesting.

Although that was remarkable enough, there seemed to be more to the situation that I didn't understand. She was acting like she knew me, not just that I wasn't human. I decided to speak plainly. I looked into her eyes and hoped that the illusory mask I wore expressed my sincerity. "I'm sorry, I don't mean to frighten you. I will not harm either of you. I am Kane. Milady...um...ma'am, I don't believe I know you."

She stared at me with eyes gone sea-green in anger, her jaw clenched. Then she replied in a low, menacing voice that did little for my confidence. "It was a long time ago. You killed my grandfather. I should shoot you right now and be done with it."

At her side, her partner scoffed before he could stop himself. "Avery, are you kidding? Your grandfather died when you were a little kid. This guy doesn't look more than 35. What are you thinking?"

60

Her eyes never left mine, and the steel in her voice left no doubt that she believed what she was saying. "It was him. I can feel it, Jim."

"What does that even mean, you can feel it?"

I kept my voice low and calm as I answered him. "She is...special." I saw the recognition in Jim's face, and I turned my attention back to Avery. "You are...aren't you? You know things. You see things. You always have. Am I right?"

At first, she said nothing, but she lowered her eyes as if to consider, and when she raised them back to mine there was something in them besides the cold anger that had risen upon my arrival. "Maybe," she whispered.

Ariana quietly spoke up. "That's rare. We know what it is. We can help you understand it. Yes, it sounds completely crazy, but if you can feel things, if you know that Kane is...different...then it's true. You have power in you."

I could see Avery turning things over in her head. Then she glared back at me, the gun barrel aimed at my left eye. "But you killed him. You slashed him open with your..." she glanced at my hands and frowned when she didn't see what she expected, "with your claws. I was there."

I have to admit, Ariana's voice actually sounded amused in my mind, *that does sound like you.*

Would you shut up? I replied. *If I did kill her grandfather, I must have had a perfectly good reason for doing so. I don't kill just for fun.* I paused. *Anymore.* Ariana rolled her eyes at me but stayed quiet. *I don't know, though. Maybe I did, but I can't be sure.*

"Ma'am, I don't know anything about your grandfather." That much was true. I've slain humans beyond counting in my time, and although there was a possibility that I might have killed the man, I had absolutely no idea if that was actually the case. "I'm a kind of private investigator, specializing in these kinds of cases. We're here to find the one responsible for hurting those innocent people. The man you apprehended was only a contractor, working for someone else. We're after that person. We have a feeling she may do something soon that will hurt a lot more people, but we don't know what."

"She?" Jim's eyebrows rose. "You think a woman was behind these...whatever these pills are doing to those people?"

Ariana nodded. "Yep. We know that and little else. We were hoping to find out something here, but when we saw you'd gotten here ahead of us, we knew we needed to stop you before you did something to get yourselves hurt. There's dangerous stuff in a place like this." She looked at Avery, who was still staring at me with those gray-green eyes. "C'mon, we're here to help. If you shoot him, you'll probably just piss him off anyway. Please, let us help you." Then she added, "Look, can't you feel that he's not here to hurt you? Look with your heart. What do you think?"

"Look with your heart?" Jim mocked Ariana's tone. "What kind of bullshit is this? Let's see some ID!"

"Wait a minute, Jim." Avery's voice was quiet but firm, and although he was still confused, Jim shut his mouth with a snap.

Avery's eyes never left mine. I could feel the energy around her, slowly rising and swirling as she stared at me. Her power had an unusual feel to it, and although I couldn't put my finger on where, it dawned on me that I'd felt it before. I remained still as she regarded me, my hands raised, my stance unthreatening. Ordinarily, I'd be frustrated with anything that got in the way of our investigation. I was built to kill bad guys, and I love my work. Cops tend to run in slow motion compared to what I'm used to, and they just get in the way. That

62

said, everything in me felt that it was important to make peace with this woman. When I get a feeling that strong, I've learned that it's foolish, even dangerous, for me to ignore it. All I could do was wait and hope that she came to the understanding that we were on the same team. More or less.

The moment stretched on forever, and I felt her power tentatively reach out for me, gently caressing me, getting a sense of who I was. I doubt she even knew how she was doing it. I let her energy mingle with mine for a few seconds, and then felt it retreat. It was strong, as strong as any I'd felt in a long while. I heard her sigh, and her gun finally lowered. Keeping her eyes on me, she slowly shook her head, then slipped her gun back in its holster.

"All right," she sighed, "Let's just say that I believe you two about all of this. What now?" She nodded to Jim, and he also put away his gun. He still didn't look thrilled about it.

My eyes flicked over to Ariana and we both relaxed and slowly lowered our hands. "We'll look around and see what we can find. You already stumbled across his computer files," I said. "Ariana can look at those safely without triggering any of the spells that might be present in the text."

"Seriously?" Jim scoffed. "You were talking about actual magical spells?"

"Yep!" Ariana said brightly. "Look, I told you that you might not believe it at first. There is an awfully big world out there that you don't know anything about. We would leave you out of it if we could, but unless you're willing to walk away from this right now, you're about to have your eyes opened to some very interesting and scary stuff. But you'll have to trust that what we say is true. What'll it be?"

Jim's expression remained skeptical. Pretty much what I expected from him. I glanced at Ariana and sent my thoughts to her. *I think it's best if they don't know what I am until it's absolutely necessary for them to know.*

Gotcha, Ariana replied quickly, *I'll be the witchy one. Hey, can you help me out a little here? Help me put on a little show for them? Most of my good stuff isn't very flashy, and might be dangerous in here.*

I smiled. *Sure. Hold up one hand and say something fancy. I'll do the rest.*

Ariana slowly raised her right hand as if she was about to swear an oath. "I'm going to cast a small spell. It won't hurt you. Ready?" Without waiting for their response, she uttered a few sharp words in old German, something about a cat in a doghouse. I cast a simple glamour around her raised hand, and it suddenly burst into intense flames. Avery and Jim gasped at the sight and took a step back, but did not draw their guns again. Their eyes were wide as they stared at her hand, a brightly flaming torch. Ariana let it burn for a few seconds, slowly gesturing for effect. When she figured they'd seen enough, she said another few words, shaking her hand as if to put the fire out. I let the illusion die, and watched the two detectives try to wrap their minds around the fact that magick was actually a thing.

I began to speak, gently lacing my words with a calming enchantment. Jim responded right away, as I saw the tension leave his body. I didn't know how much of it would get through to Avery, but she was no longer on the defensive, and whatever natural shield she had against my power might have fallen away when she relaxed. At least, I hoped so. "Magick is real. A great many of the creatures you believe to be myths and bedtime stories are also real. You don't see them because they don't wish you to, and they use illusions to keep themselves hidden from humans. Many of those creatures are harmless, some are quite dangerous. There are real witches out there as well. Most of them are good, very much so, in fact. They use their skills and talents to help others at every opportunity." I gestured at Ariana, "She is one of the good ones." Ariana smiled and gave a little salute. I continued, "Unfortunately, there are also those who would use magick to harm others for their own benefit, or amusement. Very bad people. Evil witches and sorcerers dabble in dark arts that are not only dangerous, but they corrupt those who use them. Where they might have only been assholes before, they become truly evil, and can cause a lot of pain and suffering for innocents who get in their way. I'm sworn to stop those assholes wherever I can."

Avery's grey-green eyes bored into me as I spoke. When I fell silent, she glanced at her partner, who was already looking at her to get her take on this new information. His brows furrowed, and then he spoke in a low voice, "Witches? Magick? How exactly do you suggest we write that up in the report?"

Avery paused in thought, then started to speak. I don't know what she was going to say, though, because that's when the back door was ripped off its hinges and an impossibly loud hissing filled the room like a thousand angry cobras on steroids. My eyes darted to the now-open doorway and what I saw there...what's that they say...? Oh, yes...shit just got real.

Chapter 10

The moment he stepped into view, Avery felt the icy-cold shock of recognition. *It's him, it's him, oh God, it's him*, and the little girl that lived deep inside her started screaming.

She had always felt things about people. Her intuition was always dead on, even when she'd initially been confused about what it was telling her. She'd learned to trust it over the years without thinking too hard about it. It was just a part of her, like the sound of her heart beating or the way she breathed hard when she trained. Most of the time, that intuition was present but not overpowering. But when Kane appeared in the open doorway, her senses almost overwhelmed her. His power, the sheer force of his presence, buffeted her and penetrated her.

She staggered back a step. She'd have known the feel of that power anywhere on earth, even though there was no way it should have been possible. Nearly forty years had passed since she had last felt it, and the ensuing nightmares had spanned that same amount of time. Her grandfather had been talking with a man that night, a man with Kane's face. There had been angry words and then suddenly, the man had blurred, then vanished. In his place, there had stood...something else.

Her grandfather had been killed, his chest and body slashed open before her eyes by a shadowy, man-sized shape. Its claws glinted under the full moon's light and its eyes shone silver when it turned to see the young Avery, clenching her fists to her mouth to keep from screaming. It hadn't worked. When the shape turned toward her, she had screamed with everything she had. All of her terror, all of her anger, everything that had welled up inside her when she saw the blood on her grandfather's face, it had all flowed into that scream. The figure jerked as though struck, and she remembered it had sprinted away from her and vaulted a fence to disappear into the night. She had passed out, exhausted beyond reason, and only awakened when her parents found her lying in the grass the next morning.

That night had scarred her, but all scars fade over time. And then, impossibly, he had appeared before her again, unchanged. His features had blurred somewhat in her mind, but the feel of him was clear as ever. It was *him*. Wasn't it?

Now, though, she was confused. It couldn't be him; he looked the same. And although he felt like the man from back then, she sensed just as strongly that he meant her no harm. In fact, there was a solid thread of...nobility...in her sense of the man standing before her.

Kane stood there with his hands raised, calm and quiet, radiating that odd sense of power. Everything in her said that he was there to help. His words, and those of the woman called Ariana, matched everything she felt from both of them. She looked at Jim, who inquired as to the strategy of the inevitable paperwork, and then her world went off the rails as something ripped open the back door and brought chaos to them all.

A loud hissing filled the room, almost unbearable in its intensity. At first, it was all she could do to press her hands to her ears to shut it out, but then she got a look at what was coming in the door, and one hand pulled her gun from its holster again.

Two greenish, scaled hands gripped the sides of the open doorway, black talons digging into the wood of the doorframe. The hissing came again, even louder, and the head of the creature became visible as it entered the room. Any nightmare Avery had ever had suddenly seemed like a cartoon in comparison.

The creature was an insane hybrid of snake and man—a hugely muscular man, at that. Its thick torso was covered with greenish scales on its back and yellow along its front, but it was distinctly humanoid. Below the waist, its body was that of a giant serpent, most of which was still outside the room. Its head was a horror show, scarlet slitted eyes in a frighteningly human face, framed by a flaring cobra's hood. Its mouth opened, and hinged impossibly wide, brandishing two daggerlike fangs longer than her fingers. The creature hissed, and thin green droplets fell from the fangs to spit and smoke where they hit the wooden floor. Its blood-colored eyes fastened on her and widened a touch, as though recognizing her.

Avery squeezed off several shots at the thing's center of mass. Beside her, Jim fired repeatedly as well, and her ears rang as the gunshots echoed in the small room. The creature jerked with each impact but didn't go down. In fact, although it had taken several shots to the chest and torso, there was no blood to be seen. The beast shook its head, then flexed its mighty arms and chest, demonstrating its invulnerability to their weapons. Avery heard the clanking sound of metal hitting wood and stared incredulously at the flattened bullets that fell from its thick skin onto the floor. Their aim had been true, but none of the rounds had penetrated. In fact, they appeared only to have upset the beast. Avery's mind raced as she tried to come up with a new plan, but shock and surprise were having their way with her and she drew a blank. Opening its deadly jaws wide, the snake-creature flung itself at her and Jim with impossible speed.

Something slammed into her, and the air exploded from her lungs as she was knocked to the floor along with Jim. Kane had somehow tackled them both an instant before the unnaturally quick creature could reach them. She struggled to sit up, but a strong hand pushed her back down. She met his eyes for an instant that seemed to last an eternity.

"Stay down!" he growled. Authority and power infused his words, and she found herself complying. With animal quickness, he turned towards the creature and crouched protectively over both detectives.

The monster's attack had missed them completely, thanks to Kane. Ariana had somehow gotten around behind the creature and wrapped one of her arms around its throat. It was struggling mightily to free itself, but its heavily muscled arms were not flexible enough to reach her.

"Kane!" she yelled, "get the knife! From my backpack!" The snake-thing snarled and thrashed, but it could not dislodge Ariana from its back. She managed to slip the hand of her choking arm into the crook of her other elbow, intensifying her hold tenfold as she wrapped her legs around the creature's scaly torso. Avery recognized the move from her Brazilian Jiu Jitsu training, wondering if it would work on such a beast. "The silvery one with the emerald!" Ariana yelled through clenched teeth. "Hurry it up, you slacker!" The creature slammed her bodily into the nearest wall. Sheetrock broke and buckled, and Ariana grunted in pain, but she held on.

Faster than a thought, Kane darted to the fallen backpack, dug inside, and produced a wicked looking dagger with a gleaming emerald embedded in the pommel. The beast suddenly whipped its tail upwards and struck Ariana in the head with it. Her eyes rolled back in her head and she fell limply to the floor, unconscious. Seizing the opportunity, the snake-creature balled up both enormous fists and lifted them high, intending to slam them down on her head. Avery reached out and latched onto Ariana's wrist, yanking her body clear. The powerful strike slammed into the floor like a wrecking ball, sending broken planks and shards of wood everywhere. Avery and

Jim quickly pulled Ariana's inert body as close to them as possible, shrinking against the wall as they tried to put more distance between them, but there was none to be had.

The snake-thing saw the three helpless humans backed into a corner and hissed in triumph. It slowly reared until its flared hood nearly touched the ceiling as it towered over them. It opened its mouth wide and extended its dagger-like fangs in preparation for the first strike.

"Hey! Ugly!" Kane's voice thundered, striking like a physical force in the small room. The monster flinched and turned towards the sound. Kane stood a few yards away, glaring balefully at the creature as if daring it to strike. It stared at him, its tongue flicking out to test the air once, then again. Its bloody scarlet eyes lingered on Kane for a long moment, then shifted to the cowering humans in the corner. It chose the corner.

Avery screamed as she emptied the last few rounds of her handgun into the beast, but it did not slow. Its mouth opened wide once more, then lashed out, striking faster than her eyes could follow as it sought to pierce her body. Avery flinched and closed her eyes at the last instant, awaiting the impact of its fangs. It never came.

When her eyes sprang open again, she saw Kane standing between her and the snake-thing. *My God, how could he be so fast?* He had his left hand on the beast's throat, his fingers buried deeply into the scales just beneath its chin. Huge, three-fingered hands struck at his unprotected face, but he somehow rolled with each strike and avoided its sharp talons. Its thick tail curled around his body, trying to crush the life out of him, but he stood fast, tensing against the ropy, steel-like coils. The creature began to panic, hissing frantically as its mutated windpipe slowly crumpled under Kane's powerful fingers.

70

Without saying a word, he raised the dagger high and then stabbed it down into the top of the snake-thing's head, slamming the blade deeply into its skull. The beast convulsed and emitted a loud, gargling rasp that quickly faded. Kane held it in an iron grip, staring into its glowing crimson eyes as the gleam of power slowly dwindled and disappeared. The coils continued to undulate and move, but there was no intent in them anymore, only nerves and muscles misfiring as the creature died. When the light had gone completely, leaving eyes of dull green glass in the thing's slack face, Kane walked to the open doorway that led to the back yard. He yanked the dagger from its skull and then contemptuously threw the upper torso of the monster's corpse out onto the grass. A few coils of its long body remained in the room, but he ignored them as he stepped over to the two detectives.

Both Avery and Jim still had their guns out, but lowered them as Kane approached. He went down on one knee next to them and gently placed the dagger on the floor nearby. Its blade was coated with a slimy red substance far too thick to be ordinary blood. He carefully examined Ariana, who moaned softly, but seemed to be largely uninjured. Avery was still in shock to some extent. Nothing at the police academy, nor anything she had encountered on the streets, could possibly have prepared her for what she had just witnessed. Some part of her wondered if others might be driven mad by such a thing.

"Are you two all right?" Kane said quietly. His voice soothed and warmed her. "It didn't hurt you at all?"

She stared at him blankly at first, then her powers of speech finally came back online. "No...I think we're all right," she said, glancing at the coils that remained inside the house. "What was *that*?"

Kane tossed a quick look over his shoulder before cracking the faintest of grins. "Lesser demon."

71

Jim spoke up at last, his voice cracking, "*That* was a *lesser* demon?"

Kane's smile widened, "Indeed. Admittedly, it was higher up on the scale of lessers, but still not even close to the greater demons. Those are some real heavy hitters." Kane paused and thought for a moment before continuing, "If you want to get a better look at it before it's gone, you'd better hurry."

"Gone?" Avery asked, confused. "It's dead, right? Where's it going?"

"Just trust me. Hurry it up. I'll see to Ariana; she's all right."

Avery pushed herself to her feet, and she and Jim carefully traversed the damaged floor on their way out the back door to examine the snake-thing. The backyard was overgrown and unkempt, and the beast's upper torso lay in the tall grass just outside the yawning doorway. A security light winked on, triggered by their movement as they stepped outside onto the few irregular stepping-stones that lay there. Avery felt a chill run down her spine as she moved away from the house, but shrugged it off and kept her eye on the demon.

"We already know our guns won't work on this thing," Jim muttered, even though he kept his aimed at the unmoving, scaly creature.

"Granted, but being able to shoot it anyway makes me feel better," Avery responded as she worked her way towards the front of the body, slipping a fresh magazine into her gun as she went. The demon's corpse stayed still and silent, and she strongly hoped it would remain so. She worked her way around near its head, which she nudged with the toe of her boot. There was no movement, and she finally let out a sigh of relief. She holstered her weapon and pulled out her phone. "Okay, he was right. It's definitely dead."

"You calling it in?" Jim asked as he tucked his own sidearm away and pulled out his notepad.

"Oh, hell no," Avery laughed. She pointed her phone at the creature and began taking pictures. "I have way too many questions at this point to even think about calling in the team. What are we supposed to tell them? 'We were attacked by a lesser demon in a sorcerer's house?' They'll laugh us right out of the precinct!"

Jim jotted some notes on his pad, more to help himself settle down than to record any real information. The action calmed him. "Yeah, I see what you mean. Still, we're going to have to call them in at some point." He looked around the overgrown yard, sheltered on all sides by tall trees and thick hedges. "Honestly, I'm surprised we haven't heard any sirens by now. Someone had to have heard the gunshots."

Avery froze as she processed. She frowned and looked back at the house. "Jim, go stand next to the house, would you? Just for a second."

Jim's eyebrows went up, but he tucked his pad back in its customary pocket and moved away from her until he was standing right next to the house. He turned and spoke. Avery could not hear his words.

"Hey, can you hear me over there?" Avery asked, raising her voice. Jim rolled his eyes and she saw him silently answer in the affirmative, somewhat testily. She gestured him closer, and he approached. "Stay here," she ordered. He did as he was bid as she walked over to stand where he had been a moment before, and a chill crawled down her spine at that same spot as she approached the house. She stood on the back step and turned to face her partner, who had folded his arms in annoyance. Avery took a deep breath and screamed as loudly as she could. Jim suddenly looked astonished, confirming her suspicion. She moved to rejoin him, this time expecting the chill that hit her a few feet away from the house. When she paid attention to the sensation, it felt almost like walking through a thin, cold waterfall. "You couldn't hear me just now, could you?"

Jim stared at her in surprise. "No, not at all. Were you actually screaming?"

"Mmm hmmm," she nodded. "I know it sounds crazy, but there's some kind of field around the back of the house. I could feel it. It seems to be magickal soundproofing, if you can believe that."

Jim looked at her, shifted his gaze rather pointedly towards the deceased demon, and then brought it back to her. "At this point, I'm inclined to believe pretty much anything."

Avery nodded slowly. "Yeah, me too. I'm feeling pretty damned open-minded right about now. Let's go talk to our new friends."

In unison, they both gasped. They had left Kane and Ariana alone. In the crime scene. Not only was that against police procedure, both of them damn well knew better. They bolted for the open doorway, Avery in the lead, only to find the room empty. Kane and Ariana had gone.

Jim leaned in to look over her shoulder. "What the hell were we thinking, leaving them alone like that?"

Avery remembered Kane's voice, how comforting it had felt, how reassuring, and she knew. "He cast some kind of spell on us. I'm sure of it. You know we'd never have left them alone otherwise."

Jim didn't answer at first, and instead, stepped back inside and looked around. "Something is missing. Several things, actually." He jabbed a finger in the direction of the now darkened monitors at the computer desk. "They took the computer," he swept his gaze around the room, "and there were more books here before. Several of the old-looking ones are gone now."

Avery's eyes were drawn to the black-painted floor in the corner, where lay the golden wire pentacle. Four deep gouges ran through the center of the design, breaking the wires in several places. A piece of paper lay in the center of the star, apparently torn from one of the newer reference books that lay nearby, and hastily written upon.

"They left a note," she said as she picked it up. Jim walked over and looked over her shoulder so they could read it together.

Officers,

Please forgive our hasty exit. We know you have questions, and we'll answer them ASAP. The sorceress who sent the demon is dangerous, and will kill you if you get too close. Obviously, you're not ready to face her. Let us deal with her. Cover this up as best you can and we'll find you afterward. It's asking a lot, we know, but it's for your own safety. Trust us.

A & K

P.S. Don't poke around in this room too much. It's not safe.

Both detectives were silent for a full minute after reading the note. Then a quiet sizzling sound arose behind them, accompanied by a wavering reddish-orange light. They quickly turned only to see the serpentine coils of the demon disappearing in flames that cast no heat. In less than a minute, the enormous body had completely vanished, leaving no trace whatsoever. The two partners slowly looked at each other. Jim swallowed. "As much as I hate to say it, I am inclined to believe them. What do you think?"

Avery's eyes narrowed. "We could lose our jobs, or worse, if anyone finds out. You know procedure, Jim."

Jim nodded, then pulled a handkerchief from his pocket and mopped it over his face. "You know I do, Avie, but this, ah, this is...look, these are some extenuating circumstances if I've ever seen them." He leaned forward and whispered, "Demons, Avie. Demons are extenuating."

Avery looked down at the paper in her hand. The handwriting had a definite feminine quality to it, but the 'K' was different. He had signed it himself, leaving a single letter that swirled and flourished elegantly into an archaic symbol.

"You got another evidence bag on you?" Avery said quietly.

Jim produced one from somewhere. He was like a magician with those things. "Duh. We're taking that with us?"

"Yep."

"You think they left prints?"

"Nope," she replied as she slipped the note into the bag and sealed it. "But I want it anyway." Then she sighed and looked around. "Whatever else we do, we need to pick up our spent rounds and casings. Then I want to poke around a tiny bit more." She saw concern flood his face, and added, "I know, I know. It's dangerous in here. Even so, I want to know a little more before we get out of here."

Jim frowned, but pulled out another bag and began searching the floor for the flattened bullets that had failed to penetrate the snake-demon's tough hide. He found one and deposited it in the bag along with a couple of brass casings. "All right, then. I don't like it, but I'm in."

"I thought you said I'd be taking the heat on this one if something went wrong?"

He squatted to look under the desk and came up with another mushroomed bullet. "Not a chance, sweetheart. We're both in this up to our necks." He stood to his full height and looked down at his partner, finally cracking a weary smile. "Well, your neck and my sternum, anyway."

She smiled faintly, but her mind was elsewhere. Kane was definitely more than he seemed, far more than he had told them. Setting her jaw, she determined that she'd find out who he was. This wasn't the last he had seen of Avery Lynne. *Not by a longshot,* she thought.

Chapter 11

"Hey, penny for your thoughts," Ariana's voice drifted over to me, distracting me from my musing. I turned and glanced at her, only to find her staring at one of her monitors. Upon returning to her house, she had plugged Raymond's mini-tower into her enormous computer, circumvented its meager security measures, and was now browsing through his files at top speed.

"Find anything yet?" I said, ignoring her question.

"Oh, yup," she answered brightly. "Our guy Raymond was a daring sorcerer in his way, but otherwise, pretty boring. Liked blondes, though."

I shook my head at that and sighed. "What did you find that helps us?"

"He's got all of his formulas on here. Everything connected to the pills; how to make them, how to infuse them with the bonding spell to make them call the demon, everything. It's quite impressive, actually. And really twisted."

"Anything tell you why he did it?" I asked.

"Unfortunately, no," she sighed. "I checked his emails and social media messages, there was nothing there. He was pretty isolated. Few friends, no relatives that I can see. I'm checking one more thing, though, and I bet that'll get us somewhere."

I stood and walked over to stand behind her shoulder. "What's that?"

"Well, Kane, why does anyone do anything?"

I blinked at the question, then answered, "Power, money, revenge, or love."

"Precisely. At least, those seem to be the most powerful motivators for the folks we run across, right?" I nodded and she continued. "I'm digging into his bank accounts now. He's got all his passwords automatically

78

loaded, thank goodness. I checked his history for the last week, and I think I might have…" she clicked something and a new screen popped up on one of the monitors. "Yup! Look at this," she pointed at the screen. I squinted at it. "Here's a recent deposit for a hundred thousand dollars. That's way above the usual pay grade of our community college professor, don't you think?"

"I wouldn't know," I answered truthfully, "but that is a lot of money. Where did he get it?"

Her grin widened. "It was wired directly to his account from an account in the Cayman Islands. Hmmm…give me a few minutes while I dig into it." She clicked something else and another screen popped up on the other monitor. I shook my head. Her computer prowess was profoundly helpful, and not something I could begin to duplicate. I figured I'd eventually have her show me how to at least surf the internet, as she called it.

Ten minutes passed, then she sat back in her chair and triumphantly pointed at the screen. "Ha! I knew this rig we got from Max would pay off! My old computer would never have been able to get through the firewalls. Anyway, look here," she tapped the glass on the monitor, "The money came from a shell corporation. It's a business that only exists on paper and on the internet, and they're often used to hide illegal activities. I followed the trail, though, and now I've got a name." She paused for dramatic effect.

"And…?" I prompted, deciding not to kill her just then.

"Diana Thornwall," Ariana clicked and typed some more. "She's got an estate in Old Katy, of all places. Looks like her parents hit it big a long time ago with a shipping business out of Houston and Baton Rouge, Thornwall Industries. She took it over. Never married, but has a daughter who's around twenty, it says here. Diana's…hang on…in her early fifties." She clicked again and a picture of a striking middle-aged woman appeared on the screen. "Wow, that's a cougar if ever I saw one!" I raised an eyebrow at her. I saw no resemblance to one of the cats and said as much. She just rolled her eyes at me and elaborated. "That's what we call an older woman who prowls for younger men." I looked more closely at the picture, which appeared to have been taken at a high society gathering. She was tall with brown hair, and had poured her curves into a sparkly red dress that matched the crimson on her lips. Jewels gleamed at her neck and wrists, and diamonds glinted on her earlobes. She had money, all right. She also had a predatory half-smile and a knowing gleam in her eye that made me think that Ariana's slang term was probably correct. She looked downright dangerous. Good. "Your fangs are showing, big guy." I turned towards Ariana, startled, but realized she'd been joking. My glamour hadn't slipped. I sighed with relief. I was closer to Ariana than I had been to anyone in over two centuries, but I had yet to show her my true face up close. I had my reasons.

"She's the one who paid him. She's probably also the one who set up the self-destruct spell, and sent the snake-demon to his house," I reasoned.

"That's a logical assumption, I'd say," Ariana agreed. "If she was watching the house, she'll have seen those cops. And us."

I frowned. That meant that Detectives Avery and Jim were probably in danger. Ariana's house was heavily warded, courtesy of years of overlaid protective spells. The detectives had no such shielding, and even less knowledge, other than what little we'd given them. "We need to move quickly."

"I hear ya." She printed out a handful of pages, then shut down her system. "Those cops won't stand a chance without us. We need to stop her before she takes them out." She walked over and picked up her guns and began to strap them back onto her legs. "Why do you think she did it, Kane?" she asked as she started reloading her magazines, replenishing them with the special bullets she reserved for such occasions. "Why pay Raymond that much to have some random guys possessed by demons? Judging by what we've seen her do, she's powerful enough to do that herself, so why hire it out? How could that possibly benefit her?"

"I don't have any idea," I answered coldly. I'd met hundreds of people like Diana over the centuries. Rich, powerful, and willing to kill anyone who got in their way. It was as if the money had scoured the decency from them somehow. Or maybe they'd just been born bad. Either way, it wasn't my place to care why they were so vile, just to make them pay if they hurt innocent people. "Let's go see if we can get her to tell us." I flexed my claws where Ariana couldn't see. They were about to get a workout.

Chapter 12

Jim sat in the passenger seat next to Avery, slowly shaking his head. "I don't like this. Nope. Not one bit."

Avery sighed and responded as calmly as she could, "Neither do I, Jim. But you know what'll happen if we take this to the Lieutenant. She'll lose her mind."

"Are you completely sure we haven't lost ours? I mean, we've seen some things in the streets, but...did we really see that?"

Without taking her eyes off the road, she whipped out her phone, thumbed it open to the photo album and pulled up the pics she'd taken of the demon. She'd been afraid they wouldn't be there, but they had not disappeared when the creature's body had. She handed it to him, and he glanced at it for a few seconds. Then he sighed in resignation. She tried to reassure him. "Yes, Jim, we did. And we would have died in that room if it hadn't been for those two. We owe them." She managed to suppress the shudder that gripped her when she thought about Kane, how he'd killed the demon with a combination of brute strength and a dagger's blade.

"How do you know they didn't call that thing, or summon it, or whatever?" Jim questioned. He pulled out his notepad out of habit and started going over his notes. She could tell he was just running through the possibilities. It was one of the things that made him a great detective. He'd keep going until he found something useful.

"They were just as surprised as we were when it showed up, and because it wiped the floor with that girl, Ariana, that's why. She's one tough bitch."

"Takes one to know one, I guess," he muttered. That made her smile. "Now, where exactly are we going?"

"We're going to my place." As soon as she said it, she groaned inwardly, knowing what came next.

"Hot damn, my prayers have been answered. I knew you couldn't resist my manliness forever. Just make sure you give me time to limber up, you know my back acts up and I've got this dodgy hip." Jim never even looked up from his notepad.

"You're killin', me, Jim. I'll tell your wife."

"Tell her, she'll be thrilled. Hell, she'll probably pay you to keep me."

She laughed at last, the horrors of the night dispelled somewhat by their long-running joke. "Look, I need to do some research, and I'd rather not do it down at the station where it's trackable."

"What, you don't want your Google search on Demon Summoning to show up on the IT logs?"

"Bingo," Avery said, "plus, I found something those two missed on their way out. I think it's a clue."

Jim looked at her. "What, are we Scooby Doo, now?"

"Shut up, you ass. Look, I have…I have a hunch." She pulled a folded piece of paper from her pocket and handed it over to him. He took it and carefully opened it up. He stared at it for a moment, frowning.

"Are you seeing something here I'm not seeing? 'Cause this is blank."

"Hold it up to the light. It's from a notepad I saw on the desk. The top sheet was gone, but he pressed hard with the pen and left impressions on the sheet beneath. Can you see the names?"

Jim pulled a small flashlight from his pocket and clicked it on, shining its beam on the paper. "I'll be damned. Those are the three guys that came down with demon-poisoning."

"Exactly. And look at the company logo."

"Thornwall Industries? But he could have picked up this pad of paper practically anywhere, Avie, it probably doesn't mean a thing."

She shook her head briskly. "You're wrong. There's something there, I can feel it." She turned and caught his gaze. "I can *feel* it, Jim. You know what I mean." She turned her eyes back to the road, but her partner continued to look at her.

"Are you..." he asked carefully, "are you a witch? Like Kane said?"

Avery scoffed, but didn't answer right away. Once she had ordered her thoughts, she began, "No, I'm not. At least, not like he said. I don't know anything about spells or demons or magick," she paused before continuing, "but I know I'm different. I see things. I feel things that others don't; I always have. And you know I'm always right."

He turned his eyes back to the road and sniffed. "Not a witch, huh? I'm not gonna lie, I'm disappointed. I was hoping you'd let me ride on your broomstick."

Avery deadpanned, "That's what she said."

Jim stared at her and burst out laughing. "All right, all right, you got me." When his chuckles died down, he continued, "I'm with you, Avery. You can count on me to see this thing through, whatever it is." He held up the paper she'd handed him. "Let's go run this down and see where it takes us."

Chapter 13

Avenue D was an old road that led through the middle of what residents called Old Katy, to distinguish it from everything else in the area that had sprung up in the last decade or so. There was a blend of new construction and cracker box houses among stately trees and historical homes that were only a few years younger than the Civil War's end. It was a quiet part of town, especially at night, though the lights at Mary Jo Peckham Park were blazing brightly so that youngsters could play their sports. Ariana drove the Jeep north until we'd passed the bright lights, then turned down a narrow road that paralleled a high, wooden fence, leaving the noise of the park behind us.

The shadows were welcoming as always. Ariana drove to the end of the fence, which marked the border of the property. She pulled the Jeep off the path and parked it beneath the shelter of a few large branches that reached over the tops of the tall, wooden boards. I squeezed out on my side and joined her as she pulled her backpack from the back seat. Once she was properly outfitted, she locked the Jeep and then stepped back from it.

I scanned the fence and decided the best place to go over it was directly under the overhanging branches, since they provided natural cover. I moved towards it, but Ariana stopped me. "Hang on, I've been working on something. Give me a second."

She looked around and found a decent-sized stick on the ground, which she picked up. She closed her eyes and slowed her breathing as she gathered her will. I felt the magick around her awaken as she began to chant quietly to herself. She slowly made her way around the Jeep, dragging the end of the stick in the dirt behind her.

Energy filled the narrow channel she carved into the dirt, flowing from within Ariana's body and directed by her intense focus. When she had completely circled the vehicle, she connected the ends of the channel and I felt the power come alive along its length, creating an invisible dome over the Jeep. She backed slowly away, keeping her focus on the spell she had created. She raised her hands, still murmuring quietly, and as I watched, shadows fell from the overhanging branches and engulfed the Jeep in almost complete darkness. She watched for a moment, then lowered her hands and turned to me with a big smile on her face.

"Ta daaaa!" she said, triumphantly gesturing toward the nearly invisible Jeep. The shadows beneath the branches had claimed it completely, leaving only a faint impression of the car's shape, if you knew where to look. "Whatcha think?"

I looked the spell over carefully, examining what I could see of its structure. It was sturdy yet subtle, an impressive illusion. "Not bad," I said simply.

Ariana raised an eyebrow, then rolled her eyes and sighed as she turned away to look at the fence.

"What?" I said. I had the feeling she expected more from me, but I just wasn't in the mood.

She kept scanning the fence, looking for cameras. "I worked on that spell a long time, you ass! Took me a couple of months to finally get it right."

I shrugged. "I've been doing illusions for centuries, Ariana. That one is pretty simple to me."

A tiny smirk crawled across her face. "But will yours still be there tomorrow?"

That got my attention. My illusions were amazing, but somewhat fleeting. They required my focus to exist, and could only survive without my direct involvement for a short time, certainly not a full day. If she could cast an illusion that would still be around for that long, she'd

86

stepped up her game considerably. I handed over a rare compliment. "Ok, I admit it. That's impressive."

Ariana beamed, "Thank you. You're still an ass, though."

"Granted," I confirmed. "Do you sense any wards around the property?" Despite the fact that my magick was far stronger than hers in many ways, and I had centuries of experience on her, she still kicked my ass in the creation of wards and shields.

"Hang on," she murmured, "I was already checking before you interrupted me." Her eyes were out of focus as she reached out with her awareness, scanning the perimeter for the telltale signs of a magickal ward. After a minute or so, she sighed and looked at me with a frown. "No, there's nothing there. You'd think someone powerful enough to roast poor Raymond like that and then send a snake-demon after us would have at least a rudimentary shield around their property, right?"

I nodded. "That's what I would expect. Maybe she's arrogant enough to think she doesn't need one." I remembered the wicked little smile she displayed in the picture Ariana had found, seductive and knowing. She looked the type. "Maybe she's got one closer to the house. Let's get moving. We'll find out when we get there."

I led the way into the shadows that concealed the Jeep and quickly heaved myself over the fence and into the yard beyond. The old tree had a wide trunk, and I stayed close to it while Ariana climbed over. Once she stood alongside me, we scanned the property to get the lay of the land.

The expansive back yard was surrounded by the same tall wooden fence on all sides, and the house sat closer to the rear of the property than to the main road. The grounds were mown, but the landscaping was otherwise minimal. Trees were plentiful away from the house, and the yard still retained a faint hint of wildness.

The porch spanned the entire back side of the house and opened onto an elegant swimming pool with a hot tub on one end and an ornate fountain on the other. There were a couple of other buildings that matched the beige stucco of the main house, and gently curving sidewalks connected them all. Off to one side, two vehicles had been parked next to the house. One was a sporty red convertible, while the other was a more sedate black SUV.

"Looks like somebody's home," Ariana whispered. The walls leading to the porch were glass, affording us a clear view into the back part of the house, and there was movement inside. The woman we had seen in the photo was clearly visible, though far less formally dressed. She wore a white bathrobe with a matching towel turban wrapped around her hair, and her face was clean of makeup. She held a cell phone up to her ear, and she stalked around the room, talking and gesturing angrily. As we watched, she walked over to a cabinet, wrenched open the doors, and proceeded to fix herself a drink. Cocktail in hand, she moved over to a thickly padded couch and flopped down on it, still talking on the phone. With frustrated finality, she thumbed the phone to disconnect the call and tossed it on the far end of the couch upon which she sat, as if to distance herself even further from the caller. She took a long sip from her drink and lay her head back with a sigh.

"She seems pretty stressed," Ariana quipped, "maybe we should come back and visit another time?" I cut my eyes over to her and frowned, only to see her smiling at me. She was having fun, as usual. I wouldn't be having fun until I could get my claws into something.

Somewhere in the house, the doorbell rang faintly. Diana glanced over her shoulder, then rolled her eyes, stood up, and headed toward the front door. She was only gone a few moments, then she appeared again, leading a man and a woman to a table next to the picture window.

She stopped along the way to refresh her drink, then slid into one of the chairs while her guests simply stood next to the table. One held a file folder.

"Are you kidding me?" Ariana whispered, surprise evident in her voice. I was surprised too. Her guests were our favorite detectives, Avery and Jim. They were all business, and had already pulled a picture out of the folder and laid it on the table in front of Diana Thornwall. She inhaled sharply at the sight of it. "Wow, I have to admire their efficiency. I'll have to ask how they found out that Diana was involved. I thought we had all of the evidence on Raymond's hard drive. I didn't see anything else there but spell supplies. How'd they find her?"

My gaze was locked on Avery. It had to be her somehow. She had talent, of that I was certain. How strong or how well-schooled she might be had yet to be determined. I had the sense that she was acting only on instinct, or else she'd have recognized the items in Raymond's summoning room in a heartbeat. *Strong, though,* I admitted. "It's that detective, the woman. She sensed it somehow."

Suddenly, Ariana looked at me in alarm. "Do you think she knows we're here?"

My eyes narrowed and I watched her through the glass. Avery's attention was focused entirely on Diana Thornwall, who looked somewhat distraught. I didn't dare reach out with my magick to pick up on their emotions. Avery would probably feel it, even if she didn't know what it was. For the moment, it looked like she was ignorant of our presence, and I figured we should keep it that way. "No," I answered, "she'd already have moved to intercept us if she knew. She's only here for Diana."

"We'd better wait until they leave, then," Ariana suggested.

I nodded in agreement, but kept my eyes on the two detectives. They were pretty stone-faced as they showed Diana the contents of the folder. She looked at the other pages briefly, but her eyes kept drifting back to the first photo they had given her. She picked it up to look at it again, and I caught a flash of it as she gestured while speaking. It was Raymond. She knew him, obviously, but something about the way she acted was bothering me. I would have expected her to deny knowing him, or to be defensive and angry when the police accused her of any involvement. I know her type pretty well, but no matter what I might have thought, she actually appeared upset and sad. I frowned as I watched her. Up close, I knew I would have been able to read her emotions much better, but if I had to go by the expression on her face, I would say that she was truly surprised and distressed.

I watched as Avery gathered up the pages and tucked them back into the folder while her partner took notes in his little notepad. I saw Diana shaking her head no a few times, but then nodding. The detectives nodded as well, as though they were coming to an understanding of sorts. Avery pulled a card from her pocket and handed it to Diana, who accepted it with another nod. She stood, then led the detectives back to the front door on the far side of the house. Apparently, the interview was now over.

"What do you make of that?" Ariana asked, sounding somewhat perplexed.

"It looks to me like they didn't have enough on her to arrest her, or even get a search warrant," I responded. "She's putting on a pretty good act. If they told her that Raymond was a suspect in a crime and that she had been implicated somehow, you would think that she would have responded more angrily. I didn't get that from her at all. She looks genuinely upset, acting more worried for Raymond than anything."

Ariana smiled. "I bet we can get more out of her than they could."

I wholeheartedly agreed with that sentiment. Police were shackled by certain rules when interrogating suspects. I had none. Although I enjoyed hurting people, I only enjoyed it if they deserved it. Whether or not Diana Thornwall deserved my special treatment remained to be seen.

Diana appeared once again, this time alone. She went straight to the cabinet and poured herself another drink, and even at that distance, I could see that her hands were shaking. For someone who had masterminded the demonic possession of three innocents for some greater purpose, she seemed pretty rattled. She walked over to the window and stared out at the back yard, obviously lost in her own thoughts. I knew she couldn't see us; it was so bright inside and dark outside that the window likely acted as a mirror to her eyes. I examined her face carefully. Gone was the knowing smirk, the arrogant tilt to her chin we had seen in the high society photos. Looking at her then, I thought she didn't seem anything like the business mogul we knew her to be. No, she looked more like a woman who was afraid of something but didn't know what it was. She stood that way for a minute longer, looking confused and sad, and then she turned away. Sipping at her drink, she ambled slowly to another part of the house, disappearing from our view.

I nudged Ariana. It was time for us to talk to Diana and maybe make some sense out of it all. We left our place behind the tree and moved around the pool to the covered porch. Once there, we quickly found the sliding glass door. I used a simple spell to quiet it as we opened it just enough to allow ourselves inside. We stood there in the dining area, getting our bearings, and that's when things went wrong. So wrong.

Chapter 14

"She doesn't know anything," Avery muttered as they walked to the car. "I'd bet my life on it."

Jim jotted something in his notes and nodded, "I'd agree with you on that, Avie. I've seen a lot of guilty people, and I've seen some good liars, but she got caught completely off-guard with this. She knew Raymond, sure, even cared about him, but I don't think she had any idea what he was up to, or why. Especially not the, uh, magick stuff." He flipped his notepad closed, slipped it into a pocket, and sighed. He turned to look at his partner. "The fact that Diana knew Raymond at all is proof that there's something to your hunch, though. But if she's not in on it, I don't know where we should go from here."

She leaned against the door of her car and folded her arms. "I'm not sure just yet," she answered, "and it's really pissing me off."

Jim took one long, deliberate step away from her, as if he had suddenly realized he was standing too close to a bomb. "There's chocolate in the glove compartment."

Avery cut her eyes towards him but felt her lips twitch into a smile before she could stop herself. Her partner always knew the right thing to say. She relaxed somewhat and ran her fingers through her hair as she rolled everything around in her mind. Diana Thornwall had been very forthcoming, and if her own intuition was to be believed, completely honest. Something nagged at her, though, and she finally managed to put it into words.

"Hey, did you smell something in there? Anything at all?"

"Like what?"

"I don't know...something in there was off to me. Maybe it wasn't so much a smell, but a feeling. It was like what I felt when I first saw Raymond, but not quite. It was pretty faint, but now that we're away from it, I can tell the difference."

"Is that another hunch?"

"Yes...no...hell, I don't know," she swore in frustration. "Dammit, this case is a mess."

"It sounds like we could both use some tacos while we sort this out. I've got some ideas. Hop in, I'll drive."

Before she could respond, they heard a car pull into the driveway. They both looked in that direction to see a pair of headlights approaching along the winding concrete drive. "Who is this, do you think?" Avery mused.

"Dunno," he muttered. "Maybe it's a clue."

Avery swatted him on the arm as she stepped away from her car and prepared to show her badge. The oncoming headlights belonged to a sporty little red Honda that pulled in next to them and went silent as the driver killed the engine. A young woman with short brown hair slid out of the driver's seat and approached them. She was dressed smartly in dark slacks and a gray blouse that flattered her, gold glinting at wrists and neck. The resemblance to the woman they had left inside was strong, but where Diana Thornwall had an elegant smoothness to her movements, the newcomer was quick and twitchy, unconsciously displaying the energy of youth. She stared at the two detectives, questions filling her eyes.

"Detectives Avery Lynne and Jim Kaley, Harris County Sherrif's Office," Avery said, showing her badge to the bewildered woman as Jim flashed his. "And you are...?"

She blinked in surprise and clutched imaginary pearls at her throat, "My goodness, is something wrong?"

"Your name?" Avery repeated, a calm note of authority seeping into her voice.

"Oh, yes, of course. I'm so sorry," the young woman stammered, "I'm Tanya Thornwall. I'm here to visit my mother. Is she all right?" she gestured to the house.

The muffled sound of gunshots, nearly a score of them in rapid succession, made them all turn wide eyes towards the house. Barely a moment later, a sharp scream from inside the house made them all flinch. The woman's scream was filled with terror, and it turned Avery's blood to ice. She burst into action before the sound of it had begun to fade, sprinting for the front door with her gun in hand, followed closely by Jim and Tanya.

Avery tried the door and found it locked. "Ms. Thornwall!" she yelled as she hammered a fist against the stout wood. "Police! Open the door!" The door was thick and imposing, and she knew she'd never batter it down without the SWAT guys and their breaching ram.

"Here, here!" Tanya shuffled frantically up to the door, jangling keys as she moved, "I've got a key!" Her hands shook so much that she dropped them, but she scooped them up, found the proper key and unlocked the deadbolt.

"Back away, let us handle this!" Jim shoved Tanya away from the door as gently as he could, then looked at Avery and nodded. She yanked the door open, allowing him to enter first. "Freeze! Police!" she heard him bellow as she followed barely a moment later. The scene that met her eyes made her gasp.

Diana Thornwall was lying in the middle of the room, her eyes staring sightlessly up at the high ceiling. Her mouth was still open, as if frozen during her final scream. Blood was everywhere, great sprays of it, and she lay in a slowly spreading puddle of crimson that stained the expensive carpet. Her body bore several vicious slashes, wide gashes that had opened her up to the bone. Standing over her was a figure she had seen in her dreams for years. His skin was the cool dark of shadows, so black it was almost blue. He cut a muscular figure, wiry rather than bulky, with too-long arms and spindly fingers that ended in wicked talons. Blood dripped from those claws, pattering on the still body of the woman at his feet.

Standing opposite them, on the far side of Diana's body, was the woman they had met earlier that evening, Ariana. She still wore her tactical gear and had a gun in her hand, but it was pointed at the ceiling. The other hand was held towards them, palm out, in what might have been a calming gesture. "No, wait!" she was saying, "it's not what you think. You need to listen!"

Avery barely heard Ariana's words. Her heart had stopped, then started again at twice its normal speed. The shadowy figure had tilted its face towards her and stared at her through its long, stringy black hair. She saw its glowing silver eyes, pools of quicksilver shining from jet black sockets. It opened its mouth, revealing far too many teeth, all of them sharp. It growled softly at her, and the little girl inside her started screaming in terror. However, the grown woman Avery had become was one tough bitch. She lifted her gun and took aim.

The figure bolted, and she followed it with the barrel of her gun, squeezing the trigger as she felt her sights come online with the target. The first shot went wide, but the second and third struck home, and she heard the shadowy thing grunt in pain. Ariana flung herself into her line of fire, and before she could stop, Avery had put two bullets in her chest. She grunted and jerked with the impacts and fell hard to the floor. Avery lowered her gun in horror.

The shadowy figure turned and howled at them, a ferocious yowl of anger and...grief? It lashed one long-fingered hand out and latched onto Ariana's lifeless body, yanking her off the ground and gathering her up in its arms faster than Avery could see. It leaped, and the back window shattered, spraying glass out onto the back patio, the shards glinting like diamonds in the dark. The room fell shockingly silent, and the smell of the recent gunfire was sharp in their noses.

Avery kept her gun pointed in the general direction the figure and Ariana had gone, then finally lowered it. Her eyes fell on the dead body of Diana Thornwall. She'd been slashed to ribbons.

"What..." Jim began, "in the HELL...was that?"

Avery looked at her partner and saw that he still had his gun out, aimed at the back window. His hand was shaking. She holstered her weapon, then gently put her hand on his arm. "They're gone, Jim. Whatever that thing was, it took Ariana, and they're gone."

He looked at her, looked at the window, then back at her, as if reassuring himself that all was quiet. Slowly, he let Avery ease his hands down, and he holstered his gun on the third try. He let his gaze fall on the body. "She's dead," he said in a flat voice.

The sound of the deadbolt locking behind them made them both frown, and they turned toward the front door. Something struck them both before they could register what they saw, and they sank to their knees before falling face first to the carpet. Avery's vision swam, and she struggled to move but her body refused her commands. She looked at Jim, but he had fallen facing away from her, and even though he was only a couple of feet away, she couldn't bring her arm to move enough to touch him.

"Yes, she certainly is," a feminine voice purred just out of her line of sight. "Sad, really. She was just about to donate an awful lot of money to several charities, too. Oh well," Tanya uttered a throaty laugh that sounded remarkably like her mother's, "they'll just have to do without. As for you two, I can't have you reporting her death right away, now can I? That'll open up a can of worms I'm not quite prepared for. No, I need to find out what you know first. Then we'll see what I need to do with you. I'm sure I'll figure something out."

Chapter 15

Sometimes, things just go to shit no matter what you do. The bullets had lodged somewhere in my left lung. They pained me more than I expected, but at least I'd only been hit twice. It was going to take some doing to get them out, and I wasn't looking forward to that at all. Still, I'd had worse.

I should have just left Ariana behind. I didn't owe her. In the old days, I probably would have. OK, that's not true. I *definitely* would have left her behind. She's a big girl, she knew the risks. Sometimes bad stuff happens, especially in my line of work. Now, she was just slowing me down.

The fence loomed in front of me and I cleared it with a jump that made my entire torso ache. Ariana wasn't heavy, even with all the gear she insisted on wearing, but gunshot wounds are bothersome like that. The Jeep was right where we'd left it, cloaked in its own shadows. I fished the key out of her pocket to unlock it and piled her in the back before jumping into the driver's seat. I cranked up the engine, put it in gear, and tried to look nonchalant as I drove back the way we'd entered. I knew the rules of the road, and yes, I knew how to drive, thank you very much. I admit, it had been a while. A long while. Even so, I kept it between the ditches and got us to the freeway, where I headed west, towards Ariana's place. Traffic was pretty light, which was a good thing.

The lights alongside the road started blurring, and exhaustion started having its way with me as the pain ramped up. *Not good,* I mused. *Bullets must have done more damage than I thought.* It was still a fair distance to Ariana's farm, and I could feel my body shutting down. *Dammit. Just a little farther.*

Things are a little sketchy in my mind after that, but I managed to get back to the farm. I stopped short of actually getting the car back into its customary spot in the barn. Instead, I pulled into the yard in front of the house and put the Jeep in park. Gathering what strength I had left, I turned off the key and exited the vehicle, intending to get Ariana into the house so I could check her injuries. I never made it.

I vaguely felt my knees hit the hard-packed earth as I lost the ability to stand. My body had been trying to heal itself, but everything inside my rib cage on the left side was on fire, and something was wrong. I tried to stand back up and only succeeded in falling face first on the ground. The last thing I remember was thinking that this was a stupid way to die. I'd survived a fight with a Dragon, for goddess' sake, only to be brought down centuries later by a cop's lucky shot. Hmph.

*   *   *   *   *   *

"Wow, that was interesting."

Ariana's voice disturbed me. I had been floating in the dark, warm and cozy. Frowning, I opened my eyes and let them focus until my surroundings resolved into a solid image. Ariana's living room took shape in front of me, tilted on its side. I slowly regained my bearings and realized that I was lying face down on her kitchen table. I started to get up, and felt her hands gently pressing on my back.

"Hold on there, tough guy. Let's make sure everything's in working order before you jump up and do something stupid."

I pushed against her hands and roughly sat up, swinging my legs over the side of the table. "I'm fine," I growled, irritated. *Of course everything's in working order,* I thought. *Why wouldn't it be?* My back itched ferociously, but the sensation was already beginning to fade. I took a few deep breaths and discovered a dull ache in the left side of my chest. I kept at it, and it began to fade as well. I tensed my muscles to hop down and was met with a surge of pain. As much as I hated to admit it, Ariana's advice sounded prudent to me. I sighed and relaxed, letting my body continue to repair itself. It just needed a few more minutes. As the aches dissipated, I finally turned and looked at her only to find her glaring at me with her arms folded.

"Feeling better?" she asked with sarcastic sweetness.

"I am." I paused and stared back at her. Her annoyance radiated from her in waves, and I tried to figure out what I had done wrong. I had, after all, dragged her out of the Thornwall house after she had been shot. At that memory, my eyebrows rose in surprise. "Hey," I began, "you were shot. Are you all right?"

She didn't answer me right away, only continued to glare at me. "Oh, you remember that, do you?" Then she sighed, unfolded her arms and ran one hand through her hair. "Yes, I sure was." She had removed her tactical gear and was clad in a tank top and cargo pants. Her left hand rose, hooked the fabric of her top, and gently pulled it down. Beneath it, I could see the enormous bruise that had risen where the bullets had impacted. I looked at it and frowned, and then my gaze rose back to hers as she continued, "Idiot that I am, I got in the way of a couple of bullets that were meant for you. Fortunately, I wear a vest for just such an emergency." She let go of the top and moved her left arm around a little bit, testing its range of motion and wincing as she did so. "Still sucks, though. I'm going to feel that for a long time."

I blinked at her while I took in that information. I had not asked her to do that. I'd survived bullet wounds before, many times, but I had no idea what she was so upset about. I glanced over my shoulder at the table and was surprised to see an array of medical supplies laid out there. Amidst the bloody towels and stainless-steel surgical tools from her first aid kit, I noticed a pair of misshapen lumps of metal.

She followed my gaze and explained, "I dug those out of you. When I came to in the back of the Jeep, you had passed out in the yard. You were bleeding a lot, and the wounds weren't closing like you told me they usually do." She shrugged and looked away. "I was worried about you, so I dragged you in here and went to work." She turned and walked to the kitchen sink, where she began scrubbing my blood off her hands. "I guess you didn't need my help. Stupid of me."

I was about to open my mouth and agree with her, but I held my tongue. Ordinarily, my body just spits out whatever gets stuck inside it. It hurts like hell, and takes a while, but I've never passed out during that process. This was a first. Moving slowly, I reached over and picked up one of the mushroom-shaped bullets that Ariana had removed from my torso. The moment my fingers touched the metal, they began to tingle and ache. There was magick in those rounds. It had already dissipated, but there was enough left for me to feel how potent it must've been when it entered my body. I reassessed everything Ariana had done.

"You did the right thing," I admitted. "In fact, you may have saved my life." She stopped in the middle of drying her hands and turned to look at me in surprise. I decided to surprise her a little more. "Thank you. I appreciate it." Her mouth did not drop open as I thought it might, but I still detected a faint sense of startlement from her. Inwardly, I rolled my eyes, and reminded myself that maybe I could be a little nicer. Just once in a while.

I held up the nugget of metal so she could see it. "These rounds have power in them. That detective, Avery Lynne, she's the one that shot me?"

Ariana's eyes widened as she quickly stepped forward to take the bullet in her fingers, examining it more closely. "Yes, that's the one. When she saw you there standing over the body, she obviously thought you were the bad guy and she opened fire. She's quick, that one. I didn't have a chance to explain what happened." She rolled the bullet around in her palm and opened her senses to it, then declared, "Hey, there it is! I wasn't paying attention when I dug them out of you, but if I focus, I can feel what you mean. She *did* put some extra stank on these things." She looked at me with questions in her eyes. "But she's not a witch. She wouldn't even know how to do it, and it's difficult enough that even I don't do it like this. My mother made a ton of special bullets before she...left...and she always said it was easier to work the magick into the metal *before* forming the bullets. This feels like a regular bullet that's been enchanted. Could she be more witchy than she's telling us, more skilled?"

I thought that over briefly, then shook my head. "No, I honestly don't think so. She does have power, that's a fact. But from what I can tell, her skill set is extremely limited. She didn't even know witches existed until we told her. I'm betting she did this on instinct. Her emotions were running high, her adrenaline at its peak. When she entered the house and saw us there..." I came to the only logical conclusion that I could, "I think she did it by accident."

Ariana let out a low whistle. "Seriously? Wow. That's impressive. We'll have to be careful with her from now on, then. If she can enchant a magazine full of bullets by accident, there's no telling what else she might be able to do." Finally, she cracked a grin. "At least she's one of the good guys!"

I nodded. In my time, I'd been beaten, stabbed, and shot by bad guys and good guys alike. Detective Avery Lynne really did strike me as the latter. She was in a profession meant to help people, and her aura confirmed that. Even so, she now thought I was a murderer, and would deal with me accordingly. With her unknowingly souped up firepower and heightened senses, that would be a problem. *Oh well,* I thought, *it could be worse. She could have been an evil politician or something.* "A 'good guy,' yes, she is that. On the side of the Light." I agreed.

"Ok, now that you're all better," Ariana began as she moved to the far side of the table to clean up the mess she had made while repairing me, "you can tell me what the hell that thing was at the Thornwall house."

I shook my head in dismay. "That was a lesser demon more commonly called a Gray Beast."

Ariana's eyes widened in surprise. "Lesser? Really?"

I shrugged. "Admittedly, they're on the higher end, but still technically lesser. They're pretty rare. They're generally summoned to perform a single task, usually to kill someone." I remembered the moments before it had appeared in Diana Thornwall's living room.

She had just come back down the hall from escorting the detectives out, and was surprised to find us standing there, calmly awaiting her. She kept her composure admirably for one who had just been grilled by a couple of detectives, found out an old family friend was missing, then stumbled across two strangers in her living room. She had closed her robe more tightly around herself and stood her ground. "I don't keep money here at the house. Whatever else you want, just take it and go."

More than anything she looked annoyed. That gained my respect. She was upset, but not afraid.

I reached out with my magick to calm her, and was surprised to find that it worked easily. She sighed and unfolded her arms immediately, putting her hands on her hips as she waited for one of us to speak. For a witch capable of summoning the snake demon at Raymond's and setting up the self-destruct spell that had burned him to ashes, I'd have thought she'd be harder to influence. I looked over at Ariana, who immediately started speaking.

"We need to talk about Raymond," she began.

"I already told the police, I don't know anything about that, about whatever he was doing," Diana said, a touch of exasperation coloring her words. "He's an old friend of ours, but I haven't seen him in ages. He teaches at the community college, but beyond that, I had no idea he was up to...whatever that was. Drugs?" She shook her head, "I still can't believe it." Her words rang true to me. My senses were all over her, and she wasn't hiding a damned thing. Which was problematic and confusing. She didn't have so much as a hint of magick in her. Not a drop.

I looked at Ariana and shrugged, then nodded in agreement. She opened her mouth to speak again when an alien stillness suddenly settled on the room. The air felt thick, and the temperature began to drop. We both tensed while Diana looked around in confusion. It was strong enough that she felt it too.

"Hey, what's that...?" Ariana began, one hand slowly edging towards one of the Glocks on her thighs. Before she could draw it, a sphere of roiling black fire burst into being in the middle of the room between us and Diana. It swelled until it nearly reached the ceiling, then it disappeared, leaving a monster in its place.

The demon was easily seven feet tall, over four hundred pounds of bulky muscle, and covered with leathery gray skin. Its hands had only three clawed fingers and a thumb, reminding me of the goblin race, but the resemblance ended there. Where goblins were small, but ridiculously strong, this thing was enormous and made them look like feeble children. The skin of its bald head was scarred from untold battles, and both batwing ears were ragged and torn. Baleful and menacing eyes glowed yellow in the dim light, set deep into a grotesque mask dominated by a squashed nose and a pair of rubbery lips. It turned towards me, bared a mouthful of fangs, and growled.

I growled back. I don't like demons.

It turned away from me and fastened its gaze on Diana, who had frozen in utter terror. The beast grunted and lumbered towards her.

Ariana had already drawn her sidearm by then, and she expertly emptied her magazine into the creature's wide back. It growled and flinched with each impact, and dark scarlet blood emerged from the wounds, steaming from contact with her special bullets. But it didn't go down. It was too big, too strong. And it was headed right for Diana. She screamed, her eyes wide with fright.

Bullets wouldn't work. It was my turn. I pushed the razor-sharp claws from my fingertips and launched myself at the thing. I landed on its back, dug my claws deeply into its left shoulder and reached my right hand around to rip out its throat. A beefy right hand darted up and caught my wrist. For such a big thing, it was awfully fast. I had an instant to realize that things were about to go bad, then it whipped me off its back and slammed my body down onto the coffee table with a crash, shattering the sturdy wood into splinters. That hurt a lot. The demon didn't let go, though. It just reversed direction and swung me over its head to slam my body into the floor on its other side. *At least there's carpet there,* I thought as I tried to ignore the bright shards of pain that exploded inside my body from all my broken bones.

I felt the creature gear up for another swing, but I'd had enough of that bullshit. I reached up with my free hand and slashed deeply through the creature's bicep, then lashed out at his legs as well, leaving deep, painful furrows in its bulging thigh muscles. It grunted and reflexively released me. I twisted and got to my feet in a blink, then continued slashing at its exposed torso.

I opened up four bleeding gashes in its abdomen, but it shielded itself with its thick arms, and my next attacks were ineffective. It opened up both hands as if to push me, and I saw a grin crawl across its ugly face.

Shit, I thought.

It mumbled a word I didn't recognize, and an invisible wave of force slammed into me, heaving me across the room and into a curio cabinet. There was a lot of glass and porcelain that got broken, and when I fell to the floor, the heavy wooden shelving unit fell right on top of me. It hurt, yes, but more than that, it was embarrassing. Especially because I could hear the thing laughing at me, a deep, bass chuckle. Thoroughly pissed off, I heaved myself up and flung the broken furniture away, letting it crash to the floor nearby. I crouched, staring at the creature, who still faced me, laughing. I growled low in my throat as I prepared to launch myself at him.

"That's a pretty suit you're wearing, Fae," it rumbled at me, "it makes you look almost human." It sniffed the air, then ran its warty tongue over its lips. "Your magick tastes sweet. I think I'll take it." It reached one hand towards me, closed its fist, and then *yanked*.

Fatigue washed over me in an icy wave as the very energy of my life suddenly diminished, somehow pulled out of me by the demon's spell. I gasped, then fell to one knee, unable to do anything else. My vision fell out of focus and my head swam as I struggled to find whatever strength I could, but there was none. I leaned over and put my hands on the floor as I panted, desperately searching for a plan of action.

"Puny Grim," it muttered, then it turned towards Ariana. She'd holstered her gun and was muttering a spell of some kind, doing a good job of it too. Her hands were glowing, and as I watched, they grew almost too bright to see. Unfortunately, the demon didn't want to play with her. It grabbed a big chunk of the hardwood coffee table and flung it at her. The thick boards hit her hard, and she crumpled to the floor beneath them, the light around her hands extinguished, her spell uncast. It watched her momentarily, but when she didn't rise, the demon turned to Diana, who had been frozen like a hare under the gaze of a wolf. The beast's broad back faced me again.

That was my chance. I was weak, but that didn't matter. Whether I was ready or not, it had to be now. I came unsteadily to my feet and hurled myself at the beast. This time, I went for its neck with both hands as I grabbed it from behind. My claws dug in under its throat and I wrenched them through the tough cartilage and muscle that lay there, first with one hand, then again with the other, spraying crimson everywhere. It tried to scream, but only succeeded in uttering an obscene gargle as its ruined throat filled with blood. I raked my dagger-tipped fingers across its face, blinding it, then I went back to work on its burly neck. It staggered, but I had its measure now, and I held on with everything I had. With a savage wrench, I twisted its misshapen head around and heard its neck crack. I slashed through the last of its thick neck muscles, then yanked the head free with a sickening pop. The body shuddered, then began to topple. I leaped aside as it collapsed heavily to the carpet, its mangled body twitching. I stood next to it, still holding its grotesque head in my hands as I stared at its settling corpse.

I looked down at it, concerned it might not be truly dead, but it stayed down. Then, cold, black flames sprouted from the creature's leathery skin. They spread until the body was immersed in shadowy fire. The head in my hands burst into flame as well, and I tossed it onto the body, which was rapidly being consumed. Within a handful of seconds, the creature had disappeared entirely, back to the Etherworld from which it had come. I sighed in relief. At least until I looked down at myself and saw that my glamour was *gone*. I no longer looked like an ordinary, unmemorable human. My true self was on full display, claws, fangs, and all.

Ariana grunted and shoved a chunk of debris out of the way. She stumbled to her feet and drew her gun, but she was still unsteady. I quickly turned away from her to hide my true face and my gaze fell on Diana Thornwall.

"Dammit," I muttered.

She was dead. I hadn't been fast enough. She lay on the carpet, her eyes wide and staring at nothing, her chest and abdomen slashed open by the Gray Beast's claws. Her white robe, and the carpet beneath her, was stained crimson with her blood. I stepped towards her and cursed again. We'd never get any information from her now. That was my first thought. My next surprised me. I felt...sad? Was that what that feeling was? If Diana had been innocent, then her death was meaningless. *So what?* I thought, and rightfully so. *Just another dead human. Why does that even matter?* Even so, I still felt that hollow, cold feeling in my gut.

That's when the detectives burst in and the shooting started. Between Detective Avery's unknowingly enhanced rounds and the magick I'd lost to the Gray Beast, I'd been more vulnerable than I cared to admit.

Ariana's voice brought me back to the present. "A Gray Beast, huh? Tough customers, it seems. I'm glad you got the better of him; I wasn't too much help."

I glanced over my shoulder at her, hesitant to ask. "What did you see? After it hit you with that table?"

She gave me an odd look, then replied, "What do you mean, what did I see? I saw the cops come in and start shooting at you!" She frowned, then continued, "It's a good thing you covered yourself with…whatever that was. That shadowy thing. They'd never identify you."

Good, I thought, *she thought* that *was the illusion.* "Right," I said, then quickly changed the subject. "You're going to be all right, then, I assume?"

She nodded, then headed for the refrigerator to grab a beer. "Yeah, I'll live. Nothing a bath with some Epsom salts and some witchy poultices won't fix right up." She popped the top on the bottle, tossed the cap and opener on the counter, then plopped into a kitchen chair and propped her feet up on the table. "Well, now that we know we'll survive, what do we do?"

To be honest, I had no idea.

Chapter 16

Avery's head ached abominably. Slowly she began to drift towards wakefulness, climbing out of the cool dark in which she had floated for what seemed like forever. After a few experimental blinks, she opened her eyes and tried to focus. She found herself looking at her hands in her lap, wrists bound firmly with sturdy shackles of black leather. She tried to speak but found that her words couldn't make it out around the rubber ball strapped in her mouth. She was limited to little more than a muffled grunt. Her eyes widened in outrage and she raised her head to take stock of her situation.

She found herself in the back of her own car, bound and secured with a seat belt, with Jim alongside her. He was still unconscious, his head slumped forward onto his chest, the seatbelt keeping him upright. He, too, had a ball gag strapped to his head, the red rubber sphere protruding between his lips, leather straps and tiny chrome buckles holding it firmly in place. His wrists were shackled the same as hers, and his biceps were pinned to his torso by a wide belt of black leather. A quick shrug of her shoulders confirmed that she was also bound at the upper arms. Her ankles felt similarly restrained, though she couldn't see how.

Shock and anger fought for dominance in her mind, mostly so that fear wouldn't have room to play. She knew they were in deep trouble, and she had no idea how they were going to escape. She strained against the shackles at her wrists, but they were well-made and strong, and she found no give in them. Breathing deeply as she could through her nose to calm herself, she looked out through the windows of the car to see where they were.

It was night, although she didn't know if it was the same night or another. They were still at the Thornwall estate, and the car had been driven around to the back side of the house, where it now sat on the lawn on the far side of the swimming pool. She craned her neck and saw two squat stones, waist-high chunks of granite that hinted at human-like shapes facing each other, sitting in the grass a few yards in front of the car. She moved her head from side to side to ease the ache in her neck.

She guessed she'd be far more stiff and sore had she been insensible for longer, so it had probably been only an hour or two since they'd been knocked out by...what? Her brows furrowed as she tried to remember exactly what had happened. The woman, Tanya, had been behind them. She had spoken, and then they'd both blacked out, though not from anything so obvious as a blow to the head. Avery struggled to recall the scene, and finally remembered catching a glimpse of the young woman's eyes. They had flashed brightly before they'd passed out.

That's impossible, she reasoned, even as she also admitted that was wrong. She'd already seen enough that night to stretch the boundaries of her belief far beyond what they'd once been. Tanya had used some kind of power to subdue them both.

"Comfy in there?" Avery snapped her head to the left to see Tanya's face in Jim's window, her eyes wide over a pretty smile that held more than a hint of a leer. She blinked thick eyelashes at Avery as the detective glared silently back at her. "Oh, so sorry. I forgot, you won't have much to say for a while." Her smile widened. "Sorry about the ball gags. I had them around, and since the occasion presented itself, I figured I'd put them to good use. Don't worry, I washed them first." She winked slyly, "The pink one looks good on you."

I hate pink, Avery growled inwardly. She continued to silently stare at her captor, unwilling to give her the satisfaction of a response. *When I get free from here, I'm going to ram this damned thing right up your...*

"As you can see, you're going to be my guest for a bit," Tanya said sweetly. "However, I can't keep you here. I know they'll start looking for you sooner or later. Fortunately, I have a little hideaway that's just perfect for us. Once I get us there, we can get to know each other much better." Her smile widened, showing teeth that seemed a bit sharper, more predatory than they should have.

As Avery looked into Tanya's big, blue eyes, she suddenly felt an oily chill blossom within her. They were pretty eyes, wide and clear, and enhanced with a subtle, but effective application of makeup that would have snared a man's gaze at twenty paces. But they were dead inside. Her heightened senses felt Tanya's bone-deep madness like the cold that issued forth from an open freezer. Avery's stomach clenched in on itself at the sickly chill, and she squeezed her eyes shut. With a flex of her will, she disengaged from the foul energy that assaulted her, pulling back from Tanya's gaze and power, instinctively building a wall to keep the younger woman out. A few heartbeats later, Avery sighed at the relief her mental defenses afforded her. When she opened her eyes again, Tanya was still looking at her, but now, the smile had vanished, and a look of uncertainty had taken its place. Tanya stared at her for several seconds, silent and appraising.

"You," Tanya's voice had lost its flirty tone, "you're trouble."

Avery returned her stare, then nodded deliberately. *You bet I am, you bitch.* She held Tanya's gaze, but this time, Avery released the tight control she

112

usually held on her emotions, allowing her anger to boil into her eyes. Tanya blinked.

Then the younger woman sniffed and tossed her head. "No matter. You can't hurt me. Once I get you both to my little getaway, I'll find out what you know. Then I'll put you to good use." Her lips compressed into a tight, red line, then she left the window.

Avery watched her lithe form as she walked in front of the car and stood before it, facing forward. She stood silently, unmoving, for nearly a full minute. Tanya raised her arms slowly to either side of her, palms up, and Avery felt a tingle on her skin, a stinging, nauseating sensation that burrowed into her guts. She took as deep a breath as she could to steel herself against it, and kept watching, fascinated.

A singsong chant drifted through the air to reach her ears. It wasn't a song so much as a series of syllables that formed no words she could understand. It dawned on her that it resembled something a Native American might utter as part of a ritual or war dance. Low and insistent, Tanya's pulsing voice increased the tingling in Avery's body, and her eyes widened as the air around Tanya's hands began to glow a bright and ugly red.

The radiance grew as it was echoed in the large stones that sat in front of the car. They shone in the cool dark, squatty scarlet monoliths bleeding their foul light into the night. Tanya pointed one hand at each of the stones, then slowly began to trace an arc that would meet in front of her, over her head. Crimson lines of eldritch force followed her gesture, drawn in the air by the power of her will and the dark sorcery at her command. As she brought her hands together, the curving lines of energy met, completing the arc. She continued her chant as she drew her hands downward, maintaining focus on her creation. The glowing energy that empowered the arc followed her gesture, falling to the ground like a ruby waterfall, a wavering, shimmering sheet of light that obscured everything behind it.

Her hands still together, she turned her palms outward, then, with a final, loud exclamation, she spread them forcefully apart as though whipping open a set of curtains. The wall of scarlet energy beneath the glowing arc vanished, leaving behind a doorway to somewhere else. A cool, dry wind blew in through the opening, and Avery peered through the windshield, her eyes wide. Illuminated by her car's headlights and the reddish glow of the energy Tanya had harnessed to create the portal, Avery saw the top of a hill sloping away into a deeper dark. The thick, lush grass of Diana Thornwall's back yard disappeared at a razor thin line of crimson that stretched between the two glowing stones, and on the far side, she saw patchy tufts of short, tough grass that barely concealed the harsh, rocky soil underneath. Beyond that, she could see little.

Tanya opened the driver's side door and tossed a small duffle inside, then slipped into the seat. She turned the key and the engine growled to life. With a glance over her shoulder, she smiled slyly. "Buckle up back there," she chuckled and put the car in gear.

Avery considered headbutting her from behind, but the seatbelt held her back. She looked at Jim, only to find he was still unconscious. Whatever whammy she had laid on them both was still working on him. Tanya eased the car forward, driving between the two glowing stones and underneath the arc of energy. Avery leaned as close to the window as she dared and watched in awe as the car passed through the portal, leaving the humid night of Katy, Texas behind them. As soon as the car passed completely through, the scarlet doorway vanished, leaving them in almost complete darkness, save for the headlights that speared into the night ahead.

The ground was bumpy and rough at first, then the ride smoothed out as Tanya guided them onto a road of crushed stone. Avery tried to note any landmarks as they drove, but the land on either side was dark as pitch without the moon overhead to illuminate it. She saw nothing but vague shapes that might have been shrubs or small trees. As the car topped a rise and began to head downhill again, she turned her eyes forward and was rewarded with the sight of an island of lights in the distance. She squinted and saw that the road of pale stone led to a group of stucco buildings, a wide, sprawling complex surrounded by a high wall.

Tanya drove up to an entryway secured by a gate of solid metal. She stopped long enough to pull a small device from her pocket, which she pointed at the gate. With a click of a button, the gate began to slide open to reveal a courtyard with an ornate concrete fountain in the center. The car drove inside and parked as the gate returned to its original position, relocking itself with a loud click. Tanya slipped out of the driver's seat and came around to Avery's door.

Avery tensed, searching for a way to fight, but her bonds were solid and unyielding. Tanya opened the door, and with surprising strength, yanked Avery out of the car and let her fall heavily to the hard, uneven ground. The air exploded out of her lungs and a sharp pain stabbed her scalp from an unseen rock. She gasped for breath, struggling to get air back into her lungs as she heard her partner being similarly pulled from his side of the car. Still wheezing, she stared into the darkness overhead, noticing the dazzling array of stars that lay above her. The night sky in Houston was far too polluted with light and exhaust to allow that many to shine so brightly. In spite of the seriousness of her predicament, she marveled at the sight. Then Tanya's smug face appeared in her line of sight as the younger woman bent over her prize.

"Welcome to New Mexico. You're not going to enjoy it. Sorry."

Avery's eyes widened in surprise. *New Mexico? What the hell?*

A tough-looking man in black tactical clothing appeared above her, frowning grimly. The last thing she saw was a set of hairy knuckles as they descended towards her face.

Chapter 17

I paused as I considered Ariana's question. We had to do something...but what? Finally, I made a decision. "We have to go back."

She raised an eyebrow. "Seriously? The Thornwall place has to be crawling with police by now!"

I shook my head, "Be that as it may, we need to have a better look around. Someone knew enough about Diana and her home to place a demon right in the middle of her living room. Everything pointed to Diana as being the one who hired Raymond, but she didn't do it. There's got to be something there to point us in the right direction."

"Well then, I'm glad I left a camera in the yard."

I blinked. "You did what?"

"I left a wireless camera in that tree, attached to one of the branches. They'll have to look pretty damned hard to find it, and it gives us a view of the back yard. It's got a chip that'll hold three days' worth of video. I can piggyback onto their WiFi and pick it up from here, so we can see if it's safe to go in." Ariana stood and took a deep, dramatic bow. "Aaand you're welcome!"

I was impressed. "That's a lot safer than asking the Pixies to help us again. Faster, too. Let's take a look."

We headed to her computer and I pulled up a chair as she logged on. It didn't take long for her to hack her way into the Thornwall's WiFi, then find the camera. A few moments later, we were looking at the back of the house we had escaped from earlier that night. The vantage point afforded us a clear view of the back yard and swimming pool, and it faced directly into the living room, displaying the picture window we'd broken upon our exit. Nothing moved, save the time stamp in the upper corner of the video. The place was deserted. *Odd,* I thought.

"Where is everyone?" Ariana echoed my thought. "Those detectives would have called in everyone but the coast guard once they saw Diana's body! There's no one there."

"Yes, and we certainly made enough noise that you'd think someone would have called the authorities." I thought for a moment, then said, "Can you show me what happened earlier?"

"Rewind it, you mean? Sure, hold on," she said, moving the animated arrow on the monitor over to what I now knew was a control panel. She clicked a left-facing arrow twice, then the numbers in the upper corner of the video began to roll backwards. A couple of minutes later, there was a flash of movement on the screen. "There's something. Just a sec." She let it roll back a bit more, then clicked the big arrow. The video began playing forward at normal speed, and the numbers indicated the time of our previous visit. I watched us slip into the back door and then meet Diana Thornwall. Then the demon arrived, battle ensued, and the detectives burst in and started shooting. I watched Ariana fling herself in front of me, taking the two shots that knocked her senseless. She glanced up at me from her chair, but I showed no reaction. Inwardly, I admitted that, although a stupid move on her part, it had been a noble gesture. We watched as I snatched her up in my arms and burst through the back window. Diana's body was clearly visible on the floor, as were the two detectives, their guns still raised.

That's when things got interesting.

The detectives began to turn, and there was a bright flash. They dropped to the floor like rag dolls, either dead or unconscious. Standing behind them was a young woman we hadn't seen before. Her hands were raised, palms out, and a grim smile was on her lips.

"Hey, who the hell is that?" Ariana paused the video and ran the tiny cursor on the screen around the newcomer's face, then looked at me for answers. Unfortunately, I had none.

"No idea. She's unknown to me. But I'm pretty sure she's up to no good."

"Did she just kill those detectives? That bitch!" She unpaused the video, and we watched the woman search the unmoving figures. Then she stood, turned, and walked out the front door, locking it behind her. Moments later, the detectives' car pulled around the corner of the house and drove onto the grass between the camera and the swimming pool. "What's she doing?"

Again, I had no answers. I just watched. The woman exited the car and reentered the house, stepping carefully through the window I'd broken. Once inside, she walked briskly out of view into another part of the house. We kept watching and were rewarded a few minutes later by the sight of her coming back into the scene with an armful of what looked like leather belts and other odd items. She knelt next to the detectives and began to bind them. "They must still be alive. She's shackling them."

Ariana leaned forward and squinted as the woman pulled Avery into a sitting position to continue her work. "Is that...? Ewww! That's bondage gear!"

"Indeed," I agreed, and then looked at her quizzically. "Why are you acting repulsed? They're just restraints."

"Most people nowadays don't have restraints lying around, Kane," she explained. "Those are for, um, sex stuff."

I blinked at her and took that in. Then I shrugged. Such intimate practices were ancient history to the Faerie, so much so that I'd nearly forgotten about them. I was just surprised that humans had finally figured it out. I shook my head and turned my attention back to the screen. "Regardless, she's binding them well. She must have used a spell to render them unconscious, and now she's taking them elsewhere."

"Why?"

"Well, I'm sure that someone will come looking for Diana Thornwall soon enough. Whomever she is, she can't leave witnesses. But I'm surprised that she hasn't killed them yet. Look, now she's dragging them to the car."

The next few minutes were quite illuminating. The young woman with the short brown hair was obviously the sorceress we'd been searching for. Once she got the two detectives situated, she went back and finished off some particularly nasty business in the house before heading back to the car. The portal she created was quite impressive, and it took less than a minute for her to drive the car into the sheet of scarlet energy, disappearing as if they'd gone into a tunnel in thin air. The reddish glow of energy vanished, and the yard fell still. We watched for a few minutes more to see if anything else happened, but the video showed nothing. Ariana clicked a button and the screen's timestamp snapped back to the current time, and all was still quiet.

Ariana stared at the screen, then skillfully clicked her mouse until an image of the woman appeared. She scanned through the footage until she found the clearest view of her face, then froze the video. A few more clicks and she was running a search with the captured image.

"Bingo," she announced with a flourish, "you're looking at Tanya Thornwall. That's Diana's daughter. Socialite, businesswoman, and wannabe Instagram influencer." Ariana swiveled in her chair to face and folded her arms. "Oh, and I'm pretty sure she's our murderer sorceress. How do we take her down?"

I stared at the images of our target on the monitor. She was a comely woman, fit and pretty. But it was in her eyes that I found what I was looking for. I'd seen that same darkness, that same madness, in so many pairs of eyes over the centuries. They had all died at my hands...all save one: Elias Bress. Anger surfaced at the thought of the man that had almost sacrificed me on an altar in his penthouse suite. *I'll have to remedy that the first chance I get,* I thought, then shook it off. I'd get him, too, eventually. In the meantime, I resolved to make Tanya Thornwall pay for what she'd done. With her life.

"We need to find out where she went. Where she took those detectives." I said, "As far as we know, they're still alive." I nodded toward the image of the Thornwall's back yard. "If I lay hands on those stones, I might be able to get something from them."

Ariana nodded slowly. "Want me to drive you?"

"No," I replied, "I need to move. Make sure my body is working as it should." I was feeling itchy inside, and a good run would go a long way towards putting me back to rights. Besides, I could run cross-country and make it there faster than the Jeep could navigate all the traffic stops, even at this time of night when traffic was light.

Ariana opened a drawer and pulled out a phone. She turned it on and tapped at the screen a few times, then handed it to me. "Ok, look, when you get there, take pictures of the stones. Get every angle you can, then send them to me. I can research them over the internet. Maybe I can find something. And if there's trouble, I can track the phone and come find you."

I held the phone on my palm and stared at her. She might as well have been speaking Swahili to me. When I didn't respond, she got the hint and took the phone out of my hand so she could instruct me. It took a few minutes, but when she was done, I had a rudimentary understanding of how to use the thing. I sighed. Now she'd gone and done it...I knew how to use a smartphone.

*　　　*　　　*　　　*　　　*　　　*

The night air felt cool on my face as I ran, and I reveled in the sensation of movement. My body had finally healed itself, the pain of the gunshot wounds had faded, and I ran at top speed just because I could. Much of the land I crossed was open fields, and I had to watch for the barbed wire fences that separated the arbitrary boundaries between what the humans considered their own property. I didn't care about that. None of the Fae did. We recognize our own territories, and defend them ferociously, but we hold the humans' borders in contempt. We go where we choose.

Once I hit the outskirts of Katy, I dimmed myself. No sense in ending up on YouTube, even though the likelihood of anyone recording me was remote at that time of night. I dodged through yards, crossed deserted streets, and jumped fences as I let my innate sense of direction guide me back to the Thornwall estate. I can always tell where I've been, a skill that's helped me many times over the centuries. I slowed down as I approached the Thornwall place, for even though it was supposed to be safe, it wasn't a time for throwing caution to the wind. I reached out with my magick as I walked up to the back fence where we had previously parked the Jeep, but all was quiet.

I vaulted the fence and crouched next to the tree's wide trunk. I scanned the branches above me and I picked out the camera Ariana had left there. I grinned. That had been a great move on her part. I hadn't even seen her do it.

Nothing had changed from the last time I'd been here, except the curtains had been pulled through the broken window by the breeze. I moved towards the back porch, *listening* carefully to be sure I was alone. No one was there. I could still feel the fading echoes of the dark

122

magick that had been in play earlier, grating on my senses like annoying, out-of-tune music in the air.

I've heard it said that there's no evil magick or good magick, that it's how you use it that counts. That's bullshit. Well, mostly. The raw earth-power that magick comes from is neutral in the same way electricity is neutral. But where electricity feels the same powering a lamp or shocking someone to death, magick is different. It takes intent and will to make it work. Focus and emotion. Whatever a sorcerer creates retains the attitude of its creator, the feel of his or her emotions. Evil magick feels just like you think it might: oily, creepy, and thick. A sense of dread accompanies such uses of power. It can even make ordinary humans feel goosebumps when they get near it. Good magick feels bright, airy, and warm. Humans might feel happy, or empowered when they drift close to a place where a lot of good magick was used. Either way, when someone gathers and releases a huge amount of power for good or ill, it leaves a mark.

The two stones in the yard, squat and ugly lumps, absolutely reeked of the same ill wizardry that had brought the demon to kill Diana Thornwall. Once I was sure I was alone, I stalked towards them, hoping I could find something to tell us where they had originated.

As I approached, they both flared a bright scarlet, and I backed off. *An alarm?* I thought. Other than the faint echoes of the night's previous castings, I hadn't felt a thing. It had to be something else.

The glow brightened, and a thin line of energy emerged from the top of each stone, growing taller and curving towards the other as it lengthened. I stepped off to one side and hid myself behind one of the columns that held up the porch roof. It appeared that the portal was reforming, and if that were the case, something was probably going to come out of it. I flexed my claws in anticipation. *Finally,* I thought, *a chance to have some fun.*

When the arc of energy connected, a scarlet curtain of power descended from it. I couldn't see the far side of it, but that's where the three demons emerged. All three were shorter than me, but thicker through the shoulders and more muscular. Their skin was mottled white and grey, and looked to be stretched too tightly over their bulky muscles. They were bald, with no ears that I could see, though their yellow eyes were overlarge and slitted like a viper's. Their nostrils were little more than slits as well, but their mouths were more canine, snouts pushing forward with far too many sharp teeth to be reasonable. Their three fingers ended in long claws, sharp and dangerous. I cracked my neck in each direction, limbering up for the fight that was only seconds away. Then I saw something that made me pause.

One of the demons carried a tarp under one arm and a big plastic carrier filled with cleaning supplies in the other. At second glance, I noticed another demon had an empty bucket filled with sponges and a long-handled scrub brush. OK, *that's not something even I see every day,* I thought.

I decided to wait. I just had to see what they were up to. Keeping the column between myself and the demons, I watched them make their way into the house by way of the back porch. They moved carefully through the broken glass from the window I'd shattered earlier, and the lead demon pointed to it and gurgled something at the second in line, who nodded in response. They let themselves in, and I heard some general scuffling inside. Before I could decide what to do next, one of the demons came back out on the porch with a dustpan and broom and started sweeping up the glass. I leaned over as far as I dared and got a glimpse inside the house only to see the other two demons rapidly cleaning the bloodstains out of the carpet. Something that I guessed to be Diana Thornwall's body was now rolled up in the tarp and set off to one side while the demons did their speedy work.

I thought about the situation. Obviously, Tanya Thornwall was cleaning up her mess. Which would also erase the signs of my and Ariana's presence. *Finally, something helpful!* But no way was I going to let them take Diana's body with them. By all accounts, the woman had been an innocent, and there are far too many things a sorceress could do with a dead body if she were deranged or evil enough. And Tanya seemed to fit that bill pretty well, seeing as how she called up a Gray Beast to kill her own mother. I refused to let her get Diana's corpse, too.

The sweeping demon finished his chore with unnatural speed, then laid the broom aside and disappeared around the corner of the house. Moments later, it reappeared, carrying a large piece of plywood. In one hand, it also held a hammer, and several nails were clamped carefully between its thin lips. With admirable efficiency, it nailed the board in place, covering the broken window.

The wind shifted as it finished, and it stopped suddenly. I froze in place, keeping myself behind the column on the porch. I flexed my knees just a bit, gathering myself in case I needed to fight. It slowly turned its ugly face in my direction, but its gaze never landed directly on me. It snuffled the air with big, wet sniffs, and paused as it assessed. Then with a surprisingly human shrug, it turned and reentered the house to join its brethren. *Good,* I thought. I love a good fight. I needed the exercise. But I wanted them all out here so they wouldn't hole up in the house. That wouldn't keep me out for long, but it would be troublesome.

I edged away from the column so I could get a better view and saw the three creatures flitting about inside the room, scrubbing, cleaning, putting things back in order. It looked downright tidy in there, except for the rolled up bundle off to one side. I moved over to the side of the house, where I could see the back door, but still stay out of sight until I chose to attack. From there, I could see the working side of the portal, which looked like what it was: a doorway to another place. I crept a few feet away from my hiding spot so I could see it better.

Beyond the threshold of scarlet energy, the grass became patchy and sparse, allowing the stony red soil to show through. A waist-high, spindly armed plant caught my attention. It bristled with thorns, and I could see small buds on its arms, probably flowers closed for the night. Farther away, I saw another cactus plant with thick, spiny paddles that lay closer to the ground. *Definitely desert. But where?* I realized that somewhere on the other side, I'd find Tanya. And I could end her.

I took another step towards the gate, intending to go through it, but then I stopped. When it closed behind me, I'd be cut off completely from Ariana, and I quickly decided to stay put. Just as quickly, I frowned at the choice I'd just made. I'd handled this sort of thing on my own for centuries without help. The most expedient plan was obviously for me to hustle through the portal, track the demons back to their lair, and kill the sorceress when she revealed herself. Simple, just the way I like it. I'd find my way back here eventually. *So why don't I do that?* I thought. *I could just leave her behind; that's what I've always done.*

The vision hit me with force enough to steal my breath. I'd seen it before, and it made no more sense this time than it did the last time the Goddess had seen fit to send it. Ariana appeared in my mind's eye, bleeding and bruised, wearing her battered tactical gear. We stood back to back, she and I, both ready to fight. The short sword in her right hand already had blood dripping from its razor edge, and I had the impression it wanted more. Ariana held her left hand overhead, and whatever she held in it was ablaze with power, glowing so brightly that it hurt to see. The object cast a searing circle of light that illuminated a horde of demonic creatures at its edge, dwellers of the deepest Etherworld. They growled hungrily at us, their fangs and claws gnashing and clicking in anticipation. I knew from experience that our flesh would taste sweet to them. Ariana screamed in defiance at the oncoming demons, and I heard myself screaming along with her. My eyes glowed silver as I prepared to fling myself into battle, no longer hiding my true self behind a glamour. This time, I could see my own blood seeping from a score of wounds, even as I raised one of my clawed hands to strike the first demon within reach.

The vision ended abruptly, as it always did. I staggered from the force of the sending. Man, when the Goddess sends me a message, she doesn't play around. My head throbbed, and I put one hand to my forehead as I slowed my breathing down. *OK, OK,* I replied to the Goddess I served, *I won't leave Ariana.* I got no answer, but then, I didn't need one. The vision was message enough. I backed away from the portal just as the back door opened.

The demons filed out of the house, the first holding the door open for the other two, then falling in behind them as the door swung closed. The first had the plastic carrier of cleaning supplies in one hand. Its other arm was wrapped around a bundle of wood I recognized as debris from the table I'd been thrown into earlier. The second carried the rolled-up tarp on its shoulder, presumably Diana Thornwall's body. The third held nothing, and I knew I had to take him out first. The trio marched around the swimming pool towards the glowing portal in the grass on its far side, and I gathered myself to spring at the last in line. In seconds, they passed right by, still unaware of my presence. That would cost them.

Decapitating a demon isn't the quietest thing you can do. The moment I wrenched his head from his neck, the others turned to see what was going on, just as I knew they would. I kicked the still-twitching, headless body at them to increase their confusion, and hurled the scowling head at the farthest demon for good measure. They stumbled. Capitalizing on their surprise, I lashed out and grabbed the end of the rolled-up tarp. With a yank, I snatched it from the second demon and backed away with the long bundle in my arms. Diana had been a small woman but felt oddly light in my arms. I laid her down beside the house, where the demons would have to get past me to get her.

The demons recovered quickly, as I knew they would. They crouched and hissed at me, then the farthest turned and threw the cleaners and the wood into the portal, or mostly so, as much of the wood scattered on the grass at its feet. With its hands free, it displayed its claws. *Yeah, right, I've got those too,* I thought. The two creatures began sidling away from each other, obviously thinking to come at me from both sides. The one on my right lunged at me, and I focused on him, dodging and counterattacking as I maneuvered it between me and his buddy. Only one of them could attack me at a time that way, and I knew I could kill them easily one-on-one. The demon swiped at me again, but kept back just out of my range, snarling its hatred of my kind.

I expected the other demon to go on the attack as well, but it didn't. It busied itself by gathering the pieces of wood it had dropped and throwing them through the portal. It was quick, and it didn't take long before all the broken pieces had been tossed through.

They must be following their orders, I thought, *clean everything up and escape. Which means they won't want to leave the body.*

The moment the demon finished its task, it turned back to me and got down on all fours, opening its fanged mouth wide—too wide. Its bones cracked, and it grunted as it changed shape. Two more spindly legs broke through the skin of its back, reaching for the ground on either side until the demon resembled a misshapen centaur. Its torso rose to face me, and its legs twitched and jittered like an awful spider. The thing darted to my right, then left again, and I realized that it was fast enough to be dangerous.

It knew that too, and it hissed at me with triumph and laughter somehow mingled in its hideous voice.

I gritted my teeth and bolted towards the spidery beast, intent on ripping its legs out, all of them. We met in a tangle of arms, legs, claws, and fangs, flailing furiously as we each tried to gain the upper hand. Its talons dug into my flesh, but mine dug deeper, and the demon yowled in pain.

When the other didn't join in right away, I chanced a glance in its direction, and swore. It had bolted for Diana's body the instant I'd attacked. I leaped for it, but the spider-thing reached out and grabbed my ankle in its ferocious grip. I turned and slashed through the muscle and bone of its slender arm, and nerveless fingers released me. I launched myself at the second demon, who had already dragged the body halfway to the portal. I slammed into it, and we rolled a couple of times before I came up on top. It fought hard, as demons tend to do, but I pummeled its face with brutal punches before ripping its throat completely out. Its heels drummed on the grass for an instant before it gurgled its last, fetid breath into the air.

I surged to my feet, but it was already too late. I saw the tail end of the tarp-wrapped bundle being dragged into the portal by the spidery creature. I dove for it, but the portal vanished, and I ended up landing on the grass on the far side of where the portal had been.

"Dammit," I said aloud. I hated losing. For some reason, I felt an odd sense of obligation to Diana Thornwall. She'd been ready to help us, and innocent of any wrongdoing as far as I could tell. *Just another human,* I reminded myself. *She didn't matter.* But I sighed, and couldn't shake the odd idea that maybe she did. I looked at the two stones. They didn't have much in the way of markings. It was still possible that Ariana might figure out something if she could get a look at them. Too bad I'd stowed the phone in the tarp along with Diana. There wouldn't be any pictures, but I was pretty sure Ariana could use her technical wizardry to find the location of that phone, wherever they had taken it.

Finally, I let myself smile. *We're coming for you, Tanya,* I thought, a*nd we're not gonna play nice.*

Chapter 18

Avery was thinking of investing heavily in ibuprofen stock by the time she was able to open her eyes again. The last thing she remembered was being thrown to the ground and thinking that it had hurt a lot. Moving slowly so that her head wouldn't split in two, she sat up and swung her legs over the side of the bed. Thankfully, the ball gag had been removed, as well as the shackles that had bound her ankles together. The leather restraints had been replaced with a simple pair of handcuffs, and she was grateful for the increased mobility.

She was in a small, sparsely furnished room. The bed she sat upon was expensive and well-made, and there was a desk and chair of similar make. Blankets and pillows displayed a subtle Southwestern motif. There were two doors in the room. Avery got to her feet, then moved quietly as she could to the door that looked most like an exit. She tried the knob, but it was locked. *Worth a try,* she thought as she walked over to the other door. It opened easily, revealing a small bathroom with a marble tiled shower, a toilet, a pedestal sink, and little else. Her eyes were instantly drawn to a small, frosted window in the wall opposite the shower, and she moved over to it. It was far too small for her to squeeze through and was nearly frozen in place from disuse. However, she was able to open it halfway, and she looked out to survey her new surroundings.

"Holy shit, Toto," she breathed. "This isn't Kansas...or Houston, for that matter."

The sun had risen, and the air was chillier than Avery expected as a gentle breeze came from outside to caress her face. She was on the second floor, looking out onto a wide vista of rolling hills dotted with scrubby bushes, pale green grass, and darker tufts of green that stood out in various places across the landscape. The soil she could see through the sparse grass was reddish and rocky, and here and there, spindly cholla cacti showed off yellow and pink flowers. Dark shadows of clouds crawled over the land, slowly making their way across the arid valley floor. In the distance, miles away, the dark spines of mountains lurked like sleeping dragons.

Avery's mind raced. *What did she say?* she asked herself. *Something about New Mexico?* Her eyes roved the area, and she realized that her captor had been telling the truth. The early morning was calm and quiet, save for the soft birdsong and distant lowing of cattle. She leaned to one side and saw the land rise sharply into a peak of red-tinted stone off to the east of the building. It was breathtaking...at first. As she looked at it, a cold chill worked its way up and down her spine. *Something bad is over there.* The thought came unbidden, but she had no reason to disbelieve it. The sense of unease that shivered inside her was strong enough that she finally had to look away from the ruddy rock formation.

The sound of the door opening in the room beyond got her attention, and she quickly shut the door to the bathroom, swearing when she saw there was no lock. She heard a few sets of footsteps enter the room, and she waited.

"Sorry to disturb you, but we need to talk." Tanya's voice was cool and polite. Avery stayed silent, her mind racing as she tried to come up with a plan. "Look, you know I have your partner. Don't make me hurt him. Well," she laughed mockingly, "don't make me hurt him *more*, I mean. He was pretty testy when I saw him last. We had to reason with him a bit before he settled down. He should survive." There was a pause, then, "Don't make me send these guys in there after you." Avery glanced at the window. "And don't think about escaping through the window. Even if you could get through it, you'll break an ankle from this height, and you're in the middle of the New Mexico desert. There's literally nothing for miles. My people will pick you up before you get a hundred yards from the wall."

Cursing silently, Avery opened the door and reentered the room. Tanya sat on the bed, her legs primly crossed. She'd changed into faded blue jeans, a white blouse and a pair of sturdy boots. Two large men stood on either side of the door in black tactical pants and matching button-down shirts, guns visible on their hips. Avery looked them over. *I could probably take the one on the left,* she thought. He was the smaller of the two. She looked at the second man, a thickly-built fellow with a crew cut and meaty hands. He flexed them as she watched, and she caught a flash in her mind of some of the things he had done with them. A sliver of fear ran through her before she quelled it. *I'll need to put a bullet or two in that one,* she thought. She turned her attention back to the woman. "What do you want?"

Tanya's smile widened. "Right to the point. I like that." She stretched, taking her time about it and enjoying herself. "Who knows I was involved with Raymond?"

Avery stared at her, calculating the wisdom of giving Tanya any information at all. In the end, she decided to default to her usual plan...be a pain in the ass. "Everyone. I told everyone at the station. The mayor, too. She knows. Oh, and the guy at the Stop and Go. He seemed really excited about it, too."

Tanya sighed and shook her head. "Why do you have to act like that? I was trying to be nice."

Avery raised an eyebrow. "You knock us out, kidnap us, hold us prisoner, beat up Jim, and that's being nice?"

Tanya's smile returned. "Oh, yes indeed. I guess you'll have to learn the hard way. I suppose it doesn't really matter who knows anyway, they'll never believe it." She folded her arms and smirked, her lips curling up on one side. "You know, I warned Raymond about you."

Avery's eyebrows rose in surprise. She remembered the little man's comment, saying that he knew her. She hadn't thought much of it at the time, thinking he'd just identified her as a cop.

Tanya laughed at her confusion. "I knew someone was coming for him, I just wasn't sure who or when. I knew it was a woman and a man, but little else." Running her fingers through her hair, she sighed again. "Divination isn't my strong suit, and dreams can be pretty fuzzy. But you?" Her smile came back in full force. "I knew it had to be you the moment I saw you." Then she frowned. "Those other two, though...they could be trouble." She shrugged, "No matter. They'll never find us here. And even if they did, I've got men with guns everywhere, as well as a few other surprises."

Glancing up at the two brutes, Tanya shifted her tone. "Gentlemen, I need you to do some heavy lifting for me. Let's go." The shorter of the two opened the door and Tanya stood. She glanced back over her shoulder at Avery, "You'll see me again soon. Get some rest; you'll need it."

Avery said nothing, but glared daggers at the three retreating figures. When the door closed, she sat on the bed, no closer to figuring out what Tanya wanted with her, but encouraged that she hadn't been killed out of hand.

She's gonna regret that, Avery vowed. And for the first time since she'd found herself in the cell, she allowed herself a smile.

*   *   *   *   *   *

Garrett strolled down the hallway towards the lady cop's room. He'd been told to be careful around her, but although he had replied, "Yes, ma'am," as expected, he had bristled at the warning. *Piece of cake,* he thought, *no short, middle-aged woman is going to give* me *trouble!* He'd been an MMA fighter before signing on to work private security, and he'd been in his share of scraps. Brimming with confidence, he unlocked the door.

Forcing politeness into his tone, he warned her as he opened the door, "Ok, lady, step away from the door. I'm coming in to get you." He pushed the door open and saw the cop on her knees in the middle of the room, her head bowed and eyes downcast. *What the...?* He put his hand on his gun. "On your feet, lady, Tanya wants you." She stayed where she was, wrists still cuffed, hands in her lap. "Hey. Hey, I'm talking to you!" No response.

Annoyed, Garrett pulled his gun and aimed it at her. "I told you to get up. I'm not playing." When she didn't raise her eyes to him, he moved closer, holding his gun in a two-handed grip. "Lady, I'm serious. Get. Up." He slowly walked forward until he was close enough to touch the barrel to her forehead. He held the cold metal there and applied a bit of pressure. "Look, I don't know what you're..."

Avery's hands flashed up and grabbed the gun, twisting it so that it pointed off to her right. Garret responded by instinctively pulling the gun away, which did nothing but help Avery to her feet as she launched herself at him. Before Garrett realized his mistake, she slammed the top of her head into his face, shattering his nose and rocking his head back.

She yanked the gun away from him and drove her shinbone into his groin, doubling him over, then she delivered a crushing knee to his already damaged face. Garrett slumped to the floor, bleeding and unconscious.

"Ow," Avery said aloud, grimacing at the pain emanating from her bruised head. *My kingdom for an ice pack,* she thought, but she brushed the pain aside and set about searching the thug's pockets. She came up with a set of keys, a folding knife, some change...and a handcuff key. "Yes!" she hissed in triumph. In seconds, she had the cuffs off her wrists. She rubbed the abraded skin briefly, relishing her freedom, then got to work. She dragged the unconscious guard to the bed and heaved his body onto it. Threading the short chain through the rail at the end of the bed, she secured his hands together behind him, clicking the cuffs closed as tightly as they would go. Just for fun, she whipped off the man's belt and bound his ankles as well. She stood to check her handiwork, then rolled up his tie and shoved it in his mouth for good measure.

She stripped him of his gun and spare ammo, then crept to the door and listened. Hearing nothing, she opened the door a crack and peered outside. Her room was at the end of an empty hallway. The corridor moved away to her right for several yards, then it turned leftwards. She heard voices from around the corner, both male. The unseen speakers chatted for a few moments, then began to walk away. She waited until she heard both voices and footsteps receding into silence, then eased the door open as quietly as she could. *I've got to find Jim,* she thought. Keeping her new gun at the ready, she slipped out of the room and locked the door behind her.

Chapter 19

"Von Gerhardt here. Hello?" The greeting was followed by a somewhat stifled yawn, a sign of the early hour. This close, I could hear the voice on Ariana's phone as though she'd put it in speaker mode.

A thrill shot through her, strong enough that I could feel it, but she seemed to put it aside. "Max! It's Ariana. Remember me?"

There was a beat of silence, then I could actually hear the smile appear in his deep, resonant voice. "Oh, it may be frightfully early in the day, but I'd never forget you, my dear. It's a pleasure to hear your voice again, truly." There was a slight pause, then, "Are you well? Is Kane still with you?"

"Yes, we're still working together," Ariana replied, quickly, I might add. The emphasis on the *working* part wasn't lost on me, and I found it amusing. I'd told her long ago she should just tell the werewolf king that she was attracted to him, but to my knowledge, she had not. I doubted she was intimidated by his vast wealth and power, so her reluctance to mate with him befuddled me. *Humans,* I thought, slowly shaking my head. "Hey, I've got something going on here, and I need to ask for help." Her voice was steady once more.

I heard Max's voice perk up with eagerness. "Absolutely. Just tell me what you need, and it's yours." Another slight pause, then, "You know I'm always at your service, Ariana." His voice dropped lower when he said it. Her heart started thumping with extra gusto and I worried she might have an attack.

Flustered, she tried to sound cool. And failed. "Um, right. Yes, ah…we need a helicopter to take us to New Mexico. Like, right away."

"Done," Max instantly agreed, "I'll have my man Edge fly out to you, and he'll take you wherever you need to go. He's in Fort Worth, so he should be able to get to you by..." there was a moment of silence as he apparently did some calculation, "noon or so. He can probably have you where you need to go before nightfall. What's going on?" Ariana took a few minutes to fill him in on what we knew so far. When she had finished, Max stayed silent for a moment before responding. "Interesting. I'll have Edge prepare accordingly. He's a good man in a fight, so make use of him however you see fit. I'd come myself, but I'm embroiled in a rather tricky affair in Alaska right now. One of mine has gone rogue, and I need to handle it myself. Family business." Max's voice hardened at the last, and I felt his true nature assert itself. Maximus was a cultured and charming individual, impressively intelligent and highly educated. He was also a werewolf. Not only that, he was considered the king of them all. Beneath his polished exterior was a ferocious and deadly creature, a nearly unkillable beast that I would hate to meet in combat. And I don't scare easily. Fortunately, we had sprung him from captivity some time back, so we were all on very friendly terms. He'd especially taken a shine to Ariana.

"Sure, gotcha. Good luck with that." Ariana's disappointment was noticeable, but not pitiful. "Hey, thanks for everything. You've been awfully generous. I really..." she cast a quick glance at me, "I mean *we* really appreciate it."

The laugh that jumped out of the phone's tiny speaker was warm and genuine. "Ariana, you and Kane saved my life. I wouldn't even be here if you two hadn't gotten me out of that tower. Anything I have, any resources I command, they are yours, you only need to ask."

She blushed. I rolled my eyes, and she reached over and swatted me for it. I shook my head slowly and folded my arms as I got comfortable in the kitchen chair, but I kept silent. She turned her back on me and returned her attention to the phone. "Well, thanks. You're all right, Max. Really."

"Dinner when I return?"

"Um…wait, what?"

"You know, dinner. That's when two people get together and enjoy an evening meal and conversation." He paused, and I could imagine the huge, wolfish smile he had to be wearing as he said, "You can bring Kane if you like, but I doubt he'd mind if I escorted you myself."

She unconsciously reached up and found a lock of hair to twirl around her fingers. "Dinner? Um…sure. Sounds fun." Her heart was thumping like it was in a rock band, though her voice was anything but excited. "Right. Yeah, just, um, let me know when you're back in town."

"I will. I look forward to it." His voice became all business once again. "Edge will text you when he's getting close. Oh, and Ariana?"

"Yes?"

"You and Kane be careful. New Mexico is beautiful, but it can be harsh and unforgiving. There's old magick out there, as well as a few things you may not have dealt with before. Stay safe."

"Will do. Bye." She tapped the phone and disconnected the call before slowly turning to give me the side-eye. "What are you looking at?"

"You," I said, stating the obvious. "Why not just tell him you want him? You're a witch. A warrior. And he obviously wants you as well, why not just say it? Are you afraid?"

Ariana straightened to her full height, which was a hair taller than I, and glared at me. Just when I thought she'd lay into me, she sighed and ran a hand through her hair. "Look, I'm not afraid of him. It's just...it's been a long time, and my last relationship didn't exactly end well. It got complicated." She pulled a beer out of the refrigerator, popped the cap off, and headed for the stairs. "No, I don't want to talk about it. See you in a few hours, I'm catching a nap before Edge gets here."

I watched her muscular bottom disappear as she ascended, then looked away when she reached the landing and turned down the hall towards her bedroom. I thought she was just being unnecessarily bashful, but when she had mentioned her last relationship, her normally blue aura had suddenly swirled with reds, yellows, and greens. Her emotions had become so intense, they were visible to my Faerie sight without my urging. *Complicated...and awfully interesting.* I shrugged and decided that she'd talk about it when she felt the need. I could wait.

Usually, I don't need sleep. Every now and again, I'll shut down for a few hours of true slumber, but that was only on occasion. I stretched, feeling the tension that remained in my back and chest from the night's challenges, and thought it might be one of those occasions. We had a few hours before Edge would arrive to ferry us to New Mexico, so I wandered over to one of Ariana's old, overstuffed chairs and sank into it. There was a lever on the side, which I pulled, and it leaned the whole chair back into a reclining position. As much as I hate to admit it, I loved that chair. I slept.

Chapter 20

Avery pressed her body up against the wall and slid as close to the corner as she dared. She held her gun at the ready, though she was reluctant to use it, knowing full well that even a single gunshot would bring Tanya's security forces down on her in a swarm. She calmed her breathing and listened for the sounds of activity in the hallway beyond, but heard nothing.

The building seemed new; the freshly-painted walls lacked even a hint of dust. The floors were polished wood, and she was thankful for the quiet rubber soles on her semi-fashionable shoes. Jim had always given her a hard time about them, but she'd had to run or fight far too many times to feel comfortable wearing fancier footwear, and they were proving their worth again.

The walls were topped with elegant wooden molding that matched the floors, and the entire building smelled faintly of potpourri. Sconces in the walls held Native American pottery and other items that complemented the Southwestern theme throughout the house. Avery passed a few locked doors, as well as a plush theater room that boasted several leather reclining chairs and the biggest curved TV screen she had ever seen. She had been fortunate enough to find that door unlocked when some of Tanya's security thugs approached, and she hid there until they passed. Now, she neared the end of a hallway that mirrored the one that had housed her cell. It had the same bare walls and unadorned but sturdy doors, and she had a strong feeling that her partner was near. If she'd learned anything during her time as a cop, she'd learned to trust her intuition, and recent events had only strengthened that trust. She checked to see that no one was in view, then she turned the corner.

The feeling that Jim was close only intensified as she approached the door, and she carefully reached for the knob. A shock of static snapped at her fingers and she stifled a yelp, but then tried again only to find the door locked. *Glad I grabbed those keys from that knucklehead back there,* she thought, and she shifted her gun to her left hand so she could dig in her pocket for the keyring with her right.

The air around her went cold. The temperature drop was sudden and intense, and she stopped moving as her senses went on high alert. There was no sound, but when she exhaled, she could see her breath as it steamed in the cold air. Alarmed, she put her back up against the wall next to the door and scanned the hall in either direction, but saw nothing. When nothing further occurred, she steeled herself against the feelings of dread that had arisen in her and went back to the door to unlock it.

"Jim!" she whispered. "Hey, man, you in there? I'm here to get you out!" She opened the door as quietly as she could and eased her head inside. The room was furnished much as hers had been, and to her relief, Jim was seated at the end of the bed facing the room's small window, one wrist handcuffed to the bedframe. He remained silent, his head down on his chest, as if dozing. *Dammit, I bet they drugged him,* she thought. She could only see his back, but he seemed to be uninjured, which was a relief considering what Tanya had implied. She sighed and slipped into the room, leaving the door open a crack behind her as she approached her old friend. "Jim! Hey, we've gotta go!"

A sharp hissing sound made her flinch, which saved her life. Something whistled through the air less than an inch above her head as she ducked, and she instinctively tucked and rolled to get away from her unseen attacker. When she came up to one knee facing the doorway with her gun aimed, she froze in disbelief.

The thing that faced her was straight out of a horror film, and if it meant to scare her, it was doing its job. It was only a bit taller than her, and wiry. Its ropy muscles bunched and moved, easily visible beneath its skin, which was a wet, mottled red and black. Its arms were longer than they needed to be, and where its left hand should have been, a long and jagged blade of bone protruded at least a foot beyond where its fingers would have reached. The other hand's fingers were long and grasping, and also tipped with razor-sharp bone talons. Its face was dominated by a wide, lipless mouth that held far too many needle-like, bloody teeth. Its nose was no more than a pair of wet slits in its horrid face, and it had no eyes that Avery could see. Nevertheless, it faced her squarely, its attention fully on her as its head twitched sporadically. It hissed again, and then emitted a guttural chuckle that frightened her for a moment...then pissed her off quite thoroughly.

"After the day I've had, you wanna go, ugly? Fine. Bring it. I'm gonna kick your scrawny ass up into your throat." Mindful of the noise the gunshots would make, and the danger to Jim, she deliberately holstered her gun. She had to get her partner out before anyone caught them, and shooting the creature, however enticing the idea, would bring security running. Instead, Avery cracked her neck left, then right, then assumed a fighting stance with her hands open. "Let's go, slimeball."

The creature hesitated as it sensed its prey's emotions switch from fear to outright aggression. Its smile widened, then it lunged with its bone blade, intending to skewer the smaller woman and burst her heart.

Avery parried the thrust with the palm of her right hand even as she turned her body sideways to avoid the attack, already moving forward to counter. Her left fist

143

pistoned out and struck the oncoming demon directly in its wet nostrils, rocking its head back with a loud crack as bones broke. She slipped alongside the creature as it staggered, grabbed it behind its neck and shoulder, and slammed a brutal knee into its unprotected ribs, then another. It wheezed and buckled in surprise, and she hammered the bottom of her left fist into the back of its misshapen skull as hard as she could before shoving the thing away to fall in a tangle of bloody limbs on the floor.

A human would have fallen unconscious from the rabbit punch alone. The thing on the floor, however, was not human. It shook its hideous head, then rose to its feet as it turned its never-ending grin back to her. It chuckled again.

"Yesssssss..." it rasped, "againnnn!" Avery's eyes widened as the beast lashed out with its blade and caught her left arm, just above the elbow. She clutched it and took a step back in shock, grimacing as the pain hit her. The creature took a step forward, beckoning her to rejoin the fight.

She stared at the demon for a beat, then said, "Oh, hell no." She reached over to the bed and snatched up one of the big pillows that lay there. Lightly batting aside the creature's bone blade, she covered the distance between them in an instant and jammed the pillow over the surprised creature's face. She drew her gun with the smoothness of a thousand practice draws, pressed its barrel deep into the pillow's muffling softness, and pulled the trigger. The demon's head rocked back with a new bullet hole in the center of its wide forehead, and it fell to the floor in a twitching heap. "Cut my favorite shirt...what the hell is wrong with you? Asshole..." she mumbled, venting her anger even as she holstered her sidearm. Avery stepped on the creature's right wrist with her left foot, then knelt across its bony torso, pinning its body to the floor with her right knee. She grabbed its blade and efficiently tucked the point up under its chin. With a grunt, she shoved the point well up into its skull before it could regroup. Beneath the weight of her knee, the body of the demon convulsed, twitched, and fell completely limp. She held her position until she was confident the creature would not be getting up, then she sighed in relief.

She stayed still, listening. The sound of the gunshot had been muffled well by the pillow, but if anyone was nearby, they'd have heard it, not to mention the sounds of the scuffle. When nothing materialized, she sighed again and rose to her feet to check on her partner. He had not moved during the fight, and still sat on the end of the bed with his eyes closed, silent and immobile.

"Jim," she said again as she sat beside him and laid a hand on his arm. "Come on, let's get out of here. We've got to hurry before they catch us. Jim? Hey, are you all right?"

Jim's eyes snapped open and his head turned to Avery. A wide, maniacal grin slowly appeared on his face as Avery registered his bloodshot eyes. More importantly, Jim's brown eyes were now urine yellow, their pupils little more than pinpoints in the center.

"Jim's not here right now, little girl," a rasping caricature of Jim's voice taunted her, "but I'm more than happy to play with you."

Frozen in shock, Avery heard the door burst open behind her, then strong hands grabbed her from behind. Jim cackled in a voice she'd never heard before, and as a fabric hood was slammed over her head, plunging her into darkness, she knew she was too late.

Chapter 21

The whirling blades beat the air into submission with every stroke as Edge guided the copter towards the sunset. The Goddess had painted the sky with great swaths of pink, purple, and grey, and even I thought it was beautiful work. Glancing away from the display, I let my eyes rove the land that flowed beneath us as we passed the Texas border and entered New Mexico territory. Cities were far apart out here, and if I opened myself to it, I could feel the power of the vast, open land all around me, uncluttered by the noise that accompanied so many people crushed together. It had a pure, clean feel to it, an ancient and untainted strength that could create incredible wonders, or unimaginable horrors, depending on the spirit of the being who tapped into it.

"We should reach the coordinates you gave me within the hour," Edge's voice drawled over our headsets. Ariana smiled at his thick accent. Although born and raised in Texas, her own voice had only a faint twang, while Edge sounded like he'd walked out of a rodeo ten minutes ago.

"Yeehaw, partner. We appreciate it," she replied, exaggerating her own accent. Edge turned to look at her over his shoulder, mirrored sunglasses shining over an enormous grin.

"Well, howdy, y'all know we aim to please, ma'am," he replied, pleasure evident in his voice. He'd been all over the world, but his heart had always remained in Texas, it seemed. I liked few people, but I liked Edge. His firm adherence to a gentlemanly code of behavior sat well with my Fae side, and I had a strong sense that he would be capable in combat. Something about him bespoke a strength that ran deep, and I'd seen him handle a firearm. The man knew his business. He spoke again, "There's an estate not far from where the tracking system last saw your phone. It stands to reason that's where your creepies were headed."

"Agreed," I replied over the intercom system. I never liked having the headphones on, but it did make communication easier. "Set us down close to the place, but not too much so. We stand a better chance of getting in unseen on foot if we're not right on top of them." I looked at Ariana and continued, "We don't know what we're walking into here. What little we know of Tanya's powers is impressive. She's already using some pretty tough demons to do her bidding. We'll need to be careful."

Ariana patted the guns strapped firmly to her thighs and grinned. "You know I'm a careful sort, Kane. We'll be quiet until it's time to make some noise."

I nodded, then looked back out the window into the evening sky that was quickly growing darker. We had to take out Tanya. She was making trouble enough that I just couldn't have her out there. If the cops were still alive, it would probably be a good thing to find them, too. In years past, I'd likely have given them up for dead already, but I had a strong feeling that helping them was the right thing to do, in spite of the fact that the woman's bullets had damn near killed me. I sighed, vaguely disgusted with myself. *Getting soft in my old age,* I thought.

Something rippled across my senses, at the same time Ariana spoke up. "Hey, what was that?" she asked, squinting at something over my left shoulder.

I whirled towards the window, my Fae eyes narrowing in an attempt to see what she saw. There was nothing at first, but then, I spied a scarlet flicker in the distance, twin pinpoints of ugly crimson that snaked across the dark in a sinuous path. I saw another pair not far from the first. *Those are eyes,* I thought, *but of what?* Then recognition hit me.

"Edge," I said, "they're coming in on your left. Two of them."

"Copy that," Edge replied, and I saw him glance out the window, then do a double-take. "Y'all buckle up. It's about to get busy up here."

Ariana checked her harness and asked, "What is it?"

Something slammed into the side of the helicopter, rocking the entire vehicle and leaving a huge dent. Edge expertly compensated, and the engines ramped up as he began evasive maneuvers. We were thrown against our harnesses as the copter bucked and rolled.

"Wyverns," I replied.

"Gotcha. Wait, what?" She was about to say more but another lurch made her grunt instead. I focused on staying in my seat, waiting to see what Edge would come up with. Moments later, the wall on Ariana's side buckled inward as the force of another powerful blow rocked the copter. Six-inch talons pierced the metal in two groups of four as the creature outside latched on with powerful claws. I heard its reptilian hissing, even over the noise of the copter's blades, and it dragged one set of claws downward, cutting through the metal and leaving deep furrows behind. Its barbed tail burst through the wall, then disappeared, leaving a hole the size of a cantaloupe behind. Edge jerked the copter left, then right, then dropped downwards fast enough that I saw Ariana's face turn green. The thing outside shrieked again, retracted its claws and disappeared. The copter leveled out and began to rise.

"Y'all all right back there?" Edge's voice was tight, laced with concern.

"Fine," I quickly replied. "Is there anything you can do about those things?"

Edge shook his head. Wyverns were similar to baby dragons, except they were a different breed altogether.

They weighed about a ton and averaged fifteen to twenty feet long. Their brown, scaly hides resembled those of an alligator, but were much tougher. As a rule, they were quick, strong, and vicious. They weren't nearly as smart and didn't have the extra set of arms that true Dragonkind had. They lacked the intelligence to use magick, and couldn't shapeshift either, which was a plus. Even so, they were cunning and dangerous, and would destroy the copter with us inside if they put their mind to it. I heard a loud screech from outside and realized that they probably planned to do just that.

"What can you do?" I asked, hoping that Edge had something up his sleeve.

As if in answer, he jerked the controls and the copter veered to the left, slamming me into the back of my seat while Ariana tested the strength of her harness opposite me. She grunted as the straps dug into her body. Edge climbed, then dove, then circled back to the right. Something slammed into us closer to the tail, and we spun crazily for a few moments, but Edge brought the copter back under control.

"Not much," he finally replied. "We don't have enough firepower to be able to hit them in the air; they're too damned nimble."

Another impact shook the copter as one of the Wyverns slammed into its underside. Its claws poked up through the floor and the entire vehicle shook as the beast howled its victory.

I sighed, knowing what I was going to have to do. It pissed me off, having to deal with these things. I looked at Ariana and said, "You have that ridiculously huge knife on you?"

Although a look of confusion appeared briefly on her face, she responded immediately, "Duh, of course. Why?"

I held out a hand, "May I?" She narrowed her eyes, but drew the knife, a razor-sharp kukri as long as my forearm. I'm still not sure where she'd been hiding it. She handed it to me without a word. I accepted it and pulled off my headset as I unbuckled my harness, then bolted to the door. Before she could protest, I flung the door open and heaved myself out into the howling void. Hey, it's a living.

I grabbed the bottom of the doorway with my left hand and swung myself feet first into the Wyvern attached to the bottom of our helicopter. As my feet hammered into its side, I felt bones snap beneath them, but it seemed to have plenty of ribs to spare. The creature howled in pain, but didn't let go. Its wings were similar to the bat-like wings of gargoyles, but much larger. They flapped and slapped at me as it tried to retain its hold on the copter while I wrapped my arms around its body and dug the claws of my left hand into its side. Its reptilian head, eyes glowing red and sharp fangs filling a crocodile's snout, regarded me with hatred and anger as I gripped its long torso with my legs just above its wings. As I raised the kukri to strike, the Wyvern released the copter and exploded into the air, taking me with it. I retained my grip, but just barely. The thing was powerful, and able to change direction almost instantly, which made it difficult to hang on. Its wings flapped in big, strong strokes as it slithered through the air, folding its two muscular legs up underneath itself, and it began a series of impressive aerial gymnastics in an attempt to throw me off. I gripped its serpentine body for all I was worth as I tried to bring the kukri to bear. I finally caught my balance just long enough to stab the Wyvern with the oversized blade. The creature bucked and thrashed, but there was no escape. I stabbed it a couple more times before I finally hit something important. The Wyvern went limp. There was a moment of weightlessness as it stopped flying and began to fall.

Shit. That's when I remembered I was several hundred feet in the air. And I'd just killed the thing that was keeping me up there. The fall wouldn't kill me, but it would probably hurt. A lot.

Fortunately, the other Wyvern hadn't taken kindly to me killing its mate, buddy, or whatever it was. In the growing dark, its twin crimson eyes glowered at me as it closed the distance, its fanged snout open wide to rip me in half.

I decided on a slightly different approach for this one, although it was a bit more dangerous. I waited until it was almost on me, intent on snatching me off the falling Wyvern's back like a bird munching on a dragonfly. As it came close, I arched my body just enough that its jaws slid past me, and I wrapped both arms around its sinuous neck, dropping the kukri in the process. The force of impact nearly yanked my arms out of their sockets, but I managed to hang on to the beast as it flew on. Clinging tightly, I used my legs to maneuver myself up onto its shoulders, where I settled in front of its wings. I dug my claws into either side of its neck before it could reach around to snap at me and extended them into its scaly hide, not enough to damage it, but more than enough to cause it pain. The Wyvern shook its head, screeching in frustration.

"Yield!" I bellowed. I knew that it wouldn't hear me, but the magick I sent into the beast clearly conveyed my meaning. "Obey me, and live!" It shook its head again and yowled in frustration, and I dug my claws in a little deeper. It screeched once more, but this time, I felt its resignation. The fight went out of it as it recognized a new, if temporary, master. Its flight leveled out and I knew I'd gained its acquiescence. I added a little pressure with my right hand and squeezed with my knees, and the Wvyern responded by banking in that direction.

Now that I wasn't fighting for my life, I looked around and saw that Edge had already landed the copter in a small valley below. Smoke was coming out of it in a couple of places, and I could see the damage the Wyverns had inflicted, great gashes and rents in the steel. The rotors were slowing, but still appeared to be fully functional, although some of the smoke came from the engine below the rotor hub.

With a combination of claws and will, I guided the Wyvern to the ground not far from where the copter had settled, and it touched down with impressive grace. I conferred with it for a few moments before removing my claws from its neck, letting it know that although I harbored no ill will towards it, I'd kill it if it acted up. Surprisingly, I caught a sense of respect from the beast along with its agreement. I slid off its neck, and was surprised when it leaned over and rubbed its rough, scaly head up against my arm. I sensed...affection? Wyverns are weird. I shook my head and took a moment to scratch it between its eyes.

Ariana came out of the copter first, handguns at the ready. I held my palms out in a calming gesture and spoke to her mind-to-mind as the noise from the rotors came down to tolerable levels.

It's OK, I thought at her, *this thing's with me now. At least, for the moment. He won't hurt us.* It nudged me again and I gave it a shove with my elbow before giving in and scratching it once more. Its eyes closed and it made a gurgling sound of pleasure.

Ariana looked from me to the Wyvern and back to me again before holstering her guns and shaking her head. Then she raised an eyebrow. *Wait, where's my knife?*

I shrugged. *I dropped it. Sorry. I think it fell over there somewhere.* I gestured eastward.

She said some very unladylike things as she turned and walked off in that direction, stumbling at first as she figured out how to walk across the desert's uneven ground, then smoothing out her gait as she compensated. She pulled a headlamp from some pocket or other and switched it on as she marched in search of her beloved kukri, muttering all the while. I couldn't help it. I smiled.

The rotors finally fell silent, and our brave pilot climbed out from under the copter where he'd been working. Wiping his oily hands on a rag as he approached, Edge kept a wary eye on my new, scaly friend. When it was clear that it wasn't going to attempt to bite him, he relaxed and turned to me.

"Well, this is gonna take a while for me to fix," Edge nodded towards the downed helicopter, "but I can handle it. And we're almost to where I was going to set us down anyway. The signal from the phone is less than a mile from here." He threw a glance over his shoulder at Ariana, whose bobbing headlamp was slowly receding in the distance. "She should watch for snakes out here. It's dangerous."

"Honestly, I think they should watch out for her," I replied. A muffled gunshot reached us as Ariana killed something in the distance. "See?"

Chapter 22

"I was right," Tanya purred, the sound of her voice irritating Avery's every nerve, "you *are* trouble."

Avery stumbled, but the rough hands of one of Tanya's mercenaries grabbed her until she got her feet under her again. The ground was uneven enough that she would have had trouble walking on it without a cloth sack on her head, but blindfolded as she was, she tripped about every fifth step. She'd already fallen twice, further skinning her knees, but she had refused to make a sound.

When I get loose, I'm gonna make that bitch pay for whatever she did to Jim, I swear it, she thought. Anger kept her moving towards whatever fate Tanya had planned for her, though Avery was determined to fight tooth and nail given half a chance. For the moment, her hands were securely bound behind her back, and fighting would have done her no good since she couldn't see a thing. She went along grudgingly, biding her time. *I just need one chance,* she thought, *and I'm ripping her head off.* After several minutes of walking, the ground evened out, and the sound of their footsteps began to echo all around her. *A tunnel?* A cold chill ran down her spine, an oily sense of dread that made her stomach turn.

"Garrett, take her over there," Tanya directed. "Chain her to that post. That should keep her out of my hair until I need her."

The guards manhandled Avery until she felt a solid post against her back. One of them pressed the barrel of a gun up under her chin, painfully enough that she raised her head up to get away from it. "If you so much as twitch when he uncuffs you, I'll blow your brains all over the wall. Got me?" His voice was low and menacing, but sounded as though his nose was clogged.

Avery sighed and gave one short nod. It sounded like the thug she'd overcome in her cell. His nose was broken, and it was doubtful that he harbored any warm feelings for her. She stayed still while the other thug quickly uncuffed her, raised her arms over her head one at a time, then clicked a new pair of cold, metal manacles in place on her wrists. She pulled against them but found no give whatsoever. She was stuck.

The bag was yanked from her head and she blinked in the sudden light, dim though it was. Sure enough, the man holding the cloth bag was the one she'd subdued in her cell. He glared at her angrily, both his eyes already raccooned with bruises, and a bandage across the bridge of his nose. She returned his stare with her own, unflinching and intense. As her anger rose, a tingling sensation erupted from her core, a warmth that startled her. It spread out from deep within her body, flowing down through her legs, and up through her chest and into her arms. Avery felt the rising of her power without knowing what it was, but as it washed away some of her hurts and fatigue, she welcomed it. Holding Garrett's gaze, she let a cold smile appear on her face, and she enjoyed seeing him blink.

Then she kicked him in the balls as hard as she could. Garrett doubled over with an agonized wheeze and then slumped to the floor, clutching his groin.

Tanya's laughter echoed from the stone walls that surrounded them. "Oh my, you're just delightful, aren't you? My kind of girl. If you weren't a cop, we could be friends."

Avery didn't answer. She was staring at the sheer walls of red stone that surrounded them. They were in a circular stone chamber that appeared to be several stories high. She craned her neck upwards and saw a circular opening far overhead, allowing her a view of the starry heavens above. Torches burned in sconces in the walls,

155

which were covered with what looked like Native American drawings. Some were obviously animals and humans, but others were more difficult to discern, looking more like a combination of the two. The sense of dread that seemed to permeate the entire place deepened as she took in some of the more macabre designs. Three tunnels led away from the central chamber, one larger than the others, and Avery had a strong feeling that they had entered through that passage. Small stones had been placed in a wide circle in the center of the chamber, and within that circular border, a bundle of wood had been laid in a pyramid, a fire waiting to be lit.

"Garrett, could you please remove yourself? You're annoying me with all that groaning. Go back to the main house and sit on an ice pack or something. Thomas, go ahead and take him. When you return, stay at the entrance and make sure I'm undisturbed here until morning." Tanya spoke with the calm assurance that her orders would be obeyed, not bothering to look up at her men. "I'm not expecting any trouble, but I've worked a long time for this, and I don't need any interruptions."

"What do you want us to do with the other cop?" Thomas, a leanly-muscled fellow with a dark crew cut and a beard, inquired.

"I don't need him. Set him loose in the desert. Tell the demon to walk until the body dies beneath him."

"Yes, ma'am," Thomas pulled Garrett to his feet, and helped him towards the largest of the connecting passageways. Their footsteps stirred up reddish dust as they shuffled out, leaving Avery alone with Tanya. Silence fell on the ancient chamber, broken only by Avery's breathing and the crackling of the torch flames. Tanya wandered over to a huge, wooden trunk and knelt before it. Its hasp was secured by an impressive padlock, and she produced a key from a chain around her neck that unlocked it with a loud click.

"You're wondering about all this, aren't you?" Tanya's voice was low, but the words were clear in the silence. She laid the lock aside and opened the trunk. "You know, I hadn't planned to bring you into this, but I couldn't have you running around town back home and calling attention to my mother's death. And using a police officer for my ritual will increase the credibility of my petition. I've already got more than enough as it is, but a cop?" She clicked her tongue, "That'll clinch it."

"Clinch what?" Avery asked, both disgust and curiosity in her voice. "What could you possibly be doing here, in the middle of some cave in New Mexico? This is crazy!"

Tanya laughed, a low, throaty chuckle that echoed from the stone walls. "Wow, you really don't know anything about magick, do you? Even though you're so strong with it that I can feel it from here. Well, that is an oddity. Most people who have powers like yours either figure out how to use them or they go insane and kill themselves. But you did neither, did you? No, you probably just squashed it down inside yourself and pretended it wasn't there. Am I right?" Tanya stood and turned away from the trunk, stalking slowly towards Avery as she spoke. "That's it isn't it? You just denied it. Ignored it. Even when it was screaming to come out." She stopped a few feet away, safely out of range of Avery's feet. "That's more impressive than you know, officer."

"It's Detective," Avery corrected. She could feel Tanya's approaching presence, a tingling pressure, a sense of power tightly contained, as the lithe woman came closer. "And I don't know what you're talking about."

Tanya smiled and shook her head, but kept her emerald green eyes locked on Avery's. "Delude yourself if you want to. The power is there, inside you. Not my fault you never figured out what to do with it. I, on the other

157

hand, knew early on that I could feel magick. I could move things. I knew things. And that was only the start of it." She looked off to one side of the cave, where a black duffle bag lay against the wall. She reached a hand towards it and murmured a few words Avery didn't recognize. Suddenly, Avery's skin broke out in gooseflesh as she felt an unmistakable energy rising from Tanya's elegant hand, accompanied by a low hum of power. The bag stirred, rose from the cavern floor, and drifted lazily over to Tanya, who took hold of the strap and ended her spell. The energy vanished, and Avery stared at the sorceress, who only smiled. "Magick is handy for so many things. I had a touch of power, no more than that. But time and practice has served me well, and now, I'm almost a match for...well, you wouldn't know them. But I'm capable of many extraordinary things."

"Like calling demons to kill your own mother?"

Tanya's eyes widened. "My, my, I guess you are a detective! I'd hoped you'd think that witch and her friend were responsible for that." She circled around to Avery's side before moving closer, making it more difficult for Avery to kick her, and slipped up right next to the detective. "Who was the shadowy one? The one you shot? I've heard of Ariana, at least. He was a stranger to me, though, and his energy was something I've never felt before."

Avery turned to glare at Tanya, and the thought of head-butting her was becoming quite attractive. But then, Tanya waggled a finger in admonition and made a claw with one hand. Instantly, the power rose again and Avery's throat began to constrict. She tried to remain calm, but soon, the pressure had her wheezing.

"Now, now, keep your temper under control," Tanya purred. "Don't try anything foolish, or it will be more difficult for you than it has to be. Do we understand each other?" She clenched her fingers tighter, and Avery's face began turning red with the strain. She gasped and choked a few moments more, then relented and managed to agree. Tanya lowered her hand and the pressure evaporated, leaving Avery to heave great lungfuls of air as she recovered. "Now answer me. Who was the other being in the house?"

"I don't know," Avery lied, keeping her eyes cast down as though defeated. "I thought he was killing your mother, so I shot him. I know I hit him. He might be dead."

Tanya laughed, "Oh, I doubt that. I saw what he did to my Gray Beast. Whatever did that won't keel over for something as trifling as a couple of your bullets, Detective. You're sure you don't know?"

Avery took a deep breath before replying. There was a faint tingle of power coming from Tanya, subtle, but noticeable. Avery had the strongest feeling that Tanya was listening with more than just her ears. Not wanting to give her any more information than absolutely necessary, Avery focused on the image of the shadowy figure that she had seen in the Thornhill house, the same thing she had seen as a little girl. Kane, she knew, if only from a brief meeting. But that creature, the one with the glowing eyes and flashing claws, she truly did not know what that was. She held to that truth with all her might. "No. I don't know. And I'd only met Ariana once before when we searched Raymond's house. Some strange stuff went down there, and now I know that you were behind it all." She finally picked up her gaze and leveled it at Tanya. "Weren't you?"

Tanya's smile widened until Avery could see most of her teeth. They looked sharp. "Well, of course! Yes, I had to deal with Raymond, and then I couldn't have anyone poking around his things. That might have incriminated me. I was quite surprised when I felt the snake-demon's death. He was supposed to kill anyone he met and then destroy a few things in Raymond's conjuring room, but someone dispatched him pretty quickly. I presume that was Ariana's doing?"

Aha, so she doesn't know everything, now does she? Avery thought to herself. She hesitated for a moment, then agreed, "Yes. She stabbed him with some kind of knife."

Tanya clucked her tongue. "Oh, well. I can continue that little experiment at another time. Raymond was useful, but a bit twitchy. I'll find someone else for that."

"Why those men?" Avery asked, "and what in the world were you trying to do to them?"

At first, Tanya seemed confused, then she laughed. "You mean the men that took Raymond's pills? They were nothing to me, just random test subjects. I suspect that Raymond might have had some issue with each of them that aided his choice, but I left that up to him. I just needed to see if the drug would work. And it did! Each pill opened up a path for a demon to inhabit that person's body. It was magnificent!"

Avery's brows furrowed. "Why in the world would you want a drug that induces demon possession? They just go berserk until they're either put down or exorcised...what good is that?"

"Well, firstly, it's just fun to watch," Tanya purred with a smile. "I get off on it." Avery grimaced in disgust, but before she could retort, Tanya continued, "Secondly, they don't go berserk if someone strong enough to compel their obedience holds the reins."

"Someone like you, I'm guessing?" Avery's voice dripped with revulsion.

"Oh, you're a smart one, aren't you?" Tanya walked up and ran a delicate finger along the line of Avery's jaw only to yank it back when the detective tried to bite it off. Unfazed, Tanya laughed, then slapped her hard enough to split her lip. "Feisty...I like that. Anyway, yes, that would be me. Or it will be, once I complete this ritual."

Avery ran her tongue over her swollen lip, tasting blood there, but kept her eyes on her captor. "And what is this ritual supposed to do?"

Tanya laughed. "It's going to give me powers beyond anything you've ever dreamed, little witch."

"I'm not a witch," Avery responded without thinking.

Tanya raised an eyebrow, then shrugged. "Whatever you say. I can feel your power, and it's impressive. If you're not a witch, then you've been missing out on an awful lot of fun. Too bad you won't have a chance to experience that. Now, unless you want me to replace the ball-gag, keep quiet while I set this up."

Avery thought about being a smart-ass, but decided that she could learn more by watching. And since Tanya seemed to love talking about herself, she might be able to learn more that way. She nodded her agreement.

Satisfied, Tanya turned to walk across the circle of stones, dropping the bag near the middle as she passed through on her way to the trunk.

She bent over and reached inside. When she stood upright, she held something that looked like a three-legged, wooden stool, save that it was far too small to sit on, and had a slender metal spike sticking out of it. Moving back to the circle, she knelt next to the bag and set the stool on the ground just inside the circle's boundary. The spike glinted in the torchlight, sticking straight up about six inches from the wooden disk. Then she unzipped the bag, reached inside, and produced an object that made Avery's blood run cold.

"Don't act so shocked," Tanya said, her tone mocking. She smoothed the hair away from her mother's face to reveal her wide, staring eyes and a gaping mouth.

Turning the severed head slightly in her hands, she traced one finger along the cold skin of its cheekbone, then pushed the chin upwards so the lips came together. "This kind of thing is just part of the deal when you treat with the spirits that I do. And the reward is well worth the price." She jammed the head down onto the spike and arranged the stool so that it faced outwards. "There...facing north, just as required," she said, sitting back on her heels.

"What in the hell are you doing?" Avery could keep silent no longer. She'd been a cop for years, had seen things that would turn most people's hair white, but seeing Diana's head impaled so callously on a spike both shocked and disgusted her. "She was your *mother*! How could you *do* something like that?"

Tanya stood and wiped her hands on her pants, leaving faint crimson smears on the denim fabric. As she walked back over to the chest, she replied, "I must say, it was harder than I'd thought, sending the demon over to kill her like that. She had her good points. But we'd long since had a falling out anyway, and she'd cut me out of her life completely. When I found this path, I knew she'd be the perfect sacrifice. I used my talents to get her will amended, so now all that was once hers, is mine. And with her death, I'll gain SO much power..." Tanya's voice had a faraway sound as her ambitions and dreams swelled to the fore. Then she shook herself and continued to root around in the chest as her voice returned to normal. "You see, little detective, I'm going to be a Skinwalker. I've done all that's required over the years, and the death of my mother and this ritual were all that remained." She began to pick up items from inside the chest, and when she had an armful, she walked back into the circle to lay them in their proper places. Avery discerned pieces of several different animals: the pelt of a wolf, feathers from a crow, the paws of a bear, and the head of a mountain lion were easiest to identify, while others were a mystery to her.

"What's a Skinwalker?" Avery was puzzled. She'd heard the term, but it had been long ago, and she had no idea.

"It means that I can change my shape into anything I wish. An animal, a bird, anything. With enough practice, I can even look like another person. Glamours and illusions are one thing, but this," she shook her head slowly, "this is several orders of magnitude above that. Along with the ability to shapeshift, I'll also be granted power far beyond my current magickal skills. Spells and workings that are beyond me right now will become easy. I'll be able to destroy my enemies at my whim, melting their internal organs while they scream for mercy." She looked over at Avery and smiled. Her madness glinted in her too-wide eyes, and it chilled Avery to the bone. "Won't that be fun?"

Chapter 23

Riding a Wyvern is a pretty sketchy endeavor. It's not like riding a motorcycle, which I rarely do, but thoroughly enjoy. For one thing, they fly, so there's that whole falling out of the sky possibility. And since Wyverns are basically enormous snakes with huge bat-like wings and powerful back legs, they don't fly smoothly at all. Their bodies undulate somewhat as they move, and it takes getting used to. Not only that, the flapping of their wings also gives them a sharp up and down motion. All of this wiggling around makes staying on board difficult without anything to hold onto, and it's not like you can buy a Wyvern saddle in your local tack shop. I mean, I know a guy, but he's never available when you need him. The whole thing is a challenge, but it beats walking, and the speed...ok, I totally dig that.

The strap I'd cut from the cargo area of the helicopter worked well as a rudimentary bridle and reins, so holding those helped me stay upright, but seated right behind me as she was, Ariana had nothing to hold on to but me. I don't think she enjoyed the flight the way I did. She hadn't complained once, but her grip was tighter than you'd think. If I were human, I'd probably have bruises. I smiled as I guided the reptilian beast through the night sky and away from where Edge was still working on the helicopter.

Edge said we should go due west, Ariana's voice echoed in my mind. *I'm guessing towards those lights over there.* She released her iron grip on my midsection just long enough to point towards the tiny island of bright spots in the otherwise dark vista that spread out beneath us, then she clutched me again. *That woman, Tanya, has the money to build a spread out here, that's for sure. I'm guessing whatever she's up to requires a high degree of privacy.*

It's never helpful to be disturbed when summoning demons and whatnot, I agreed, *it causes trouble.*

We drew closer to the lights, and I saw a cluster of small adobe buildings situated around a central, larger one, all surrounded by a solid wall. The compound sat in a wide valley, and the land rose gently away from it on all sides save the north. Less than a mile from the wall, a small mountain loomed, its sides nearly vertical. It radiated a sense of dread, a foul and oily pressure that would have turned my stomach had I not been used to such things. This was an old power, but still vibrant and strong. I knew that bad things had happened in, on, and under that giant fist of stone. Of course, as a practitioner of evil magick, Tanya would have sought out such a place for her home away from home. I sighed. Whatever she was doing was pretty high level, and if she was using the power I felt from whatever was inside the mountain, it told me that she was even more dangerous than I'd thought.

Hey, what's that down there? A guard? He doesn't look right. Ariana's mental voice pulled my attention from the mountain for the time being. She was pointing again, and I looked where she indicated. Sure enough, a lone figure, a man, appeared to be stumbling in our direction. He was on foot and appeared unarmed. He also looked familiar. Even with my Fae sight, I needed to be a bit closer, so I pulled on the reins and applied pressure with my knees, guiding the Wyvern into a wide, sweeping turn so we could come in a bit lower. Although Ariana had spotted the shambling figure, I could see much better than she in the darkness. I nudged the Wyvern and sent a mental image of a glide, and the beast complied, catching the wind beneath its membranous wings and smoothing out our ride. As we approached, the figure stumbled and fell face first onto the hard, uneven ground, then stayed there, unmoving.

I had the Wyvern touch down several yards away from the prone figure, as quietly as possible. A glance towards the compound showed no activity whatsoever, and I felt reasonably sure we'd see any trouble in time to escape if necessary. Ariana practically fell off the Wyvern's back, then scrambled to her feet, embarrassed. I slid down somewhat more gracefully and patted the huge reptile's neck. It gurgled at me, then stepped away, sat down, and folded its wings and tail around itself to wait. I looked at the downed figure and finally recognized his clothes and the top of his balding head.

"It's that detective," I informed Ariana, "Jim, I think." As a precaution, I cast a dimness over the Wyvern so that it wouldn't spook the detective, and we approached the prone man.

Ariana had already drawn one of her handguns and had it pointed at him as she crept closer. Unwilling to risk a light so close to the compound, she squinted into the darkness, watching closely for signs of movement. "Detective?" she called softly. "Are you all right? What are you doing out here? It's me, Ariana."

When no answer was forthcoming, she holstered her weapon and knelt beside the man's body, gently touching his throat with her fingers. She looked up at me with relief. "He's alive! Help me roll him over."

I complied and we turned him over on his back. He looked worn and dirty, but otherwise unharmed. His eyes were closed, but his breathing was steady. I knelt next to him, Ariana opposite. Not wanting to waste too much time, I reached over and slapped him smartly across the face.

"Hey!" Ariana gasped in surprise.

166

I shrugged. "Why waste time? Gotta wake him up so we can figure out what to do with him. And maybe he can tell us something."

That's when his left hand shot up and almost grabbed Ariana by the throat. Almost. Mine shot out and intercepted his, grabbing him by the wrist before he could close his grip. Ariana lurched backwards, and fell on her butt, drawing one of her sidearms on the way. I quickly shifted my knee to pin his body down and grabbed his other wrist to keep him from attacking me with that hand. When I looked down into his face, I knew what I'd see, but even so, it pissed me off.

Jim's eyes, now wide demon's eyes, had snapped open, and his lips were skinned back to reveal far too many teeth. He struggled, but I'd been more prepared for this one. I could hold him down all day like this. As long as he didn't know Jiu Jitsu, which would just make it more difficult for me. Fortunately, neither Jim nor the demon had a clue, and they continued to flail about ineffectively.

"What the hell?" Ariana bellowed as she jumped to her feet, her gun pointed at the detective's head. "Is that what they look like when they go all demonized?"

"Yup," I replied. "Do you have that stuff we put together?" Demon-Jim struggled and grunted, but otherwise stayed silent. Ariana blinked at me, then holstered her gun and whipped her backpack off her back and proceeded to dig into it. It only looked half-full, as always, but I knew that she probably had a kitchen sink in there amongst all her other toys. She'd cast one hell of a spell on it years ago, and its capacity was impressive, even to me.

"You think you can banish me, GrimFaerieeee?" The demon that rode inside Jim's body finally spoke in a grating hiss. "I'm too strong for that!"

I ignored his comment and focused on keeping him securely pinned. Ariana produced a wide-mouthed jar and laid her backpack on the ground. She unscrewed the lid and dipped her fingers inside, coming out with a dollop of clear gel. Without direction from me, she leaned in, slapped the goo on Jim's face, and smeared it around, being careful to avoid his snapping teeth.

"What's that?" Jim's demon hissed in alarm. "What're you...GAAAHH!" He suddenly screamed as if we'd set him on fire. I shifted to pin his left arm with my other leg, then clamped my free hand over his mouth. The desert air was still, and I knew the sound would travel. He yowled and screeched beneath my hand, struggling in vain to escape. After thrashing ferociously for a few seconds, his body convulsed and arched beneath me. A fiery glow blossomed in his body, an ugly reddish-orange light that shone from within, then quickly extinguished. Jim's body fell back to the stony soil, limp and quiet, his eyes closed. I waited half a minute, then removed my hand from his mouth, taking time to wipe it clean of Ariana's demon-expunging goo on Jim's shirt. I figured he wouldn't mind.

"Wow, that looked like it worked!" Ariana whispered, her eyes wide with excitement. "Awesome!"

I didn't respond, keeping my attention on the detective. He remained quiet for a few moments, then heaved in a huge breath of air that he let out with a low moan. His eyelids fluttered open and he scowled up into the night sky. "Ow," he wheezed. "Ow. Hey, what happened?" He focused on me, kneeling as I was on his midsection, and grimaced, "Can...can you get off me, please?"

His eyes had returned to normal. "Sorry, Detective," I offered, "but you'd been possessed by a demon. We had to restrain you until we could get it out." I stood up, and he heaved a relieved sigh as my weight left his body. I helped him to his feet, which took some time. He moved stiffly, still unsteady after whatever the demon had put his body through, and he favored his left leg. I let him compose himself, then urged him gently, "Tell us what happened."

Jim pulled a handkerchief from his pocket and wiped Ariana's anti-demon gunk from his face. When he was done, he was about to put the cloth square back in his pocket, but then hesitated, looking at it with disgust. Ariana stepped forward, palm out.

"I'll take that. I can still use some of it, I think."

"Um…thanks," Jim said, gingerly handing the sodden cloth over. "What was that stuff, anyway?"

Ariana wrapped his handkerchief in another cloth from her backpack before depositing it inside. "It's kind of an instant-exorcism gel," she smiled proudly in the darkness as she donned her backpack again. "It's just aloe vera with a whole bunch of other stuff thrown in, then imbued with magick. Tough to make, but with Kane's help, we pulled it off. We weren't sure it would work, but it certainly did the trick."

Jim frowned. "That was…wow…am I hearing you correctly? I was possessed? By a demon?"

"Yes," I affirmed, "that woman, Tanya, is a sorceress. She's the one who hired Raymond to make those pills. Anyone who takes them opens themselves instantly to a particular type of demon, kind of a soldier. You took one of the pills?"

Jim nodded, rubbing the back of his neck in embarrassment. "Not by choice, but yes. When we broke back into the Thornwall house and saw…whatever that was standing over Diana's body, Avery shot at it." His eyes flicked to Ariana and narrowed in suspicion. "And you. She shot you!"

"She did, yes. My vest kept me safe. Look, we didn't kill Diana. A demon did that. It vanished afterwards, just like the snake-thing at Raymond's, moments before you two came in. I swear, we were there to talk to Diana, that's all. The trail led straight to her, as I'm sure you discovered as well."

Jim stared at her, assessing, then turned to look at me and tensed as he put it together. He saw me as I usually presented myself: an average guy with unruly dark hair and a forgettable face. My glamour was meant to keep me under most people's radar, as they say. Nothing memorable about me. And now, Jim was trying to reconcile that with the monster that he had seen standing over Diana's body. My true self. That had scared him. I raised my hands slowly, carefully, to show him I meant no harm.

"Yes, that was me," I admitted. "I'm a GrimFaerie. I'm one of the good guys. The demon killed Diana, and I killed the demon, just like at Raymond's place. I'm on your side, Detective. My oath on it."

He stared at me, then seemed to come to a decision and finally relaxed. "All right. I don't know what a GrimFaerie is, but you did save us from that snake-thing. And I can't say that you've tried to hurt us." Then he cut his eyes to Ariana, "Although you did knee me in the balls."

"Hey, we didn't know each other yet!" Ariana protested. "I gave your gun back and everything, didn't I?"

Jim nodded reluctantly at that, and I cut in, "What happened after Avery shot at us?"

"You two vanished, Tanya locked the door behind us, and then we went lights out. I woke up locked in a room in the big house over there, I'm guessing." He waved a hand towards the complex in the distance. "Everything after that is pretty fuzzy, but I remember Tanya and her goons jammed a pill in my mouth not long after I woke up." Suddenly, his eyes opened wide. "Avery! They must still have Avery in there somewhere!" He reached inside his coat for the gun that wasn't there as he took a lurching step towards the complex. My hand on his chest stopped him.

"Hey," I said quietly, "you need to let us handle this."

"Like hell, I will!" He tried to slap my hand away, but nearly fell when his injured leg gave out on him. He ended up clutching my arm to stay on his feet.

Ariana came and put a calming hand on his arm. In his way, he was fierce. I sent a gentle touch of reassuring magick into him. When my power touched him this time, I felt his strong affection for his partner. In a blink, I knew there was nothing romantic between them, but even so, he would willingly die for her. It took more energy than I'd expected to finally soothe him.

"You're injured," Ariana stated simply, "and you're only going to slow us down. We're ready for this. We're heavily armed and have experience with this kind of thing." He tried to protest, but she caught his gaze with her own and held it. Emotions warred on his face as he battled his urge to go to Avery's aid, but Ariana's eyes held a promise, and he finally clung to it. She added softly, "We'll get her."

"We have a man over the ridge," I kept my voice quiet, but firm. "Edge is fixing the helicopter. He'll patch you up and wait for us to return."

Jim looked in that direction, still uncertain, then spoke barely above a whisper, "You have to get her. She's my friend. I…"

Ariana squeezed his arm in reassurance, "We know. We'll get her back, I promise."

I frowned at her and sent, *We might not be able to keep that promise, you know that.*

Without shifting her gaze away from Jim, she replied, *Up yours, Kane. We'll get her.*

I sighed. Oh, well. I do enjoy a challenge.

Chapter 24

Blood from Avery's chafed wrists crawled down her forearms. The pain from the cold steel manacles had faded to a dull ache as she'd become accustomed to it. Her shoulders burned unbearably from the strain, but she ignored that agony as best she could. Instead, she focused her anger on the woman who had captured her. Her gray-green eyes observed everything, taking it all in, even though she struggled to make sense of what she was seeing.

The ceremony had begun. Tanya's chant echoed from the walls, low, wavering syllables that Avery didn't understand, but felt all the way into her bones. Tanya had lit the fire in the center of the ritual circle, then altered her tone as she tossed several handfuls of powders and herbs into the flames. Her voice became harsher, more guttural, and the fire responded. The flames crackled higher and a thick, ebony and scarlet column of smoke arose, orange sparks swirling up on the heated air within. Avery's eyes stung, and she angrily blinked away the tears. Tanya ignored her and continued her chant as she raised her hands, imploring the fire to burn higher. It obeyed her command, and Avery felt its heat on her skin, unwelcome and hateful. Without warning, the heat turned to cold as something unseen emerged from the depths of the flames, and she recoiled as she sensed an intelligence where there had been none before.

Moving with graceful elegance, the sorceress stepped over to the wooden chest against the wall, never wavering in her song. Taking her time, she slowly undressed, folding her clothes and depositing them in the chest until she stood naked, the hellish light wavering on her tanned skin. Her constant chanting rose and fell to create a hypnotic rhythm that filled Avery with dread, and Tanya began to sway gently in time with her song.

A pressure had been rising in the room ever since Tanya had lit the fire, and Avery felt something pushing at her, pressing at her. The unseen force felt oily and oddly cold on her skin, but she saw nothing as it touched and probed as if it were trying to gain entrance to her body. She steeled herself against it and tried not to panic. Desperate, she took a breath, and sent her focus inwards, away from the encroaching force.

The strange tingling that had arisen within her beckoned, a welcome warmth within her core that was both alien to her and familiar. She took a shuddering breath and moved her awareness deeper into her own body. She found the power there, a burbling vitality that invigorated and energized her. For the first time, she reveled in it, accepted it, became one with it.

With a thought, she imagined it pressing outward, repelling the unhealthy presence that sought to corrupt her. She was quickly rewarded as the questing tendrils of energy snapped back, leaving her alone. Her mind reeled. Power swelled inside her, but she had no idea how to use it. She opened her eyes again and saw Tanya in the center of the circle, her gaze locked on Avery, her song never wavering.

She had painted her face white and black to mimic a skull, and the rest of her nude body was covered with swirls and sigils, red and black expressions of Tanya's mad desires. Somehow, the designs made Avery's mind itch, and she tried not to dwell on them. Tanya smiled a death's-head grin when she saw Avery's disgusted expression, then she slowly turned to face the fire again and knelt before it, placing a small stone bowl and a flint knife on the ground before her. Then she sat back on her heels, swaying gently from side to side as she deepened her song.

In spite of the fire's brightness, shadows appeared along the high walls of the cavern, their alien shapes implying horrors that made Avery want to scream before her anger asserted itself again. She clamped her mouth shut and forced herself to watch as the ritual progressed. Her power began to roil inside her, protective and strong. She grunted in frustration, desperately trying to figure out what to do.

The dancing shadows began moving with purpose. Like living things, they crawled across the ruddy cave walls, making their way to a wide blank space surrounded by ill-favored and ancient designs. They slithered and moved, though nothing in the room could possibly have cast such shadows, moving as they did of their own accord. Within moments, they gathered themselves together into an inky blot of darkest midnight on the wall, far larger than Avery's two arms could span, and half again as tall as she. The shape seethed for a moment, then took shape. Something coalesced from the shadows, gaining substance in the ruddy light, and Tanya's song intensified as she poured her energy into the ritual.

Two yellow orbs appeared, wide, staring eyes that glared malevolently from within the darkness. Long, stringy hair sprouted from a grotesquely large head, surrounding a reddish, swollen face. Tusks stuck out from between rubbery lips, and its lower jaw thrust forward belligerently. Thick muscular shoulders led to brawny arms that hung down nearly to the ground. One enormous fist clutched a flint axe, and the other held a wicked-looking flint dagger. Black and white scales dusted the creature's arms and torso, while the thick mane of a buffalo covered his neck and upper back. The huge, hulking thing flexed its powerful arms, then unthinkingly used the knife in its left hand to swipe at the lank hair that hung down into its face, gashing its own forehead. Thick blood trickled down from the wound, but the creature paid it no attention. Its unblinking, bulbous eyes fastened on Tanya, who finally ceased her chant.

When it spoke, the power of its voice made Avery shudder. It wasn't loud, but she felt the intensity of it in her bones. It sounded as though it was several versions of the same voice speaking at once. At first, the words were incomprehensible to her, clipped syllables that made no sense. Then something shifted inside her, and although she still heard the unknown words on the air, she began to grasp their meaning.

You are foolish, the demon said, addressing Tanya.

Atahasia, I desire the power of the yee naldlooshi. I have earned it.

The demon, Atahasia, grunted and kept its unblinking eyes on her. Its gaze fell on Diana's disembodied head, which had been placed facing him. It clucked its tongue.

Your mother?

Exactly so. Her head serves as proof of my intent.

It turned an appraising glance at Avery, who felt the full weight of Atahasia's attention for the first time. It was immensely powerful, harsh and dangerous, and she shied away from it. At first. Then her anger rose and she pushed back with her newfound power, repelling the demon's intrusive energy. There was a sense of surprise from the being, and then it laughed and dismissed her as it turned back to Tanya. Avery was relieved, but also terrified. In the instant before it had turned away, she had felt an inkling of its true power, and it could have killed her with a thought.

And that one?

An additional sacrifice. A peacekeeper, possessed of her own magick.

Atahasia laughed, a low, grating chuckle. *She is not needed. But I will enjoy her nonetheless.* It raised the bloody dagger in its left hand and gestured towards the pieces and parts Tanya had laid out all around the circle. *To gain the power to walk in their skin, you must take something of them inside you. Eat.*

Tanya obediently rose to her feet, bringing the knife and bowl with her. Moving slowly and deliberately, she moved to each item around the circle, cutting a piece from each and placing it into the bowl. When she cut a piece of the skin from Diana's head, Avery thought she would throw up, but she managed to keep from heaving. Tanya was about to return to the center of the circle when she paused, then looked at Avery. A wicked smile appeared on her face. She placed the bowl gently on the ground near the fire, then approached Avery from one side, wary of her legs.

Tanya's left hand reached out and grabbed Avery's throat in a viselike grip while she displayed the sharp flint knife, now covered in bits of black and red gore.

"Hold still, now. I don't want you to hurt yourself."

Before Avery could respond, she felt a sharp pain in the skin of her neck, just below her left ear. Tanya quickly released her and stepped away, narrowly avoiding Avery's infuriated kick. Smiling wickedly, she showed Avery her prize, a tiny chunk of flesh balanced on the tip of the blade. "Just a precaution," Tanya murmured, "might come in handy." Still smiling, she returned to the circle to add the bit of flesh to the bowl.

"I'm going to kill you, you bitch!" Straining against her shackles, Avery had never been so angry, felt so violated in her life as now. She had a good idea where this was all going, and it both sickened and infuriated her. She had to stop it. *But how?*

Chapter 25

Jim was pretty startled when I revealed the Wyvern to him, but he took it in stride. I guess he'd seen enough weird stuff the last few days that a Wyvern was just another drop in the bucket. He held on just as tightly as Ariana when I flew him back to Edge at the downed copter and seemed relieved when I dropped him off. Edge said he'd almost got it running, but there were still some issues. It didn't matter that much until it was time for us to head home. Provided, of course, that we survived.

What do you think, the roof of the big house? I could hear the eagerness in Ariana's voice as it echoed in my mind.

That's my thought, I agreed. *I'll dim us until we land.*

The illusion of dimness is one of my most handy. It doesn't make me completely invisible, but instead, makes me unremarkable. Unnoticeable. You can still see me if you know exactly where I am and you look really hard, but most people can't do that. For all intents and purposes, it's as good as being transparent. Casting it over myself, Ariana, and the Wyvern would take a little extra muscle, but I was more than up to it. The darkness would pretty much assure that no one would see us.

As we approached, I cast the illusion and examined the layout of the compound. A paved road led from the front gate off to the west, then south, likely heading for the distant highway, but a pair of ruts also led from there to the top of a hill nearby. I opened my senses and detected the same kind of energy that I'd felt in Diana Thornhill's back yard. The portal had to be there. *Good to know.* There were five buildings in total, all surrounded by a ten-foot-high wall. I didn't see any guard towers, so that helped some. Even so, I could already see a couple of men in black fatigues moving around down below. I narrowed my eyes a little and saw they were heavily armed. *Of course they are,* I thought. I smiled. I liked fighting with armed guards. They always thought they were invincible until my claws came out.

The buildings all had flat roofs, which made our landing much easier. Half the roof of the main house was an open patio with a smattering of outdoor furniture, as well as a covered patio attached to the main house. That looked like the perfect entry point. It was empty of guards as far as I could tell, so I guided the Wyvern towards it, keeping an eye on the guards that occasionally drifted into sight elsewhere on the property. For the moment, we remained undetected. The Wyvern glided down until it was only a few yards above the gravel-covered surface of the roof, then it alighted as gently as a hummingbird.

Ariana slid off first, then I followed. I removed the strap from its snout, rubbed its neck, then told it to go.

You're free, I sent the mental image of the Wyvern flying away. *I release you. Now, go.* It snorted quietly and rubbed its head against me, nearly knocking me down, before it turned to go. It looked at the sky, then back at me again, almost seeming reluctant to leave. *What?* I asked, more surprised than anything. I had assumed control of this one by brute force; I thought it would be glad to be rid of me.

The Wyvern ducked its head under its wing, gnawed briefly, then plucked out one of its own scales. It leaned over to me, offering it from between its teeth.

I'd never heard of anything like this. Wyverns are wild. They obey only if subdued and dominated, which I had. This one was offering me...friendship? I reached out and took the scale, which was about the size of my palm. It shone in the faint moonlight, and I could see its rough beauty. I looked up into the beast's eyes, and nodded my

178

thanks, not sure of what else to do. It snorted, satisfied, and flung itself into the air, winging off to parts unknown.

What're you, the Wyvern whisperer? Ariana spoke up.

I shook my head in bemusement and handed her the scale, which she quickly stowed away in her backpack. *I have no idea. Nothing like that's ever happened to me before. Those things don't make friends.*

She grinned as she settled her backpack in place again. *Looks like that one does. I'm pretty sure it was sweet on you. You ready?*

I nodded, and we headed towards the glass doors that led to what I guessed would be Tanya's quarters. Lights were on inside, revealing an ornate bedroom with a canopy bed and cherrywood furniture. Ariana slowed as she walked towards the door, then stopped. She raised one hand as if touching an invisible wall, which I figured she probably was.

There's a ward here, she confirmed. *It's a good one, too. Stronger than the ones at Bress Tower.* She turned to look at me and I saw a smile creep onto her face. *But I'm better. Give me a sec.*

Wards are tricky things, something of an art within an art. To be perfectly honest, I'm not that good at them. They take years of disciplined practice and having talent for them doesn't hurt. Although I've certainly had the time, I've generally been able to break through most wards, survive the consequences, and then cause my particular brand of trouble, so I saw no need to practice them. Even so, that approach is not always the best way, especially if you want to get through the ward without letting its owner know you're there.

Despite her youth, Ariana was a literal master of wards. Her mother had apparently trained her young daughter's ass off, and to very good effect. The shield around her home was pretty much impassable to all but a ridiculous amount of high explosives. She could feel wards that others would most certainly miss, and she could find a way through barriers that might fry a buffalo to a crisp. Wards were difficult to create on the fly, even for her, but given a couple of minutes, she could do some impressive work. She stood silently for a few moments, gathering her energy, then she began chanting a series of soft syllables, imploring the ward to allow us entry. That always seemed to work for her, coaxing a ward to act the way she wished. It was effective this time as well, for she moved her hands as though parting a curtain and nodded at me.

Ok, go quickly, it's a strong one.

I ducked through the ward at the spot she indicated and felt a tingling sensation all around me as I passed through the aperture she had made. She stepped in behind me and let the ward close itself once more. Then we approached the back door, a wide glass fixture that was probably bulletproof. I gently tried the handle, and found it locked. I reached in with my magick and clicked the tumblers into position, then eased the door open. Within moments, we were inside, and I closed the door.

The room smelled of potpourri and musk. An enormous canopy bed was to our left, and on the wall facing it was an open fireplace, its flames crackling merrily. The walls were a pale brown, accented by rich wood molding that matched the furniture in the room. The bed was unmade, and clothing from both sexes was strewn across the floor, along with an adult toy or two. Ariana made a face and stepped carefully across the carpet, avoiding some of the more interesting items.

"Well, at least Tanya seems to have a healthy sex life," she muttered.

The far corner of the room opened out into a large, plush sitting area, and to our right, enormous double doors stood open to reveal a richly appointed bathroom with gold fixtures and a huge shower chamber. A large desk sat in the opposite corner of the bedroom, covered in neatly arranged piles of papers which contrasted the rest of the bedroom's disarray. Ariana moved towards the desk and scanned the items displayed there. Suddenly, she froze.

"Kane," she called, alarm plain in her voice, "you need to look at this."

I stepped up next to her and said, "Ok, what is it?" I looked over her shoulder and saw one of the pages she was pointing to. My skin began to crawl.

The book had been bound in leather by someone with little skill for such tasks, and it looked to be a couple hundred years old. The paper was brittle and yellowed, and the handwriting was a thin but elegant scrawl that spidered its way across the page. It was in English, but spattered with words I recognized as coming from various Native American tribes. The language was formal and poetic, but clear enough in expressing its intent. I pointed at two words I recognized and wished I hadn't. I sounded it out, "*Yee naldlooshi.*"

"What's that?" Ariana asked. She had sensed the play of foul energies across the entire desktop. The old papers and books had seen enough action to pick up a lasting residue of fell magick that remained long after it should have faded. That was a very bad sign.

"That's a Skinwalker," I said, wishing I had anything else to say. "They're no joke. They're shapeshifters, among other things. The contract they make with the evil spirits to gain their powers requires them to perform atrocities any normal human would find repulsive."

Ariana frowned, flipping pages and unconsciously wiping her hands on her tac vest each time, trying to rid herself of the gritty, horrid feel of them. Where there were drawings, they depicted horrors that surprised and disgusted her. "Why would anyone want to do any of this? It's abhorrent! I mean look at this!" She pointed at one particularly detailed sketch of a beheading.

I sighed before explaining. Ariana was young, especially compared to me. I had seen things over the centuries that appalled even me, and nothing really surprised me anymore. Disgusted, yes, but not surprised. Human beings were capable of extreme selflessness at times, such kindness that would bring tears to your eyes. I've seen it. And yes, I might have been moved a time or two as a result. My heart is black as pitch, yes, but it still beats. I still feel.

That said, I've much more often bore witness to the evils that humans are capable of inflicting on each other. I've seen things, terrible things. Centuries upon centuries of them. Discovering that Tanya most likely was trying to become a Skinwalker didn't surprise me at all.

"A Skinwalker is a kind of witch that gains the power to change their shape into any animal they choose, but they're far more than that."

"So what, they're like werewolves?" Ariana asked. I knew she was thinking of Maximus, the King of the Werewolves. He had made something positive of his affliction, but that's still what it was: an affliction. He hadn't asked for it. No werewolf had. Lycanthropy often been thrust upon them, the result of being at the wrong place at the wrong time. One bite, and they were cursed forever. They either adapted or they went insane until someone hunted them down and killed them.

"Not exactly, no. Yes, Skinwalkers can change shape, but it's because they're willing to do awful things to gain that power. They control what they become, and they gain several additional powers as well, none of them good."

"Like what?"

I scanned the documents before us to confirm what I already knew, "Some have control over the weather in a small area. Others can enter people's minds to control them. They actually feed on fear, so they'll often terrorize their victims to increase their strength. When they've fed sufficiently, they kill them. And in terms of magick, they're extremely strong. It would be like comparing an ordinary human to Hercules."

"That sounds faaabulous," Ariana drawled. "How do we kill something like that?"

I turned to look her in the eyes, and I grinned. My eagerness must have overcome my control for a beat, and my glamour slipped enough to show my eyes. Ariana shuddered. She was tough, but my true face isn't exactly nice to see.

"I'm going to rip her throat out. That should work."

She was silent briefly, then nodded. "Yeah," she said, "yeah, I guess that'll do it. Let's find that bitch and get this over with."

Ariana looked at the desk again, then started stacking all the books and papers into one pile. She gathered her focus and murmured a few words, gesturing over the materials as she did so. She cast her spell over the items and I felt their foul emanations vanish as she wrapped them safely within her power. She sighed, "That's better. These things are dangerous, no way I'm leaving them here!" She whipped off her pack and deposited everything inside. The pile was bigger than the backpack, but as always, when Ariana slipped her arms through the straps once more, the pack still looked barely half-full. "All right, let's go find that detective and put Tanya out of our misery!"

That's when the door opened. A guard was backing into the room, carrying something in both hands. He was tall and brawny, with long hair done up in a man-bun, dressed in black cargo pants and a black polo shirt, probably the standard uniform for all of Tanya's hired help. He had a hefty handgun strapped to one thigh, and a tattoo of a serpent slithering out of his shirt collar to wrap around the back of his neck. His eyes were on the burden he carried, and he was faintly whistling as he entered.

I grabbed Ariana's arm and held her still. *Don't move.* I felt a mental nod of assent from her. We'd worked together enough to act well on each other's signals. Technically, we were in plain view in front of the desk, but the dimness I cast over us both would probably hide us from the goon's eyes. We stayed frozen and watched him closely, hoping for the best.

The man turned as he entered the room and let the door shut behind him. He didn't notice us, only walked over to the bed and laid a laundry basket filled with folded clothes on it. He turned and opened the bottom drawer of a nearby chest and then began transferring the clothes into the waiting drawer, still idly whistling as he did so.

You want him? I silently asked Ariana.

There was a slight pause, then she answered, *Nah. He's cute and all, but he's a bad guy. Plus, that man-bun looks ridiculous on him.*

I closed my eyes for a moment. *No, do you want to take him out or do you want me to do it?*

Oh, right! No, I got him, just give me two seconds. Without another word, she silently moved forward. Man-bun didn't look away from his work until he heard her whip out the collapsible baton she'd produced from somewhere. He turned and registered Ariana's presence as her baton flew through the air on its way to his temple. Too late.

I'll say this for him, he was tough. The first shot dropped him to one knee and I thought he was done, but he shook it off and came up with a furious growl. He grabbed Ariana's arms at the biceps in an attempt to keep her from hitting him again, his fingers digging painfully into her flesh. She grunted, but it wasn't from fear. It was anger.

The guard was even stronger than he looked, and Ariana dropped her baton as her fingers went numb. He grinned at her, but he'd forgotten about her legs. She drove her shinbone into his groin, doubling him over and loosening his grip. She shrugged loose and grabbed one of his arms, shifted his hand out of the way, and performed a beautiful arm-drag that brought her around behind him. She wasted no time in wrapping her arm around his throat and locking in a solid chokehold worthy of a UFC champion. His face purpled, and he flailed ineffectually for a few seconds. Even though Ariana wasn't nearly as big or strong as he, she knew what she was doing. He slumped in her arms, unconscious, and she guided him to the floor.

"Nice job," I commented.

"Thanks! I've been working out," she responded. She found a pair of handcuffs on his belt and cuffed his hands behind his back, then pulled some thick zip-ties from her own pocket and secured his ankles. With a sigh, she sat back on her heels and closed her eyes. Her breathing slowed, and she raised her hands over the unconscious man's body. She began chanting quietly, a low murmur that carried the weight of power in it, but it was a subtle, gentle magick. The man on the floor exhaled softly and relaxed into a deep sleep. Ariana's eyes opened again, and she stood, retrieving her collapsible baton as she did so. "He'll sleep the rest of the night, at least. Now what?"

"Let's go find Tanya, and hopefully, the detective as well. We need one dead, and the other still breathing."

We walked over to the door and eased it open. A hallway led off to the left, and I could see a couple of doors down there before the corridor turned to the right. Directly in front of us was a set of stairs that led to the next level below. Voices drifted up to us, and I counted two speakers, both male. Keeping us dim, I led the way down the stairs, Ariana following close behind.

Two guards were in the great room, which sported a vaulted ceiling and an impressive chandelier. The men stood in front of an incredibly wide TV screen, absorbed in some sporting event that required a ball and helmets. I thought about subduing them right away, but I figured leaving them alone would buy us a few more minutes to look around, so we slipped past them and down the hall. At the far end, we found a small bedroom that looked recently lived in, and I felt something familiar.

"There's energy here," I whispered to Ariana. "I think they kept our detective in here."

"Oh, so now she's *our* detective?" she needled me. She seemed to love doing that when she got the chance. "I didn't realize that your relationship had gotten that far. She shot you, remember?"

"She had good reason," I said.

"If you say so," she shook her head. "Can you tell anything else?"

I opened my senses to the full and shifted my perception, trying to hone in on Avery's distinctive energy. She had been here for hours before being moved, so her aura was still visible to me. Its intense residue was fading, but I interpreted it the best I could.

There had been a scuffle in the room, but then she'd left. I motioned for Ariana to follow me and I eased back out of the room, tracking the faint trail of her energy. Once in the hallway, I saw it move away from us, stop at another room, then head out into the great room and towards the big staircase that led to the ground floor. Which meant we'd have to pass the guards. I smiled...I needed some exercise. I looked at Ariana and sent, *I'll take these two, then we follow Avery's trail. It heads downstairs. Give me a moment.* Ariana drew one of her guns, screwed a silencer on the end, then nodded at me. We moved silently down the hall, and I was already relishing the fight.

Ariana and I stopped at the edge of the hallway before entering the great room. We heard the two men roar at something they heard on the TV, and I readied myself to slide around the corner and take them both. Just then, a tinny voice blared in the room. One of them had a walkie talkie.

"Main House, this is Guard Shack, over."

We heard one of them click the button on the device and reply, "Main House, copy."

"One of the drones spotted a downed copter couple of miles out. We're sending a squad on bikes, over."

"Copy that, Shack," the guard replied. "All's quiet here. Queen's taken the guest into the mountain, over." The man let go of the button on the device, then spoke to his comrade, "Sounds like we're going to be digging more graves in the back yard."

The second man swore, "Dammit. I hate that. Those guys get to ride those bikes out there and shoot up shit. That's way more fun than being stuck in here."

"Yeah, well, at least we've got all the sports channels, right?"

Number two mumbled something, still sulking.

Great. They were sending a crew after Edge and Jim. With motorcycles, they'd be there in minutes, even accounting for the dark and the rough terrain. I idly hoped Edge brought some heavy armament with him, then I shifted my focus to the task at hand.

Kane! Ariana interrupted my thought process by shouting in my mind, *they're going after Edge! We've got to stop them!*

I gave her a look. *No we don't. Edge and Jim are on their own. We've got a job to do.* Even as I mentally sent her the words, I realized that wasn't going to fly with her.

Like Hell! she responded. *We've got to do something! Those are our people out there. We can't just let them die!* She reached out to grab my arm for emphasis. She never did that. I didn't particularly care for it, but I could read it all in her aura. Responsibility, caring, affection, fear, and anger all boiled around her like the corona of the sun in that moment, and I knew adjustments needed to be made. Of course, I could have just ignored her and gone ahead on my own...nah, that wouldn't do. The Goddess had already expressed her desire for us to work together, and clearly so. I sighed.

Hold on one second, I paused our conversation and bolted around the corner. The two men died without a sound, except for a faint gurgling as I gashed their throats with my claws. I didn't have time to baby them, and they weren't worth it anyway. They slumped to the ground with surprised looks on their faces, guns still in their holsters. That task completed, I found the dimmer switch on the wall and lowered the lights so we could see out of the big window. Then I called Ariana over and pointed.

"All right, fine. See those lights?" I began, "That road leads into the mountain. There's seriously bad juju in there, judging by the feel of it, and I'm pretty sure that's where they've taken Avery." I pointed off to the east. I could hear the high-pitched noise of dirt bike engines revving up, and several headlights were visible in the courtyard below. "Those guys are leaving any second. I can catch them. You can't. But you can get into that mountain and put a few bullets in Tanya before she does something monumentally bad."

She looked out into the darkness, taking in the imposing mountain, and shaking off the dread she felt come over her when she looked too long at it. Then she looked at the motorcycles in the courtyard. As she watched, the main gates began to open. They'd be leaving in moments.

"All right. Go save Edge. I'll take care of that hussy, Tanya." Ariana's voice was hard and her head held high, confident as always, but then she paused. The tiniest doubt wriggled its way into her, and it showed on her face. Almost too quiet for me to hear, she asked, "What if I'm too late?"

The Goddess still speaks to me on occasion. Not nearly often enough that I can count on her for any real assistance, but she's come through for me a time or three. She never speaks to me in words, but in visions and feelings. Just then, she showed me a few tiny flashes, just enough for me to be sure of our path.

"You're not too late, not yet. Avery's alive, and there's still time, but not much. Kill anything that gets in your way, just get to that mountain and find the Detective. I'll handle those assholes down there and get back as soon as I can."

Ariana looked at me, her mouth clamped into a thin line, and she nodded. She glanced down at the bodies of the thugs I'd just killed, then she knelt beside one of them. He'd been carrying an assault rifle with a folding wire stock and a long, curved magazine. She appropriated this, then relieved the dead man of several other magazines, which she stuffed in her pockets. When she rose to her feet, she jacked a round into the chamber and nodded firmly at me. Then her smile returned.

"Look, it's an AK-47," she explained. "I've always wanted one of these. You can beat them to death and they'll still shoot. Never hurts to be prepared, right?"

Chapter 26

The window shattered as I crashed through it, making a pretty sound that I always enjoyed. My trajectory took me beyond the falling shards of glass, and I landed in the flagstone courtyard in a shoulder roll that allowed me to come up running. The motorcycles had only just left, and the automatic door was sliding shut. I lowered my shoulder and slammed into the moving metal plate, knocking it off its track before it could lock into place. The gate mechanism sputtered and sparked before it finally ground to a halt, leaving a six-foot gap between the door and the wall.

Good, I thought, *that'll make it easier to get back in.* I slipped through the opening and saw the headlights of the motorcycles up ahead, shakily spearing into the night as the bikes navigated the rough terrain.

They were fast, sure. But so was I. And I'm better in the dark. It looks almost like daylight to me. I took off at a run, dodging ruts and cacti along with way, reveling in the feel of the cool air as it rushed past my face. The riders up ahead didn't know I was coming, had no idea their death was approaching with each passing moment. I knew I had to act fast; they would reach the downed copter in short order.

The riders topped a ridge and caught some air as they left the desert floor, showing off a little for each other. I crested the same ridge a moment later, and was dismayed to see the copter in the distance. Neither Edge nor Jim were in sight, so I hoped they'd stay that way until I was finished with the bad guys. I pushed myself a little harder and closed the distance on the rearmost rider.

I came up alongside him and lashed out with my claws, intending to lay him completely open. To my surprise, my claws scraped across some kind of armor, and only ripped wide gashes in the leather of the protective jacket the guy wore. He wobbled a bit, but quickly regained control of his bike. Utterly surprised, he whipped his head in my direction, but couldn't quite make me out in the dark, dim as I was. Without missing a beat, he pulled a small submachine gun from a holster on his cycle and fired a burst in my direction, narrowly missing me. I slowed a fraction so I could get behind him, then came up on his right side this time.

You want to play that way? Fine.

I put on a burst of speed and angled towards him. When I leaped, his head was just swinging around to that side as he tried to locate me. He never even saw me. I turned an aerial cartwheel over his bike and grabbed his helmet as I hurtled over the top of him. I let my momentum aid me as I viciously wrenched his head almost all the way around. His neck made some beautiful cracking noises and his body instantly went limp as my feet hit the ground running on the far side. The bike floundered, hit a stone, and flipped end over end as the rider's body fell away. I caught a lucky break as the motorcycle clipped the back of another rider, flinging him and his bike into a bone-breaking roll.

Two down, three to go, I thought.

The others had figured out something was amiss. They broke off their original heading and began to circle my position. I tried to pick one to target next, but bullets raked the ground at my feet, forcing me to step back and regroup. Another barrage of gunfire had me diving and rolling out of the way. The bullets were coming too close. Somehow, they were able to see me, despite my glamour. *Dammit,* I thought, dodging yet again as more rounds hissed through the air next to my face. *Probably something in their helmets.*

Just as I avoided another volley of shots, I felt a searing pain across my back. I turned to see one of the riders streaking away from me. He'd come up in my blind spot while I was occupied and hit me while I wasn't looking. The pain was fierce, but manageable. I'd had far worse and could already feel the wound beginning to knit back together. I gritted my teeth and looked around until I spotted the culprit. One of those assholes had a sword.

Seriously? I thought. *Guy thinks he's a samurai or something?*

I knelt and ran my hand along the ground, coming up with a jagged, fist-sized stone. I tracked the sword-wielder as he made a lap around me, then I whipped my arm forward with blinding speed. The rock sailed through the darkness and impacted with great force on the rider's helmet, making a satisfying sound as it shattered the thick protective plastic. I've never played baseball, but I have one hell of a throw. The now-dead rider pitched sideways off his bike, dropping his sword from limp fingers. I bolted for it, snaking my way through the bullets laid down by the remaining three riders, and snatched it up.

GrimFaeries usually have no need of weapons, equipped as we are with such impressive sets of claws and teeth. However, I'd already seen that their helmets and armor were a bit tougher than usual. Three feet of steel might help me move things along. I twirled it in my hands, getting its balance. It wasn't the best made blade, but it had my blood on it. So that made it mine. I crouched and held it at the ready.

They came at me from the west, their bikes far enough apart that I could only reach one at a time. That would leave my back open to attack. I gauged the distance and decided to take my chances on the rightmost one. I planned to fling myself at him, cut him in half, then drag his body along with me and use it as a shield of sorts. Not the best plan, but I was pressed for time. I gathered my feet under me and prepared to spring. The bikes accelerated, their motors buzzing loudly in my ears, and I could see the gun barrels they had leveled on me as they approached.

Ok, here we go, I thought.

I never made that leap. The rider to my left suddenly flew off the back of his bike as though yanked by a tether. The other let his gun hang from his neck strap, and used both hands to steer his bike to a skidding stop, just out of my range. He looked at his companion in confusion, looked at me standing several yards away with a naked blade in my hand, then gunned the throttle and threw up a spray of dirt as he headed back the way he'd come. He hadn't gone ten yards when he jerked violently and fell off to one side, leaving his bike to roll forward several yards before it lazily fell over and sputtered to silence.

I was confused. I'd had nothing to do with their deaths. I was relieved, but also disappointed. I'd really looked forward to killing them. A quick check of the bodies showed me that the last two had enormous holes drilled into them.

A figure came strolling over the ridge from the east, and I recognized Edge, who was smiling widely. He was carrying an enormous rifle with an equally huge scope. I busied myself by finding the sheath for the sword and slid the blade into it as Edge approached within speaking distance.

"Heard all that racket," he said calmly, a hint of amusement coloring his words. "Used the night scope on my Barrett. Figured you might not refuse a little help."

"Thanks," I said. As much as I loved a good fight, he'd saved me time and effort. I had none to waste. "You two all right?"

"Oh, yeah, we're fine. Almost got the copter up and running. Would have finished had those knuckleheads not come around. I'll take one of these bikes to get back to the copter, finish it up." Shifting the rifle to hang across his back on its sling, he walked over to one of the motorcycles to check it over. He righted it, sat astride its seat, and kicked the starter.

I looked at the other cycles, lying forlorn in the dark, riderless.

"You know Edge, that's not a bad idea. Not bad at all."

Chapter 27

Ariana watched Kane make the diving leap out of the big picture window. She bolted to the edge to see him running for the closing gate. He slammed into it, freezing it in place, then he slipped through the opening and vanished into the night. Not two seconds later, a couple of black-clad guards rushed from somewhere below into the center of the courtyard. They carried AR-15's, and opened fire in the direction of the fleeing figure, but only let a few rounds fly. It was obvious he had already escaped, and they saw no sense in wasting ammunition. Suddenly, one turned and looked up at the window. He slapped his comrade's arm to get his attention, then pointed at Ariana, silhouetted in the window above.

"Ah, crap," she muttered, rushing across the room toward the doorway. She had to find her way downstairs, then get outside the compound and head to the mountain to find Tanya and Avery. She shouldered open the door, then skidded to a stop in the hallway as she heard the two guards from outside already thumping their way up the stairs. She looked around, but there was almost nowhere for her to hide, no other room close enough for her to duck into. Instead, she opened the door as far as it would go and hid behind it, her back to the wall. It was poor cover, but all she had. *I really need to work on my quick-draw glamour skills,* she thought as the heavy footsteps approached.

A few feet away from the open door, the men slowed. She quietly mashed herself as close to the wall as she could, hoping they would overlook her terrible hiding place. Letting out a slow breath, she reached out with her magick, searching for something she had seen in the room behind her. The invisible tentacle stretched through the wall and into the room, sending only faint signals back to her. She gritted her teeth as sweat began to drip from her forehead. She was much better at spell-casting than she was at this, a brute force use of her power. She focused on her breathing, trying to ignore the fact that the two men were now only a few feet away.

"Ok, I'll go in first," one was saying. "It's quiet in there, they may be hiding. I'll take the left, you take the right."

Before the other could respond, Ariana found what she'd been after. A glass vase was sitting on a side table, filled with glass beads, water, and calla lilies. Flexing her will, she wrapped her power around the vase and pulled. She felt it slide off the table, then heard it shatter as it struck the wooden floor.

"Dammit! Go, go, go!" the first man yelled, and they both raced into the huge living room. Shots rang out as they excitedly sprayed the room with gunfire. Moments later, they removed their fingers from their triggers and surveyed the damage. The TV was shattered, more windows were broken, and bullet holes pocked the walls in several places. It was a huge mess.

"Shit," the first man said.

"Yeah, I don't think Tanya's going to like this," murmured the second man, shaking his head slowly.

There was a meaty *thwack!* and the first gunman slumped to the floor as Ariana's baton made contact with his skull. The second jerked away in surprise, narrowly avoiding her backswing. He stumbled, fell down on his butt, then scuttled awkwardly away from her. Ariana kept her gun pointed unerringly at his head, and she took a confident step forward. His hand twitched toward the gun that still hung from his neck by its strap, but she had the drop on him.

"Freeze!" she ordered, her voice firm and loud. "Show me your hands!" She took a step closer, the barrel of her gun never wavering. Her voice dropped, cold and menacing. "I mean it. Do it now or you know what you'll get…" she narrowed her eyes and read the embroidery on his shirt, "Garrett."

Garrett looked into Ariana's bright blue eyes. Whatever he saw there kept him still. Moving carefully, he brought up his hands in surrender.

She tried not to smile and failed. She surveyed the man's two black eyes and bandaged nose and said, "Looks like you've had a tough night, there, Garrett. Wanna talk about it?"

Garrett just looked at her with a combination of anger, fear, and embarrassment. He clamped his mouth shut and shook his head.

"No? OK, suit yourself. Put that gun on the floor and slide it over. Slowly, please." Garrett carefully did as he was told and the gun slid out of his reach. "Now the Glock." Moving slowly, he pulled the handgun from its holster and slid it over to her as well. "Now roll over on your belly and put your hands on your head. I promise I won't kill you unless you do something stupid. Got it?"

He stared at her briefly, then seemed to come to a decision. With a sigh, he rolled over and laced his fingers behind his head.

"Good choice, Garrett. Now just stay still until I get you situated, and someone will come and check on you in the morning. You'll be fine." Keeping the gun in one hand, she knelt and dragged a pair of cuffs from the utility belt of the downed guard, then leaned in and clicked one side around his left wrist, intending to pull his arm around so she could cuff his hands behind his back. As she did, his right hand flashed around to his front pocket, then quickly darted up to his face before she could protest. "Hey, what're you doing, you jerk? I told you to stay still!" She pressed the barrel of her gun into the back of his head hard enough that it should have hurt. "Now don't move!"

Garrett stayed still. For a few seconds, anyway. Then his body shuddered, fell still, then shook as he started laughing. It wasn't the meathead frat boy laugh she'd expected from his appearance. No, this was a laugh that had a thick stripe of crazy in it, high-pitched and maniacal. She backed away from him, keeping the gun up.

Garrett rolled over and pushed himself to a sitting position, ignoring the guns on the floor nearby. His mouth was stretched wide in a joker's grin, and his eyes were hugely round and yellow, their pupils tiny pinpricks in the center. He cackled again, and spoke in a high, reedy voice. "Ariana, my love, I'm so glad you decided to play with us again!"

She hid her shock at the sound of her name. She knew now what she was dealing with, and it wouldn't be pretty. *Dammit, my demon-goo is in my pack!* She thought. She didn't really want to shoot Garrett, but might not have a choice.

"No comment, my love?" the demon that now inhabited Garrett teased, "but I've missed you soooo much!" Then it launched itself at her.

Too fast, too fast! she heard herself shriek in her mind as she fell backwards, instinctively trying to avoid the demon's headlong rush. Her feet came up and landed on Garrett-demon's chest, and rather than kicking him away, she bent her knees and allowed his momentum to carry his body over hers. Then, with a powerful thrust of her legs, she heaved him into the wall behind her, where he smashed into the sheetrock and then slid to the floor in a cloud of white dust.

She was on her feet in an instant, racing across the room to put some distance between them. She aimed her AK at Garrett as he stood up, then carefully popped off a round at his shoulder. The impact jerked Garrett's body to the left, but then he just smiled that insane smile and took a menacing step forward.

"Dammit Garrett, stop! I mean it!" When the demon only laughed in response, she lowered her aim and put a bullet into his left shin. He went down to one knee, but then stood and kept coming, ignoring whatever pain might be coursing through Garrett's body.

Ariana knew she only had two options. The demon-goo was in her backpack, but she'd have to drop her gun to get it. Or she could just shoot Garrett in the head and be done with it. She growled in frustration.

"Damn you Garrett, you're gonna owe me. You'd better find the cure for cancer or something after you leave here." She dropped the gun to hang on its strap, then whipped her backpack off, unzipped it, and reached inside.

That's when Garrett picked up the couch and threw it at her. She tried to dodge out of the way, but one end clipped her thigh, and she fell heavily to the ground as the couch destroyed an end table behind her. Clenching her teeth in pain, she pulled out the jar of goo and tossed her backpack aside.

Garrett was on her in a heartbeat, lashing out with a fist almost too fast to see. The blow rocked her, and she fell on her back as she tried to regain her composure. Before she could move, Garrett sat astride her torso, pinning her between his legs.

"There, there, my little pretty! Just relax, and we'll have some *real* fun!" He cackled as his demon eyes bore down into Ariana's. He knew he'd won.

Or at least, he thought so. Her right hand swept up and slammed the squatty jar of demon-goo into the side of his head, cutting off his laughter with a grunt. He slumped sideways, and she swiftly caught one of his arms and executed a sharp bridge-and-roll to put him on his back. She deftly passed his legs, then pinned his arms to the floor with her knees as she settled her weight onto his chest.

"Sorry, Garrett. You're just not my type, man. I'm swiping left." With her hands free, she unscrewed the jar and scooped up a dollop of the gunk with her fingers, then slapped it across Garret's bruised face. As she expected, he screamed horribly, arching his body and thrashing beneath her, but she relaxed and held her position, keeping him safely pinned. Soon enough, his body glowed from within, shining like an ugly jack-o-lantern, and it convulsed one last time before falling still.

Her hands flying, Ariana retrieved the handcuffs and secured his hands behind him, then zip-tied his ankles and did the same for his unconscious partner. After a moment's thought, she pulled out her first aid kit and applied a quick bandage to each gunshot wound.

"You're still an asshole, Garrett," she mumbled as she packed everything away and picked up her gun, "but there's my good deed for the day. Pass it on, you schmuck." She glanced over at the two men Kane had killed earlier and felt a passing sadness. She understood what he was, and how he did things. He'd actually become less violent since they'd begun working together, if he was to be believed. Seeing the two corpses bleeding onto the floor, their throats neatly sliced open, she felt a shudder run up her spine. Although he fought on the side of good, he sure did it in an ugly way. She shook her head, reminding herself that anyone he killed generally deserved it. Any of these guys would have shot and killed her, or worse. Even so, she felt compelled to stop and help Garrett. She sighed, feeling a little stupid, but also feeling like she did the right thing. Shouldering her backpack, and holding her gun at the ready, she moved towards the door and the hallway beyond.

Fortunately, it seemed that almost all of the guards were either dead, unconscious or in pursuit of Kane, so she met with little resistance as she made her way down the stairs and out the back door of the residence. The huge, red mountain loomed, a darker shadow in the night, and she moved towards it, as she searched for a way over or through the wall. She found a small service door in the northwest corner, and moments later, she was running for the mountain. Her feelings of dread increased with every step as she approached the sinister looking peak. *Something is in there,* she thought, *something really bad.* Fear washed over her, oppressive and overpowering, and nausea roiled in her stomach. She felt herself slowing down, felt her confidence waning. *Can I really do this?*

Then she remembered the detective. She was in there somewhere. It wasn't often that Ariana ran across someone like herself, someone who felt magick the way she did. Even if Avery didn't know how to use it, Ariana felt a kinship with her nonetheless, and her being a cop meant that she wanted to help innocent people. Ariana gritted her teeth and willed her legs to run faster, pushing herself through the unseen wall of dread and trepidation. *I've got to get to her before Tanya does something to her,* she thought.

The road was clear all the way to what looked like a reinforced cave entrance at the base of the mountain. A light post had been erected there, shining a pool of illumination on the yawning mouth of the entryway. She slowed as she neared it, then stopped entirely and knelt in the middle of the road, intent on making herself as small a target as possible. From a pocket on the side of her backpack, she pulled a small pair of night vision binoculars and scanned the cave entrance. She found the guard lurking in a shadowy alcove just to the left of the opening, and she knew she'd have missed him if she'd been less careful. She laid the binoculars on the ground and took aim with her AK, then lowered it. She was much too far away to hit him with any accuracy, and even if she were closer, she didn't share Kane's affinity for killing first and then never asking questions later. This guy was armed and likely not hired for his compassion, but even so, Ariana had reservations about killing him with no warning. Knowing Kane would have given her a hard time about the entire episode, she sighed and decided on a change of plan. Still kneeling, she pulled off her backpack and rummaged around in it. When her fingers touched a small leather pouch, she allowed herself a slight grin. *I've been wanting to try this out anyway,* she assured herself. After she carefully withdrew the pouch, she slid her arms through the straps again, let her gun hang from its lanyard, and then began working her way closer to the guard, keeping her eye on the shadowy spot that hid him.

When a light blinked on, allowing her to see his downturned face clearly, she froze. He'd pulled out his phone and was idly thumbing the screen. He looked bored. *Perfect!* she thought, *I hope this works.*

She closed her eyes and took a few deep breaths to clear her mind. Shutting out all the negativity that emanated from the looming bluff, she looked inward, finding a familiar space of stillness within herself. Once her spirit was placid and calm, she began a chant, a quiet whisper that she used to focus her will. In her mind, she created an image of the result she desired, held that picture in high definition before her mind's eye, and poured her energy into it. With careful, deliberate motions, she loosened the drawstring on the leather pouch and poured the contents into her outstretched palm. A mound of silvery powder sparkled in the moonlight, glinting in response to her magick.

When her eyes opened, she found the tiny glow of the guard's phone, revealing his shape against the darker shadows of the mountain behind him. Still holding the image strongly in her mind, she blew the powder from her palm in one long, focused exhale.

The powder didn't fly away as one might expect; it answered Ariana's call. Borne on a sinuous tendril of focused magick, the powder snaked through the cool desert air, winding its way towards the guard.

She had spent most of the last year wandering in the forested land that surrounded her family home. Dozens of species of spiders lived in that wooded area, and she had observed almost all of them. All spiders spin silk, though not all of them use it to catch their prey. Some simply use it as an ever-present safety line, leaving a single, white thread behind them wherever they go. Others build extraordinarily elaborate webs, using different kinds of silk depending on the function they needed.

Ariana had observed every spider she had run across, spending time with them, getting to know how they moved, how they hunted, and where they lived. Although she'd been scared of them as a little girl, she'd actually come to care for them as she understood them. They only wanted to be left alone, they hunted only what they needed, and their webs were often creations of stunning beauty, especially when the dew of early morning clung to the silken strands of their circular sculptures. It had been necessary for her to gain a strong sense of each spider, or else the spell she intended would never have taken shape. It had also taken a painstaking, careful effort to collect the types of silk in the quantities she desired without harming the tiny arachnids. And each time, she'd thanked them for their help.

The line of powdered silk wound its way towards the guard, drifting with purpose through the air like a serpentine ghost. Whatever he was looking at on his phone kept him occupied, and he was completely unaware of the approaching spell. The misty tendril wrapped its coils around him, a silent and gentle caress.

The guard's eyes caught a flicker of movement and he registered the ghostly tentacle that surrounded him. He frowned in confusion, but at that point, it was far too late for him.

Ariana whispered the final word of the spell and *flexed* her will, clenching her fist as tightly as she could. The phantom tendril exploded into a massive web that completely covered the guard, mummifying him in its silken, unbreakable grip. He stayed on his feet at first, teetering. His legs had been webbed together, just as his arms had been pinned tightly to his sides. His phone hand was now pressed uncomfortably to his chest as the enormous web captured him better than any straight jacket. A muffled cry barely escaped his lips, sealed shut as they were. He toppled, falling face first to the ground, raising a faint cloud of dust on impact.

Ariana crept closer, her gun at the ready as she scanned the area for additional guards. When she saw none, she walked over to her captive, rolled him over, and pulled him into a sitting position with his back against the stone wall next to the entrance. When he seemed comfortable, she knelt and looked into his wide, confused eyes. As he took in the sight of her, his eyes narrowed in an angry glare.

Excited, she whispered, "Did you know that spider silk is five times stronger than steel?" She grinned, her blue eyes twinkling in the moonlight. The guard shook his head. "Well, it is! You'll just have to be patient. The enchantment will fade when the sun hits it in the morning. You good?" His eyes narrowed as he thought about his situation. He struggled briefly, found that he truly couldn't move, other than to thrash about like a man-sized worm, then relaxed in surrender and nodded. Ariana's grin widened. "Yeah, it's my new favorite spell!" She nodded towards the entrance. "Tanya in there?" The guard glared harder at her but didn't move. "Oh, come on, we were getting along so well. Do I need to get rough with you?" She drew a six-inch throwing knife from her boot and cleaned her nails with it. She saw his eyes tracking the razor-sharp blade. She gestured with it when she spoke again. "Look, I'm a nice girl...mostly. Don't make me prove otherwise. Now let's try again. Tanya in there somewhere?"

The guard's eyes flicked towards the entrance, then back to Ariana. He sighed through his nostrils, then nodded.

"Good. She got the cop in there with her? Avery?"

He took a moment to decide whether to tell her anything, but rolled his eyes in disgust at himself, then nodded.

That's good news, at least, she thought. Then another, less pleasant thought occurred to her, and urgency found its way into her voice. "Is she all right?"

The guard shrugged his shoulders, which Ariana interpreted as meaning, "Last I knew, she was."

Relieved, she sighed. Then she raised an eyebrow at her captive. "You might want to rethink your career, man. Your boss is killing innocent people. That makes you an accomplice at the very least. You know that, right?"

The guard looked at her, then looked away. He heard Ariana say, "Karma's not a picky bitch. She'll come for you, too." He stared off into the night, contemplating. When he turned back, she was gone.

Chapter 28

Avery couldn't believe what she was seeing, and she'd seen a lot of unbelievable things the last few days. Here she was, chained to a post, forced to watch a naked sorceress make a bargain with a hideous, demonic entity that looked like something out of a nightmare. The air in the cavern was hot and cloying, and the pain in her arms and shoulders grew more intense with each passing minute. The spectacle playing out before her, though, drew her attention from the pain.

Tanya filled the bowl with pieces of each animal, as well as the bits of flesh from Avery and Diana, and carried it to the fire in the center of the ritual circle. She knelt before it and picked up a small bottle that she'd placed there. Chanting, she poured a thick, red liquid into the bowl, then dropped the empty bottle so she could hold the bowl with both hands. She leaned over the fire, holding the vessel over the flames, somehow ignoring the pain it must have caused in her hands. Her song never wavered. The demon, Atahasia, murmured in approval, then swiped its hair out of its face, again drawing its own blood with the flint knife and ignoring it.

Drink, the demon encouraged her, *follow the Witchery Way. Walk on four legs and hunt. Soar through the night sky and spy on your enemies. Through claw, talon, and tooth, through serpent's coil and cougar's bite, wreak havoc on your enemies. With the power of rain and wind, you will triumph. With the power of suggestion, you will sway others to your will. Yes, little witch, gain everything you've ever wished for,* Atahasia laughed, a low mirthless sound, *and pay the price.*

Tanya swayed in time with her chant, then stopped long enough to drink the contents of the bowl. She gagged once, then gasped as the grisly concoction made its way down her throat. Her hands went to her stomach, and she hunched over, coughing. Her breathing became harsh and ragged, and she grunted in pain. Atahasia laughed. She convulsed and fell over on her side, clenching herself around her agony as the potion began to remake her.

Her skin rippled as if something moved just beneath its surface, and she screamed. Fur pushed its way through her pores, a golden-brown pelt that soon covered her entire body. Her scream rose in pitch, becoming a feline yowl of pain, as sharp, curved talons pushed their way through her fingertips, spurting blood as they broke the skin. Tanya writhed and squirmed as bones popped and muscles reordered themselves, causing torment she could never have understood before now. Her form became more cat than human, then shifted into an enormous mountain lion. Before she recovered, another transformation began. Feathers burst through the furry skin on the huge cat's back, long and black. The cat thing curled into a tight ball as its front legs broke, healed, stretched, and changed into wings. Soon, a misshapen raven flapped frantically in the center of the circle even as another animal began to push its way to the fore. Tanya wailed in agony, her voice slowly morphing into a sharp hiss as her tongue forked and her legs began to mold themselves together, merging into one long, slender tail that thrashed and coiled as the snake emerged from somewhere in Tanya's spirit.

Again and again, the being on the floor howled and changed, its body morphing into all manner of beasts. Some were ferocious, while others were quick and furtive. Finally, Tanya's human form pushed its way to the surface again, and she lay still. Her tanned, nude limbs were now devoid of paint and glistening with sweat. She panted as though she'd just finished a marathon, her eyes open, but unseeing.

Avery frowned as she stared at her captor. She was human again, yes, but the proportions of her body were somehow...wrong. Her legs seemed just a touch too long in the calf, her feet and hands likewise longer. Tanya lay on the floor, quivering, quietly moaning with each breath. Awareness gradually returned to her eyes, and she sat up. Moving carefully as she recovered her composure, she gathered her feet beneath her. She stood slowly, as if testing her limbs for the first time. She stretched her arms out in front of her and examined them, turned her hands over and stared at the overlong palms and extended fingers. She closed her eyes and exerted her will. Bones popped, and the palms slowly adjusted, shrinking to their former lengths. Tanya looked down at her legs and repeated the process as she made similar changes to her calves and feet. When she had shrunk to her normal height, she glanced over at Avery, who was still staring at her.

"There, now," she said, beaming. "Just right."

"You're..." Avery spoke, finding it difficult to get the words out. "You're *insane!*"

Tanya laughed, dismissing Avery from her attention, looked back at Atahasia and bowed her head. "I walk with you now, Father. I walk the Witchery Way."

The demon's low chuckle echoed in the cave. "Indeed, you do, daughter. Now guard yourself. One comes who means to kill you. A fitting test for your new power."

Tanya yelped in surprise as the enormous demon burst into a cloud of thick, swirling shadows. Sinuous tentacles of darkness snaked across the walls until they found the shadows that birthed them, leaving the two women alone in the room with the crackling fire. Tanya's head whipped around towards the largest tunnel, the one that led to the surface. A low growl escaped her just before three shots rang out in rapid succession. One of the bullets clipped her shoulder, and blood flew in the air. Tanya uttered a short scream and fell to one knee, clutching the wound, then she scuttled out of view of the tunnel and pressed her body against the stone of the wall.

"Avery!" Ariana's voice echoed throughout the cavern. "Are you in there? Are you all right?"

Avery took a deep breath to reply, but Tanya extended one hand, blood still dripping from it. "Hush!" she hissed, and Avery's scream made no sound whatsoever. She glared at her captor, only to see Tanya changing. Her body roiled and shuddered. Her pixie-short hair, formerly dark brown, extended into shoulder-length black tresses. Her body shortened, grew denser with muscle, and curvier. Clothes appeared, battered slacks and a deep blue blouse, covered with stains that mirrored those on the garments Avery wore. Tanya ran her hands over herself, as if trying out her new body, then she raised both hands and gestured at the detective once more. A barrier of energy rose around Avery, making the surrounding air hazy and blurry. When Tanya next spoke, it was with the detective's own voice.

She whispered, "There now, a veil should keep you out of sight. Behave yourself!" Raising her voice, she yelled out, "Don't shoot! It's me, I'm here!" Tossing a wicked grin at the real Avery, Tanya raised her right hand, which suddenly shifted and changed, becoming a hideous hybrid between a human hand and a cougar's paw, deadly talons flashing in the firelight. Tanya called out again, putting as much fear into her stolen voice as she could. "She's hiding in the tunnels! I'm hurt...help me!" Tanya affected a limp, then staggered into the middle of the room where anyone in the tunnel could see her. Tanya-Avery stumbled and fell, grunting in feigned agony as she did so and hiding her right hand as if it were injured.

Avery's blood was boiling. Bound, silenced, and hidden, she knew Tanya would easily fool Ariana long enough for the newly-minted Skinwalker to surprise her, maybe even kill her. She tried to scream, but nothing got through Tanya's enchantment. She tried rattling her chains, but the spell kept them soundless as well. Cursing, she reached into the tingling energy she felt deep inside her, struggling to find a way to use it.

*   *   *   *   *   *

Ariana had followed the tunnel from the surface, keeping her gun at the ready. This far in, she doubted she'd have much of a chance to do anything but shoot any of Tanya's thugs if they appeared, but so far, she'd seen no one. The oppressive dread of the place hammered at her relentlessly, trying to push its way through the mental shields she'd erected.

When she'd spied Tanya standing naked in the chamber up ahead, she'd seen her opportunity. As much as she hated killing unsuspecting people, she knew without a doubt that Tanya was *bad* people. She was a cold-blooded murderess who would kill anyone who got in her way. Holding that knowledge in the front of her mind, Ariana had taken careful aim and fired off three shots. Only one had struck her target, and she cursed herself for not sticking with one of her own weapons for the longer shot as she watched Tanya duck out of sight. *Too late now,* she thought, and she stalked closer to the chamber's entrance, watching for Tanya to come back into view. When she didn't appear, Ariana took a chance and yelled out, "Avery!" She waited only briefly before calling out again, "Are you in there? Are you all right?"

After a moment's pause, she heard Avery respond, "Don't shoot! It's me, I'm here!" Pain was thick in her voice. "She's hiding in the tunnels! I'm hurt...help me!" Avery stumbled into the center of the chamber up ahead and fell to her knees, hair covering her face.

Ariana raised her gun to cover the kneeling figure as she moved into the large, circular chamber. As she stepped inside, the raw, hateful aura in the cave hit her hard, making her guts churn with nausea. She took in the wall paintings, the ceremonial items laid out around the circle, and knew she'd found the right place. *Whoa, seriously bad stuff going on in here,* she thought even as she steeled herself against it. When she saw the chamber was empty but for the two of them, she lowered her gun and rushed to Avery's side. She knelt and gently grabbed the battered detective's arm, intending to help her to her feet. Her eyes darted to the two smaller tunnels that led away from the chamber. *She's got to be in one of those, but which one?* Resolving to figure it out once she got Avery to safety, she focused her attention on the kneeling detective. "Can you walk?" Ariana asked, concerned.

Avery nodded, then turned her head slightly. A glint of scarlet flashed in her eyes, and that's all that saved Ariana's life. She flung herself backwards just as Avery lashed out with her mutated right hand, aiming for Ariana's vulnerable throat. The razor-sharp claws scored her neck and left deeper slashes in her shirt and tactical vest, but she lived. She frantically crab-walked backwards until she fetched up against the stone wall, then found her weapon still hanging on its strap around her neck. She pointed it at the scarlet-eyed detective, who now stood tall and proud in the center of the circle.

"Avery! What the hell are you doing?" Regaining her composure, she got to her feet, struggling to maintain trigger discipline. "Did she put a demon in you? Talk to me!"

Even as she asked the question, she knew that wasn't the case. The others had wide, yellow eyes. This Avery's eyes looked normal until the light hit them just so, causing them to gleam scarlet. And something about her was both wrong and familiar. She moved haughtily, with a certain arrogance that Ariana had never seen the detective display. A sly smirk tugged one corner of Avery's mouth, and Ariana recognized the expression from a hundred pictures on social media. She finally understood. She'd arrived too late; Tanya had become a Skinwalker.

Tanya laughed with Avery's lips and spoke, "Stupid little witch. My powers are now more than you can even fathom." She threw back her head as her body rippled and changed, yellowish fur pushing its way to the surface. A grunt escaped her, more feline than human. Her arms lengthened, her snout pushed forward, and fangs sprouted as she worked her jaw muscles. In moments, a lithe half-human, half-puma stood before Ariana, nearly six feet of lean muscle and deadly claws. Her voice was altered, lower and menacing. "I can taste your fear, darling, and it's delicious. Do your worst."

Ariana needed no further urging. She began firing the AK-47 in controlled bursts, making sure as many rounds hit her target as possible. With each cluster of bullets, the horrid, cat-like beast jerked and spun, blood flew on the air, and bestial howls echoed from the walls. When the magazine ran empty, she tilted the gun sideways as she pulled a full mag from her vest, knocked the empty out, jammed in the new one and racked the slide before orienting it on the target once more and resuming fire. The echoes from the shots were deafening in the cave, and she found herself screaming, her yell blending with the noise of the gunfire until her last magazine ran empty. The beast stood, wavering on its misshapen legs, then it toppled to the floor.

She stared at the creature, a mass of bloody fur and half-human limbs. As she watched, it moved. Slowly at first, it twitched and rolled over. A low growl rolled from the beast's throat as it pushed itself up. The growl became lower, deeper, and words emerged.

"If that's the best you can do, then I'm really going to have some fun with you." With frightening quickness, Tanya's body changed again as it rose, expanding, its fur becoming darker as it took on a new, larger shape. "Yes, I'm going to rip you open and pull out your intestines. I'll pull your arms off one at a time, and slowly. Then I'll break your back. I'll use my power to keep you alive while I do it. You'll feel every single thing I do to you, and you'll be powerless to do anything about it."

Within the space of a few frantic heartbeats, Tanya completed her metamorphosis, and now an enormous gray wolf fixed its scarlet gaze on her. It growled, a low, rumbling sound that sent a spear of terror through Ariana's heart. She'd killed a lot of things in her time, many of them bigger than this. But the primal power of a wolf, the sheer size and energy of it, called to some ancient part of herself, a genetic memory of being lower on the food chain than such a dangerous creature. As it bared its white fangs, she felt fear grip her tightly.

Along with fear came anger. Her eyes narrowed and she muttered, "Oh, hell, no." Dropping the empty gun and moving into a stance that would allow her to quickly dodge in either direction, Ariana's mind raced through her options. "Come on, you bitch!" she teased, trying to goad Tanya into an attack. One hand pulled a slim knife from her boot, hiding it alongside her body. "You want me? I'm right here. Come and get me!"

The attack was fast, much too fast. Three hundred pounds of wolf shot forward, wide mouth agape, intending to rip out Ariana's throat in one vicious motion. She ducked to her right and dove, slashing at its ribs with her dagger as she flew past, rolling on the hard stone floor and coming up in a crouch. The beast had trouble stopping its momentum and skidded on the stone as it howled in frustration. Its paws and their sharp nails did little good on the relatively slick surface and it fell heavily on its side.

Jumping on the chance, Ariana raised her left hand and chanted strident words of power. A bright blue glow appeared as she gathered energy in her palm, focusing her will to the task until it shone with a brilliant glare too bright to look upon. Just as the wolf sprang to its feet and turned to face her, Ariana made a throwing motion and launched the spell across the intervening space. Lightning exploded across the distance, slamming into the wolf's chest. It howled in agony as her power took it from its feet and drove it backwards. It hurtled through the air and smashed against the wall with an ominous thump, leaving a great spiderweb of cracks in the stone as it slid into a heap on the floor. Exhaustion from the casting of the spell hit her in a wave, and she dropped to one knee, but she wasn't finished. Moving with the smoothness of long practice, she pulled her sidearm, racked the slide, and took aim at the beast's shaggy head.

"That's right," she said, panting, "you've got nothing." She opened fire. Her special *kills-everything* bullets slammed into the wolf's head and body, the wounds steaming on contact with the heavily enchanted lead. The animal shuddered with each impact and did not rise. Ariana emptied her magazine, then lowered her gun when the slide locked open. Bright motes of exhaustion spun before her eyes, and she sat heavily on the floor. The lightning spell had drained her deeply, and she knew it. Taking slow, deep breaths, she exchanged the empty magazine for a loaded one and stowed the empty on her belt. Once her gun was reloaded, she relaxed. Keeping her eyes on the dead creature across the cave, she scooted backwards until she reached the wall. Leaning on it, she sighed in relief and let the silence comfort her.

As she caught her breath, she became aware of a popping sound. She brought her gun up, aiming at the wolf's corpse, and found that she was shaking. Grimacing, she added her other hand to the grip.

"Dammit," she muttered. It wasn't over.

Tanya's canine body was changing. The wolf's head turned to glare at her, its scarlet gaze revealing hatred and rage, then it turned away as the pain of its transformation overcame it. The grayish body hunched and rolled, the fur becoming a much darker brown. It rose...and kept rising. Soon, the beast stood on two legs, its bulky frame towering over Ariana's full height. It growled again, much lower, deeper than before. Her heart turned to ice at the unmistakable sound of it.

When it finally turned toward Ariana, her face paled at the sight of an enormous grizzly bear, easily a thousand pounds of hard muscle and fur. It offered a wickedly fanged smile, then launched itself at her as she scrambled to get to her feet.

She managed to fire four shots into the creature's huge chest, but they had no effect at all. She tried to duck as she had before, tried to dive away at an angle, but the bear swatted her with a massive paw, batting her across the room like a child's toy. She hit the wall hard, banging her head in the process. When her body came to rest, she had vicious gouges in her left shoulder, left by the bear's great claws, and her left arm was broken at the humerus from the sheer power of the blow. Another bright flare of pain erupted from her left ankle, only dimly registering among the pains of her head and shoulder. Her gun spun away, out of her reach, and she struggled to remain conscious.

"Seems like I've got a little more than nothing." The bear's voice was low and rumbling, yet it still had a hint of Tanya in it. The beast dropped to all fours and turned to face her downed opponent. "Whatever was in those bullets stings a bit, but you're no match for me. Poor lillle witch."

The bear ambled closer, impossibly powerful and huge. It lumbered lazily towards her, taking its time. It stood tall on both legs again, preparing to fall upon Ariana in a fury of fangs and claws.

An odd noise, almost a buzzing sound, reached Tanya's ears, and she turned her snout towards the large tunnel that led to the outside. It was coming closer, louder. The fierce whine of an engine filled the cavern.

Kane had arrived.

Chapter 29

The ride across the desert was actually kind of fun. I loved the speed, and although I can run that fast for a short while, the motorcycle could do it for much longer. The terrain was rough, but I could see perfectly well by moonlight, so I enjoyed riding the bike hard, jumping the hills when the occasion presented itself, and going as fast as the motorcycle would allow.

I half-expected to be shot at when I came close to the compound, but I saw no one. Ariana must have enjoyed herself as well. I skirted the walls, leaving a wide enough gap that I wasn't an easy target for a sniper, and then made for the mountain on the north side. The feelings of dread and nausea, the hallmarks of old, bad magick, were getting stronger all the time, and I hoped Ariana was all right.

That thought made me frown, and I shook my head. She was either alive or she wasn't. That's how it would be. I didn't need to be all mushy about it. I tried to ignore the fact that I leaned on the accelerator harder as I approached the cave.

My intention was to stash the bike and then move quietly inside, hoping to surprise any bad guys I ran up against. As I was about to turn aside, the Goddess told me not to. That was it. No vision, no flash of insight, other than the pure knowledge that I needed to be inside that cave *right now*.

Whatever you say, Lady. I'm not one to take orders from anyone. That is, unless it's Mother Nature. If she says go, I just go.

I nearly ripped the throttle off as I gunned the bike and hunched my body over the handlebars. The engine whined in my ears, complaining as I pushed it to its limits. The yawning mouth of the cave entrance beckoned, and I hit it at full speed. The stone floor of the inner passage sloped downwards, which only made me go faster. I realized I was grinning like a fool, but I didn't care. This was fun. And if Tanya was down here as I thought she must be, I'd probably get to kill her. More fun.

The tunnel leveled out and I saw it ended in a chamber up ahead. Reaching out with my magick, I felt Ariana's presence, as well as something hideous that could only have been Tanya. I'd only been near her once before, and that was when Avery had been shooting at me. However, I still recognized the feel of the younger Thornwall woman's aura, as I might have recalled the faint scent of her perfume. The only problem was that her magickal footprint was now about fifty times what I had sensed that first time. The taste of that aura was now hugely dark and powerful, and I was hard-pressed to remember when I'd felt something like that from a human. I realized that she must have completed her ritual; she'd become a Skinwalker.

Shit.

As I approached the opening, I saw an enormous...bear? It was standing in the middle of the chamber, its attention focused on a figure on the ground nearby. I glanced that way and recognized Ariana with her back up against the wall. Bright spots of pain flowed from her into my perception, and I could see her favoring her left arm. There was blood on her chest and shoulder. Oh, yeah, it was definitely time for me to join the party.

The bear turned and looked at me just as I raced into the chamber. In that instant, I yanked on the handlebars as I stepped off the back of the bike, popping a wheelie and sending two hundred fifty pounds of angry motorcycle hurtling into the bear at top speed.

The bear's angry roar was cut off by the impact, and the flying cycle bore Tanya back into the wall of the chamber, where she slammed into the stone with an immensely satisfying crash. Big bones broke, and an injured moan rolled out of the bear as it sank to the floor, still entangled with the slightly misshapen motorcycle. The machine fell to the floor and toppled over on its side, red blood smeared over some of its chrome and leather.

"Kill her, Kane!" Ariana mumbled, still groggy. I was somewhat surprised to hear that from her, and I turned to give her a quizzical look. Her voice gained strength as she urged, "Seriously! She's going to change again and walk it off. Kill her right now!"

My head snapped back to the dying bear on the floor. It growled at me, then began to twitch and convulse. Its fur rippled oddly and I realized that Ariana had the right of it. Anytime a Skinwalker changed, any wounds it might have had in its previous shape would simply vanish as its body reorganized itself into a new form. I bolted forward, my claws out, and slashed at the furry neck for all I was worth.

And I missed.

Tanya's change was faster than I expected, and by the time my claws would have opened up her throat, she'd shrunken into a slender, furry thing the length of my forearm. A ferret! My claws struck sparks from the stone as she evaded me, then she raced up my arm and onto my back. Hot bursts of pain erupted along my back and shoulders as she dug her tiny but sharp incisors into my flesh, and I spun in place, frantically trying to lay a hand on her. I heard her laugh, her voice an odd chittering from that tiny throat, and no matter how I gyrated, I couldn't get hold of her.

Something whipped around my body, pinning my arms to my sides. I looked down and saw the thickening coils of a python tightening around me. *Uh, oh.* I'm strong. I can, if properly motivated and can get a good grip, throw a car at you. But I'm limited by the laws of physics and leverage the same as humans. Pin my arms to my sides tightly enough and I might have a problem. Another coil worked its way around my neck, and I decided that I did, indeed, have a problem.

I turned my head to one side and jammed my chin to my shoulder, keeping the coil from wrapping completely around my neck. It wasn't comfortable, but it bought me some time. My mind raced as I tried to figure out what to do. Even biting her would only get me so far, and it would leave my neck vulnerable.

Out of the corner of my eye, I saw the head of the python circling around so she could see my face. Her forked tongue flicked out repeatedly, testing the air for any sign of fear it could use to gain power. I had no fear for her to use against me, though. Just anger. That was for my strength, not hers. I strained against the coils and the snake hissed laughter at me, then tightened them another couple of inches, making it harder for me to breathe.

"Let him go!" The pain was evident in Ariana's voice, and she groaned as the words left her mouth. She put her right hand to her head to steady herself, but nearly passed out instead. I watched her try to reach her gun, but the few feet that separated her from it may as well have been miles. She reached for its twin in the holster on her left thigh, but between the pain and her awkward position, it was lost to her as well. She tried again to reach the other gun, but her movements were feeble and slow.

Looks like it was all up to me this time. To be honest, I didn't like my chances.

Chapter 30

I moved backwards and slammed up against the stone wall, hoping to damage Tanya's serpentine coils enough to get her to let go, but she didn't budge. In addition, the motion finally allowed her to slip a coil under my chin. I tightened the muscles of my neck, but she was *strong.* I knew it was only a matter of time. Pressure started to build in my head and my ears started ringing. I reached out with my magick, trying to get into her head, but her mental defenses were more solid than steel. Whatever she'd gained from the dark powers when she became a Skinwalker had strengthened her magick far beyond my ability to penetrate. She had me.

No.

I strained harder against her coils, determined not to go out that way. I'm a GrimFaerie, dammit. I'm of the Fae. I grunted and strained harder, growling as my anger rose, and I gained a quarter inch of breathing room. She hissed furiously and struck at my chest with her inch-long fangs, burying them deeply into my pectoral muscle. The pain should have drained me, but it didn't. It pissed me off.

NO.

Walking this earth for centuries as I have, I've fought some things that would eat Tanya for lunch. And I killed them. All of them. I would not, could not, let this mortal sorcerer beat me, not like this. In the midst of all the pain and rage that swirled through me, I latched onto that thought, held fast to it. It steadied me. I focused my mind and gathered every bit of power I could find, along with every scrap of physical strength I possessed. With a primal shout of fury, I released it all, prying my arms away from my body with all my might. Something snapped inside the snake and coils began dropping away as she lost feeling in the lower half of her body. As my hands came free, I started throwing off the rest of her. Her fangs pulled out of my chest and I threw her across the floor into a limp, ropy mess. Tanya hissed all the while, furious. She struggled to slither away, but only the top half of her body answered her, while the rest twitched and spasmed aimlessly. I grinned at the sight, then my exertions caught up with me and the room spun. I fell to my knees, then found myself face down on the dirty stone floor, wheezing in great gulps of air as best I could.

"That'ssssss it!" Tanya's voice was barely recognizable as it came from the snake's head. "I'll kill you for that!"

I raised my head as much as I could, locked my gaze onto hers and responded, "Bring it, baby." Then I laid my head back down on the cold stone as I caught my breath. I figured I had a few seconds before she changed into whatever was coming next, and I needed every one of those seconds if I was going to meet her on my feet. My strength returned quickly at such times, but I'd unleashed a lot of my energy. It was going to be a race to see who recovered first.

Tanya's hiss became a growl, and I heard the popping sounds that accompanied the shifting of her bones as they reorganized themselves into their new configuration. I didn't bother to look. Instead, I focused on the stone in front of my face. I pulled my hands up beneath me so I could push myself up, and I sat back on my heels, vertical at least. When I saw what Tanya was becoming, I considered lying down again, but only for a millisecond. I sighed, then grinned tiredly. If ever I wanted a challenge, I was about to get one.

The creature before me was nine feet tall, and still growing. I thought it was a bear at first, but then its arms lengthened into a grotesque combination of human and bear, with long, grasping fingers tipped with dagger-like claws at least five inches long. The legs were wrong, too, not like the stubby-looking legs of a grizzly. They were longer and more muscular. I finally recognized them as those of a lion, but far larger. When she stopped growing, the hideous thing Tanya had become was nearly a dozen feet tall and had to weigh a couple thousand pounds, easily. Her bear's snout was too long, much like a wolf's, but truly belonged to neither. The finger-long fangs seemed perfectly appropriate in the gaping mouth on that monstrosity. She opened her jaws wider and growled at me, then swiped her claws at the floor, digging four deep slashes into the hard stone as though it was nothing but soft dirt. Only her eyes reminded me of Tanya, human eyes, but filled with a scarlet gleam of malevolent power.

I sighed and rose to my feet. I cracked my neck to the left, and to the right, then bared my own claws and fangs. They seemed pitiful next to those of the thing across from me. I'd never had claw envy before, but there's a first time for everything. Nevertheless, I flexed my fingers, gathered my feet beneath me, and prepared to fight for my life.

The creature's roar rattled the entire cavern, and I answered as I sprinted forward, intending for one of us to die in the next few seconds.

An intense beam of pure blue-white fire as thick as my waist slammed into the beast's left side, knocking it out of my path and into the wall with an impact so great that a wide crack crawled up the sheer rock face and dust fell from the ceiling. A rumble from within the mountain answered, as though it was displeased. I skidded to a stop as I stared at the wounded creature in astonishment.

Where the bolt had struck, Tanya's fur was blackened and burnt, and the misshapen left arm was badly broken and mangled. Flesh hung from it where it wasn't gone altogether. I could see ribs exposed through the beast's shaggy pelt on that side. The enormous creature slid slowly down the wall into a heap on the floor, completely stunned. I turned to see where the bolt of energy had come from and saw nothing at first. Then the air shimmered as a veiling spell collapsed, and I saw a battered, exhausted woman hanging from a tall wooden post by a pair of steel shackles on her wrists. Her black hair hung loosely on either side of her dirty face. When she raised her eyes to mine, they were glowing fiercely with the same bright blue energy that had struck Tanya's monstrous form. Thin tendrils of power played around her face like lightning. Her mouth was clamped in a thin, tight line, and determination was written all over her face. As I watched, the light faded from her eyes and she sagged, as if whatever energy she had conjured had been holding her up.

"Detective Avery!" I said, surprised. "What did you just do?"

"I..." she whispered, just loudly enough for me to hear, "I don't know. Got mad. Tired of her...bullshit."

I looked at Tanya and saw that her form was already changing, shrinking, her bones popping and snapping as they reordered themselves. This time, however, the wounds she had taken didn't mend. When she resumed her fully human form, her entire left side was still burnt and mangled. A faint, agonized moan escaped her, a mournful, gurgling sound. Keeping my guard up, I walked over and knelt beside her, though just out of easy reach.

The damage was extensive. The blast of magick Avery had thrown at her had devastated her left side and laid most of her rib cage open to the elements. Even if she were in a hospital's ER at that moment, there was no saving her. Her eyes fluttered open and she looked around wildly, suddenly terrified. She tried to move and grimaced in pain. Then her eyes fastened on me and I finally saw terror there. I dropped the illusion that hid my true face from the world so that she could see. If anything, her eyes widened slightly at the sight of the real me.

"The Goddess tells me that your crimes are punishable by death," I said quietly. "You've more than earned it, I think." She began to quiver, and she moaned again, quite piteously.

Of course, I have no pity in me.

Seeing no need to make her suffer further, I reached out to grab her hair. I tilted her head back slightly and sliced her throat open with my claws. They went deep, all the way to the spine. Her eyes stayed on mine until the light went out of them.

It took me another few seconds to remove her head from her shoulders. You can never be too careful with sorcerous types, especially Skinwalkers. They were a tough bunch. Couldn't have her coming back to life somehow and causing more trouble. That done, I laid the head on the floor several feet from the body and moved towards the detective. She'd been watching me the whole time, exhausted, but wary.

When I got the chains down and popped open the manacles, Avery sat down with her back against the post to rub her wrists.

"It *was* you," she said, her eyes narrowed as they regarded me. "You killed my grandfather. I'm sure of it now. I saw you that night, like this. The way you moved, the way your power feels...I felt your magick back then, but I was just a child and I didn't know what it was." She paused and looked harder at me. "It was *you*."

Before I could speak, I realized that I had yet to cover my features with my customary glamour. She was seeing my true self, just as Tanya had, but she wasn't flinching. She just sat there looking at me, waiting for me to talk. I sighed and put my 'face' back on, then spoke.

"What I said before was true, Detective. I don't remember you or your grandfather. If I killed him, I can only tell you that I had an extremely good reason for doing so. I'm an assassin, yes, but I work for the Goddess. For the Light. I keep the balance. If she pointed me towards your grandfather, then he was doing something truly evil, and that marked him. I can't tell you anything more because I don't remember off the top of my head. I've been all along the Gulf Coast during the last hundred years or so, and I've killed a lot of people. Each and every one of them was a murderer at the very least. There was evidence in plenty if you knew where to look. But although I'm a killer, and a damned good one, I don't kill innocents. Ever." I glanced over towards Ariana, who was finally sitting up. "Especially since I've been hanging out with her." I allowed myself a ghost of a grin and whispered, "I think she's a bad influence, but don't tell her I told you so."

Avery's gaze flicked towards Ariana and then locked with mine again. She didn't answer, turning my words over in her mind, I'd guess. It was a lot to take in. I'm sure she had loved her old Grandpa, but if I'd come for him, then he had to have been dirty. She was trying to remember if she'd seen anything that would indicate that.

Being that close to her, I could feel her power, depleted, yes, but still there. I reached for her with my own and slammed up against a mental ward nearly as strong as Tanya's had been. Avery's eyes flicked toward me as she felt the intrusion, momentarily concerned, but I raised my hands, palms up, and said, "It's OK, it's OK. I was only looking you over. Trying to figure out what your magick is made of, that's all. I won't hurt you." Avery relaxed at that, albeit somewhat reluctantly.

I inclined my head towards Tanya's body. "What did you do?" I asked again. "She was nearly invulnerable. How did you kill her?"

Avery finally lowered her gaze as she contemplated. "I don't know, exactly." When she looked up at me, I could tell that she had tabled the 'you killed my grandfather' discussion for another time. She had more pressing matters to talk about. "She hid me with that spell or whatever right after Ariana showed up and shot her. I could see what was going on, but no matter how much I screamed, none of you could hear me, and certainly couldn't see me." She paused and I realized how hoarse her voice was. "I watched her fight with you, and all I could think about was that she'd probably killed Jim, and now that she had those powers, she'd go back to Katy and Houston and kill more people there, too. That really pissed me off." She shrugged and allowed one side of her mouth to tip upwards into a smile, "And I'm not all that fond of being chained up like that, either. I'm a cop; I do the cuffing, not the other way 'round."

I understood that sentiment. "Will you let me examine you? With my magick? It won't hurt, I only want to figure out how strong you are, maybe figure out where your power comes from."

She thought about it, then nodded. "What do I need to do?"

"Just relax, and when you feel my presence, don't fight it. You shut me out before, so this time, just don't do that." I explained.

Avery nodded, then took a deep breath and relaxed. "OK. Hit me."

I smiled and reached for her. It took only a moment to confirm what I'd suspected: she was a natural witch...and something more. She'd never known it, never been trained. And holy goddess, she was strong. There was definitely Fae blood in her veins, and it was thick. It's a wonder it hadn't expressed itself before this, but then, it was likely she'd unconsciously held it in check all this time for fear of not being normal. Close exposure to all of the

227

magick she'd come in contact with lately had awakened it in her, relaxing her inhibitions against using it. Interesting. Very interesting.

Ariana walked over, cradling her left arm, and looking like she'd mostly regained her composure. I was sure she'd managed to block most of the pain using a carefully placed bit of magick, but what was still getting through was probably pretty stout, judging by her expression.

"What's the verdict, Kane?" she asked tiredly.

"You might want to spend some time with her," I suggested. "She can learn a lot from you, and at this point, she needs to. She's freaky strong, and she'll need guidance." I looked at Avery again, "She can teach you. And I guarantee that you'll need the skills you'll learn from her. Now that you know about our world, you're a part of it whether you like it or not. And your strength will be needed, I have no doubt."

Avery looked from me to Ariana, then nodded. "OK. When we get back, and after I clean up this..." she shook her head, "this mess, we'll get together. And you need to get that arm looked at."

Ariana glanced down at her arm and laughed, though it pained her to do so. "Yeah, I'll have to teach you one-handed for a while. But that'll do. We've got a lot of basics to cover. Being a witch is really cool, but it's a shit-ton of work."

"I'm no stranger to that," Avery replied, then her eyes widened. "Jim! They turned him into one of those demon things! We've got to find him!"

"It's OK, he found us. And we got the demon out of him; he's perfectly fine," Ariana reassured her. "He's worried about you. We nearly had to tie him up to keep him from coming with us."

Avery sighed in relief, and to my surprise, her eyes welled up and she couldn't quite stifle a sob. Just as quickly, she wiped her nose and straightened up. "Sorry. We've been friends a long time, Jim and I. He's a good man. I hated that she did that to him. He didn't deserve that."

I glanced over at Tanya's body, lying motionless across the room. "Well, at least we know it won't happen to anyone else. She's done. No more demon pills."

Just then I caught the faintest, but most welcome sound I'd heard in a while: helicopter blades.

"Ladies, I believe our ride is here. Shall we go?"

Chapter 31

I really like Edge. He happened to have a huge chunk of explosives stashed in the helicopter. "For emergencies," he said. We dropped a few bricks of C4 into the chimney at the top of the mountain on a timer, and it brought the whole thing down on top of Tanya's body, sealing up the ceremonial chamber and the entrances to the other two tunnels that led deeper into the earth from there. Whatever was down there should probably stay locked away in any event.

The shockwave rocked the helicopter a little before Edge smoothed out the ride once more. He flew us toward the rising sun, back into Texas. Jim, Avery, and Ariana were buckled safely into their seats, already dozing. Edge had splinted Ariana's arm nicely and dosed her with painkillers, so her sleep was even deeper than the others. She was snoring, mouth wide open, and she'd drooled a little. Just darling. I took a picture with her phone. I was sure she'd love that.

Movement outside the window caught my attention, and I leaned over to see better. What I saw made me smile. The Wyvern was flying alongside us, maybe a hundred yards away. Its leathery wings flapped lazily as it flew, mostly gliding on the air currents. An idea struck me, and I unbuckled my harness. Moving carefully up into the cockpit, I shut the door behind me and sat in the seat next to Edge. He saw me and nodded, before turning his attention back to his instruments and the wide-open vista before him.

"Does this thing have an autopilot?" I asked him.

He slowly turned back to face me, one eyebrow raised, his curiosity piqued. Edge nodded. "Yes sir, it does. Might I ask why you'd want to know such a thing?"

"I need you to shut the door for me after I jump out. I've got another ride home, I think. I'll meet you all back at Ariana's tonight. Fly safely, Edge."

He opened his mouth, closed it again, then simply nodded. He hit a series of switches, removed his hands from the controls, and gave me a thumbs up.

I opened the door to the cabin and jumped out, relishing the howl of the wind as I fell. At that height, it felt like flying, though I knew I was plummeting to earth instead. I looked off to my right and saw my new buddy.

The Wyvern screeched, its song piercing the air even above the rushing air in my ears. It flapped its wings and instantly changed direction to intercept me. I swear, it actually seemed excited. When it reached me it eased alongside, then drifted beneath me so that I landed softly on its shoulders. I slid my hands along its neck and found the spots where I had dug my claws in to control it before. The wounds had already healed, but I found I could grip the scales well enough that I wouldn't fall off, and I held on with my thighs as well.

Ever been to Texas? I asked the Wyvern. I got a swirl of emotions in return: eagerness and joy, mostly. I let myself go a little and grinned like fool. *Well, I think I can find a spot for you out there somewhere. And I'll see a guy about a saddle.*

The End

**For updates about new releases,
exclusive promotions,
and a complimentary short story,
visit the author's website
and sign up for the VIP mailing list
at
http://www.whitmcclendon.com**

The Fire of the Jidaan Trilogy
Boxset

*Epic Fantasy that will sweep
you away...*

"...a truly imaginative trio of books..."

"...hard to put down...I was on the
edge of my seat!"

Reyanna's Prophecy
Book 1 of the Forge Born Duology

The adventure continues...

"...an engaging, exciting and action-
packed fantasy adventure, well-
crafted...a welcome sense of humour
as well..."

233

About The Author

Whit McClendon was born on October 31, 1969 in Freeport, Tx. He grew up in Angleton Texas and was active in martial arts, track and field, and playing the clarinet in band. One year at Texas A & M proved that lacrosse was far more fun than electrical engineering, and he eventually graduated with a degree in Engineering Design Graphics from Brazosport College. After working in the petrochemical field as a CAD drafter for many years, Whit finally realized his life's dream of becoming a full-time martial arts instructor. He now lives with his family in Katy, Texas, plays lacrosse as often as possible, and runs Jade Mountain Martial Arts. He laughs a lot more now than he did when he worked at the engineering firm.

whitmcc@jidaan.com
www.whitmcclendon.com
www.jmma.org

www.ingramcontent.com/pod-product-compliance
Lightning Source LLC
Chambersburg PA
CBHW060550260626
47161CB00003B/1136